BEASTS
BRIDE

BOOK ONE
THE BRIDES OF SKYE

JAYNE
CASTEL

WINTER MIST
PRESS

The Beast's Bride, by Jayne Castel

Published by Winter Mist Press
Edited by Tim Burton
Cover designed by Winter Mist Press
Cover photography courtesy of www.shutterstock.com
Scotch thistle vector image courtesy of Wikipedia Commons.
Map of Isle of Skye by Jayne Castel

Excerpt from the poem, 'Ae Fond Kiss' by Robert Burns.

Visit Jayne's website: www.jaynecastel.com

The beauty who refuses to be wed. The beast who loves her in vain. A twist of fate that brings them together.

Rhona MacLeod is the beautiful, willful daughter of a clan-chief on the Isle of Skye. Desperate to remain free and bow to no man, she refuses all the suitors who ask for her hand.

Taran MacKinnon is one of Clan-chief MacLeod's most trusted warriors. He carries a secret passion for his chief's middle daughter. However, Rhona has never been able to see beyond his scars and forbidding appearance that have earned him the name 'The Beast of Dunvegan'.

Frustrated by Rhona's defiance, her father makes a decision that will force his daughter to take a husband—games that will bring warriors from all over the island, and from the mainland, to compete. Rhona must wed the victor. Finally, Taran has a chance to prove himself. If he wins the games, he can have the woman he wants—but can he win her heart?

Historical Romances by Jayne Castel

DARK AGES BRITAIN

The Kingdom of the East Angles series
Night Shadows (prequel novella)
Dark Under the Cover of Night (Book One)
Nightfall till Daybreak (Book Two)
The Deepening Night (Book Three)
The Kingdom of the East Angles: The Complete Series

The Kingdom of Mercia series
The Breaking Dawn (Book One)
Darkest before Dawn (Book Two)
Dawn of Wolves (Book Three)
The Kingdom of Mercia: The Complete Series

The Kingdom of Northumbria series
The Whispering Wind (Book One)
Wind Song (Book Two)
Lord of the North Wind (Book Three)
The Kingdom of Northumbria: The Complete Series

DARK AGES SCOTLAND

The Warrior Brothers of Skye series
Blood Feud (Book One)
Barbarian Slave (Book Two)
Battle Eagle (Book Three)
The Warrior Brothers of Skye: The Complete Series

The Pict Wars series
Warrior's Heart (Book One)
Warrior's Secret (Book Two)
Warrior's Wrath (Book Three)

The Pict Wars: The Complete Series

Novellas
Winter's Promise

MEDIEVAL SCOTLAND

The Brides of Skye series
The Beast's Bride (Book One)
The Outlaw's Bride (Book Two)
The Rogue's Bride (Book Three)
The Brides of Skye: The Complete Series

The Sisters of Kilbride series
Unforgotten (Book One)
Awoken (Book Two)
Fallen (Book Three)
Claimed (Epilogue novella)

The Immortal Highland Centurions series
Maximus (Book One)
Cassian (Book Two)
Draco (Book Three)
The Laird's Return (Epilogue festive novella)

Stolen Highland Hearts series
Highlander Deceived (Book One)
Highlander Entangled (Book Two)
Highlander Forbidden (Book Three)
Highlander Pledged (Book Four)

Guardians of Alba series
Nessa's Seduction (Book One)
Fyfa's Sacrifice (Book Two)
Breanna's Surrender (Book Three)

Epic Fantasy Romances by Jayne Castel

Light and Darkness series
Ruled by Shadows (Book One)
The Lost Swallow (Book Two)
Path of the Dark (Book Three)
Light and Darkness: The Complete Series

***

For Tim, who has gotten very fond of these journeys to Scotland!

***

Map

"Beauty is not in the face; beauty is a light in the heart."
—Kahlil Gibran

Chapter One

The Beauty and the Beast

Dunvegan Castle, Isle of Skye, Scotland

Early summer, 1346 AD

"YE WILL NOT wed me then?"

"I'm glad to see yer ears aren't full of porridge, Dughall MacLean. Aye, ye heard me right."

The young man—broad and muscular with a shock of peat-brown hair—glared at Lady Rhona MacLeod. Dughall folded his thick arms across his chest, staring her down.

Rhona lifted her chin and held his gaze steadily.

"So ye think ye are too good for the likes of me?" A storm gathered in his eyes as he spoke.

Despite her brave front, nervousness fluttered up from the pit of Rhona's belly. They stood alone in the gardens that lay south of the castle's curtain wall. Rhona was unarmed, and her father's men waited some distance away at the entrance to the gardens. She didn't have her sisters at her side either; their presence always made her bolder.

At her back, Rhona could feel the weight of Dunvegan Castle silently watching over them. The dove-grey fortress rose sheer from perpendicular edges of rock to the north, its massive battlements stark against the windswept sky.

In contrast to the barren moorland and craggy peaks that surrounded it, the garden was a small, sheltered spot. It was a softer world, although Rhona now regretted agreeing to take a walk with Dughall there. It was too private; a canopy of green and beds of herbs and flowers surrounded the pair.

Rhona forced herself not to shrink back from her angry suitor. Instead, she watched him, waiting for his temper to cool.

Dughall took a threatening step toward her, closing the distance between them. "A rare, fiery beauty, ye are, Rhona," he growled, "but I would tame ye."

Annoyance flared within Rhona at his presumption, making her forget her fear. "And that's why we wouldn't be suited," she countered, her tone sharpening. "Ye should find yerself a biddable wife."

He moved closer still. "Ye'd be biddable." He lowered his voice. "Once I were through with ye."

Rhona clenched her jaw. "Don't threaten me."

His face twisted—Dughall's pleasantly handsome features turning ugly in an instant. Rhona shifted back from him, but he grasped her arm. "Ye need to learn yer place. Ye are a spoilt, haughty bitch, but I still want ye. And one day ... I'll have ye."

Heart thumping, Rhona attempted to wrench her arm free. However, he held her in an iron grip. "Unhand me," she snarled, fear turning her savage.

He grinned, his dark blue eyes narrowing. "Or what?"

Rhona hissed out a breath. "Let me go."

"Beg ... and I might."

"What are ye doing, Dughall?"

A man's voice—low and powerful—interrupted them. Rhona twisted her head to see a huge warrior, with a fur mantle about his broad shoulders, striding toward them.

Relief flooded through Rhona at the sight of Taran MacKinnon. Yet even so, the warrior's formidable appearance struck her. He was a terrifying sight. Taran wore a heavy mail shirt under his mantle. His dark-blond hair was cropped short, a severe style that did nothing to soften his presence, and a rough stubble covered his strong jaw. He wore a grim expression, yet it was not that which drew Rhona's eye but the scars marring his face.

They were impossible to ignore.

One cut vertically from his forehead, missing his eye and scoring his right cheek. The other slashed sideways across his left cheek. The scars were disfiguring, and despite that Taran had served her father for a few years now, Rhona found it difficult not to stare. The cold look in his ice-blue eyes, the hard set of his mouth, warned that he was not a man to be messed with.

Her father kept this warrior at his side for a reason.

Dughall snorted, his gaze tracking Taran's arrival. But his grip on Rhona's arm released, and he moved away from her.

"The Beast of Dunvegan nears," he sneered. "Yer father's faithful hound."

"Aye." Rhona stepped back, instinctively moving toward Taran. His presence made her feel braver. "And he has a vicious bite, as ye well know."

"Lady Rhona." Taran stopped next to her, his grey-blue gaze searching for any sign of injury. "Are ye hurt?"

Rhona shook her head. "I was just explaining to Dughall that I would rather wed a stinking goat than him. He didn't take the news well."

"Bitch!" Dughall advanced, his hands fisting.

In an instant Taran had drawn the heavy sword that hung at his hip and stepped before Rhona, shielding her with his body.

"Be wise, Dughall," he warned softly, "Leave now, before I spill yer blood."

A tense silence fell. Dughall's face screwed up, and he spat on the ground at Taran's feet. "The Devil take ye both."

The man stalked from the garden, between rows of rosemary and lavender. Only when he disappeared from sight did Rhona loose the breath she'd been holding.

To her annoyance, she found that her pulse was racing. As much as it galled her to admit it, Dughall had scared her.

Feeling the weight of Taran's gaze, she inclined her head. "What?"

"Have a care, Lady Rhona," he replied, resheathing his sword. "Some men don't take kindly to being spurned."

Rhona frowned. "I don't need ye to preach to me, Taran." She huffed out a breath. "Although I'm glad ye arrived when ye did."

"I heard raised voices. I sensed trouble brewing."

Rhona sighed and pushed a heavy lock of auburn hair from her face. Now that the tension had released, her legs felt oddly weak. The sensation annoyed her. She was the daughter of a warrior. She'd been taught to fight, and yet when Dughall had seized her arm, she'd been unable to free herself. That angered her. She didn't think of herself as feeble like other women, and yet she'd been helpless.

"I'm out of practice," she muttered. "Why did we stop our fighting lessons?"

"Ye stopped them." Did she imagine it, or was there a trace of mirth in his voice? "Ye said ye were too occupied by other matters."

"Well, I'm not anymore," she replied, meeting his gaze squarely. "We shall resume them tomorrow at noon."

"Aye—as ye wish."

"Good." Rhona gathered her skirts and moved past him before flashing Taran a smile. "Next time I spurn a man, I want to be ready to geld him if he touches me."

Taran MacKinnon watched the second daughter of Malcolm MacLeod walk away from him, heading out of the garden and back toward the castle.

Now that her gaze was averted, his own devoured her.

She wore a kirtle of green plaid with a straw-colored leine underneath. The garment was fitted, highlighting her statuesque form and lush curves, and the dip of her waist. She walked with a determined stride, her long, curling dark-red hair tumbling down her back.

Taran's breathing hitched as he watched her—the fire-haired woman he'd wanted for a while now.

Only, she didn't return the sentiment. To Rhona, he was merely her father's warrior. *Scar-face*—The Beast of Dunvegan.

The name Dughall had thrown at him didn't bother Taran, he'd heard it enough times over the years for the insult to lose its sting. But he didn't want Rhona to look at him that way.

A bee buzzed by, on its lazy path to the bed of roses behind him. Taran inhaled the sweet scent of the flowers and closed his eyes for a moment.

Being near Rhona MacLeod was agony. She'd ensnared him, dug her thorns deep into his flesh. Standing close to her for a few moments had been both pleasure and pain.

He heaved in a deep breath, opened his eyes, and followed Rhona out of the garden. Sparring with her tomorrow would be sweet torture.

He could hardly wait.

Chapter Two

A Man's World

"YE WILL HAVE to choose a husband sooner or later, lass. Don't make me choose one for ye."

Malcolm, clan-chief of the MacLeods, glared at his daughter before spearing a leg of roast fowl with a knife. Next to him, his wife, Una, cast her husband a reproachful look. She'd been trying to get him to eat less of late. He was a big, bearded man with a wild mane of greying auburn hair. At fifty winters the clan-chief's girth was increasing with each year; over the past few months, gout had pained him terribly.

"Aye, Da," Rhona replied, favoring him with a contrite smile, "but let it not be Dughall MacLean. The man's a brute."

She was merely trying to appease him. Rhona had no intention of wedding anyone. She'd seen nothing of marriage in her twenty winters to make her want to shackle herself to a man. Her mother had died many years earlier, yet Rhona remembered how oppressed she'd been, how Malcolm MacLeod's word was law in all things. Her father treated his second wife no differently, although Una didn't seem as cowed as her mother had been.

Beside Rhona her elder sister, Caitrin, shifted uncomfortably on the wooden bench, a hand straying to her swollen belly. Next to Caitrin, the youngest of the three sisters, Adaira, bowed her head. Her silky brown hair fell across one cheek, her mouth twitching as she fought a smile.

"Most men are brutes," Caitrin murmured, censure in her sea-blue eyes. "I wish ye well finding one that isn't."

Rhona's gaze narrowed. "Those are fine words coming from a wedded woman with a bairn on the way."

Caitrin's gaze held hers a moment before dropping to the trencher of pottage before her. Rhona continued to watch Caitrin, her own frown deepening. Her sister would never have said such a thing if her husband, Baltair, had been present.

Fortunately for them all, he was away hunting, and Caitrin—who was heavy with bairn—had come to live in Dunvegan until after the birth. Once the child was born, she would return home to the MacDonald's broch, Duntulm, which lay upon the northern coast of the isle.

Caitrin's situation was just another reason why Rhona had no intention of choosing a husband.

Her sister had changed since wedding Baltair MacDonald two years earlier. It was as if a light had gone out within her; she seemed so distant these days.

"What kind of man would sway ye then, sister?" Adaira asked, observing Rhona over the rim of a cup of wine, her hazel eyes mischievous. "Must he be handsome, strong, or kind?"

At the head of the table, their father snorted. "Spare me the witless chatter of women."

This comment drew a snort of laughter from his son, Iain. Like his daughters, Iain was born of his first wife, who had died when Rhona was eight. He'd just reached his sixteenth summer and had recently developed a sneering attitude toward his elder sisters.

Rhona cast her brother and father a withering look before her attention shifted to her stepmother. Una was a beauty with clear skin, sharp blue eyes, and raven hair. She'd once been the wife of the chieftain of the Frasers of

Skye. Ever since she'd left her first husband for Malcolm MacLeod, there had been a rift between the two clans. Una was now favoring her husband with a simpering smile, as if he had not just insulted her sex.

Rhona gritted her teeth. She hated that it was a man's world, and that women like Una would play down their own cleverness to flatter their husbands' egos.

I'll not wed.

Picking up her cup of sloe wine, Rhona took a sip. They sat at a long table in the Great Hall. The chieftain's table took pride of place at one end, next to a hearth set into the wall. Even now, in summer, a log burned—for inside the thick walls of Dunvegan Keep the air was always cool and damp.

Above them rose a ceiling of wooden rafters, like the ribcage of a great beast, blackened with smoke. This was the grandest space in the keep, but this evening Rhona felt constrained by it.

Caitrin with her sad eyes, and Adaira with her headful of girlish fancies.

Una with her smug smile.

Iain with his smirk.

Rhona's father with his insistence that his daughters be bred like sows.

I should have been born a man.

Rhona's gaze shifted across the hall then, gliding over the tables where kin and her father's warriors ate their supper. The rumble of voices was like the sound of the surf on a shingle shore. Her gaze alighted on Taran, seated at the far end of one of the tables. Even at meal times, he was still clad in his mail shirt—ready to serve her father at a moment's notice.

He might have been scarred and ugly, but she envied him.

No one insisted *he* wed or bore sons. Taran MacKinnon was free to live as he pleased.

"Show me how to free myself from a man's grip."

"What, like Dughall had ye in yesterday?"

"Aye—I need to know how to break a hold."

Taran raised an eyebrow. "I thought ye wanted to practice at swordplay?"

Rhona shook her head, favoring him with a slow smile. "Not today. We've done that for years. I want to be able to fight without a sword or a dagger in my hand."

The pair of them stood in the training yard—a small area wedged in between the stables and the armory. Stained and pitted grey walls reared up around them, and a blue sky full of racing clouds stretched overhead. There was no one else about, Rhona had made sure of it, choosing the time when most folk would be eating their noon meal.

Like Taran, Rhona was dressed in a mail shirt today over a léine—a loose tunic that reached the knee. She had swapped her kirtle for a pair of braies and long boots, while her long hair was pulled back in a thick braid.

Taran found the sight distracting.

"Aye ... very well," he replied after a pause. Truthfully, he wasn't that keen to give her such a lesson. MacLeod wouldn't be pleased to learn that his daughter was being taught to brawl.

On the other hand, he rarely had the opportunity to be in such proximity to Rhona, or to touch her.

He approached the young woman, stopping before her so that they stood only two feet apart. "Grab me then ... like Dughall did with ye."

Rhona nodded, her lovely features tensing with concentration. She had a proud face, with high cheekbones and a slight cleft in her chin. However, it was her storm-grey eyes that caught his attention: large and limpid with long lashes.

Rhona reached out with her right hand, her fingers fastening around his left forearm. Taran inwardly cursed the leather bracer that prevented their skin from coming into contact.

"He held me like this," she explained, "and then he yanked me against him." Taran felt a tug at his arm, but he did not budge.

She frowned, huffing out a breath. "Clearly, I'm not as strong as him."

Taran smiled. "Strength will only get ye so far—agility and flexibility are just as important."

He watched her frown ease. "Really?"

"Aye ... yer mistake yesterday was to give him time. The first rule is to act quickly."

Her mouth curved, an expression that made him grow still. "So, what should I have done?"

He raised a foot, nudging her in the shin with his toe. "Kick first." He then raised the hand she held, turning the palm toward him. "Then do this ... as if ye are trying to read yer palm. See how it makes yer wrist twist and exposes the underside of yer hand?"

Rhona nodded, her gaze shifting to where she still gripped his forearm.

"Now reach under and around the arm that's caught and catch yer attacker's hand ... like this."

His fingers hooked over the heel of her hand, and the warmth and smoothness of her skin made his breathing catch. Forcing himself to concentrate, Taran stepped back from her, rotating his body in an arc while twisting her wrist.

Rhona lurched sideways, stumbling as she nearly lost her footing.

He favored her with a tight smile, trying to ignore the feel of her hand in his. "There ... easy."

Rhona gave an unladylike snort before righting herself and releasing him. "For ye, maybe ... ye are three times my size."

"I told ye before—size makes no matter. If ye move fast and loose like that, ye can bring any man down."

Her eyes lit up, her full lips stretching into a wicked smile. "Can *I* try?"

Taran nodded. "Ready?"

"Aye ... grab me."

Her words, said with earnest ignorance, made his pulse quicken. How often had he dreamed of doing just that?

Taran stepped forward, catching hold of her arm and holding tight. He thought he might have to remind Rhona of the moves—yet before he knew it, she kicked him hard in the shin. She then twisted, raised her palm, and took hold of the meat of the hand that held her. An instant later she pivoted like a dancer.

Taran, caught off guard by her swiftness, pitched forward and fell to his knees.

Male laughter rang out across the training yard, and Taran glanced up to see his friend Gordon leaning up against the armory door, observing them. The warrior's swarthy face was creased in amusement, his dark eyes twinkling.

"I never thought I'd see the day Taran MacKinnon would be brought to his knees by a maid."

Rhona glanced up and grinned. "Did ye see that, Gordon?"

"Aye ... impressive, Lady Rhona."

Taran rose to his feet. "Just teaching Lady Rhona some tricks, should any of her suitors take liberties."

The mirth left Gordon's face. "A fine idea, although I'd not let MacLeod know about this."

Or of the many sword-fighting lessons I've given her over the years, Taran thought grimly. MacLeod would skin him alive if he ever found out. It would have been worth it though, for Taran had cherished every moment he'd spent with Rhona.

"Don't worry," Rhona replied with an airy wave. "I never tell him ... and I hope the pair of ye won't either."

She turned to Taran then, those luminous eyes fixing upon him in a way that made his chest constrict.

Lord, how he wanted her. And yet he knew it was hopeless. She would never see him differently.

"Teach me more," she said, her mouth curving. "I want to learn it all."

Chapter Three

Too Far

"HOLD STILL, LADY Rhona ... I've nearly finished."

Rhona loosed an irritated breath, waiting while her hand-maid completed the final touches to her hair. She hated sitting still, especially when she felt agitated.

"There, milady." Liosa stepped back, admiring the cascade of curls and braids she'd painstakingly created. "All done."

The hand-maid, whom she and Adaira shared, looked so pleased with herself that Rhona forced herself to smile. "Thank ye, Liosa," she murmured. "That will be all ... Adaira can help me with everything else."

"Aye, milady." Liosa bounced in a curtsey, still smiling, and bustled off.

Rhona waited until the hand-maid had left the chamber, the heavy door thudding shut, before she sighed and glanced down at the silver-grey kirtle she'd chosen for today. She'd hoped the color would appear drab on her. But from the dreamy way Adaira was gazing at her, she guessed the gown had the opposite effect.

The sisters stood in the small bower they shared: a square stone room with a hearth at one end and a tiny window that looked north over the sparkling waters of Loch Dunvegan. They'd once shared this bower with

Caitrin too before she'd wed—the three of them tucked up together in the large bed, keeping each other awake at night with stories and teasing.

"Ye look breathtaking," Adaira breathed. Her sister's heart-shaped face was solemn. "I wish I was tall like ye. It must feel liberating to be able to meet a man's eye."

Rhona huffed. "Aye, although not all of them like it."

"What do ye mean?"

"Most men like to be able to look down upon a woman ... makes them feel powerful."

Adaira's brow furrowed. "I'm sure they aren't all the beasts ye make them out to be."

Rhona favored Adaira with an arch look. "And ye'd have the experience to know?"

Adaira lifted her chin, flicking her walnut-colored hair off her face. "I'll have suitors of my own soon enough."

"And for yer sake, I hope they're young and bonny ... not like the man who's been invited to eat with us today." It was impossible for Rhona to keep the sourness out of her voice. As if to punish his daughter for her stubbornness, Clan-chief MacLeod had invited the recently widowed Aonghus Budge from Islay, an isle that lay to the south of their own. Over twenty-five years her senior, Chieftain Budge was the last man in the world she wished to wed.

A gentle knock sounded on their door, and a moment later it opened to reveal Caitrin.

Their elder sister's face was pale, and she had dark circles under her eyes. Her belly—huge now—thrust out before her. She wore a loose, tent-like kirtle that accentuated just how big her stomach had grown over the last few weeks. Rhona was no midwife, yet she guessed her sister's time was near.

"Are ye ready?" Caitrin asked with a wan smile. "Da awaits."

Rhona's nostrils flared. No, she wasn't ready—and she never would be. Yet Caitrin didn't deserve the sharp edge of her tongue. Neither did Adaira. The pair of them weren't to blame for today, so Rhona merely nodded.

The aroma of roast goose and the less savory smell of cabbage, turnip, and onion pottage greeted Rhona as she led the way into the Great Hall, her sisters following close behind her. Servants carried out baskets of bread and wheels of cheese to the table; while others circled with ewers, pouring wine, ale, and mead. A lad sat next to one of the huge hearths that dominated either end of the hall and played a small harp. The happy tune didn't match Rhona's mood.

Usually, she looked forward to feasts such as these—roast goose was one of her favorite meats—but not today. Her stomach had closed. She had no appetite.

The rumble of conversation stopped when Rhona appeared. She made her way down the hall and along the aisle between the rows of tables, head held high. No one here would know how she dreaded this feast.

Her father watched her approach, as did the man seated to his right: Aonghus Budge.

The chieftain of the Budges of Islay rose to his feet, his thick lips curving into a smile. "Lady Rhona, ye have grown into a lovely lass."

Rhona forced a smile in return and curtsied. "Good day, Chieftain Budge."

She took her seat at the table, thankfully across from her suitor rather than next to him.

"Aye, Rhona's the image of my mother as a lass," Malcolm MacLeod boomed, reaching for a cup of wine. "She has the same red hair and wild temperament. It takes a rare man to tame such a woman ... yet my father did."

Rhona inhaled sharply and dropped her gaze to the empty platter before her. She hated it when her father spoke of her in such terms.

"A strong-willed girl like Rhona needs an equally strong man." Her stepmother, Una, spoke up. "A soft-hearted, weak husband would ruin her."

"Ye need not worry there," Aonghus Budge assured the clan-chief's wife, his attention still fixed upon Rhona. "I know how to handle a woman."

Rhona ground her teeth. *Aye—and I've seen how ye do.*

She remembered the soft blonde woman he'd once been wedded to. They'd visited Dunvegan around five summers earlier for Lammas—a feast that took place late in the summer, which heralded the harvest. Rhona recalled seeing the poor woman voice an opinion during the meal, she couldn't remember what about, and the way Aonghus had backhanded his wife across the face in reply.

Rhona glanced up, her gaze traveling to her suitor. He watched her under heavy lids, his florid face flushing further under her scrutiny. Like her father, he'd been strong and muscular as a younger man, yet at forty-three winters he was now growing fat. A flaccid, high-colored face ran into a short, thick neck. The ring-encrusted hand that grasped his cup of ale was blunt and coarse with grime-edged fingernails.

Rhona's bile rose. She would never let him near her. She'd sink a knife into her breast first. If her father thought to soften her attitude, this wasn't the way to go about it. More than ever she felt determined to avoid the trap that had brought many a woman misery.

The feast began, and Rhona picked at her meal. Her body had drawn taut like a bowstring as she waited for the arrow to fly. Sooner or later her suitor would bring up the subject of marriage.

Aonghus had just begun his third cup of ale when he did. "Lady Rhona ... ye will have heard that I was widowed this past winter?"

Rhona looked up, her gaze meeting his. "Aye ... and how did yer wife die?"

A shadow moved in the depths of Aonghus Budge's blue eyes. The question was impertinent, for she already knew the answer—all of Skye did. However, she continued to hold his gaze. *Good.* The sooner he realized she would make him a poor wife the better.

"She took a fall," he said after a long pause. "Down the tower stairs ... and broke her neck. God rest her soul."

Rhona pursed her lips. *Poor woman.* What hell she must have endured as this man's wife.

"As I was saying." Aonghus started again, undeterred. "I am widowed ... and in need of a wife. I'm looking for a strong, hardy woman to bear me plenty of sons. I think ye will suit me well."

Rhona clenched her jaw so hard it hurt. Her fingers tightened around the cup of wine before her. How she wished to throw it in his face. "No ... I won't suit ye at all."

Silence fell at the chieftain's table.

Everyone went still, even the servants who had been moving from feaster to feaster, refilling cups, halted their passage. Either side of Rhona, Caitrin and Adaira paled. Caitrin dropped her gaze to the table, while Adaira's eyes grew huge and frightened.

"Excuse me?" Aonghus broke the hush, his gravelly voice now harsh. "What did ye say?"

An angry breath rushed out of Rhona, a red haze obscuring her vision. Enough. She was tired of this mummery. She'd not be trapped or forced to wed this man. She'd hid her true feelings long enough.

"Ye heard me," she growled. Her heart started to race then. She was bold, yet knew when she'd taken things too far.

"Rhona." Una's voice lashed across the table. "How dare ye speak to our guest so. Apologize. Now."

Rhona ignored her stepmother. The woman didn't have—nor would she ever have—any authority over her.

Instead, Rhona held Aonghus Budges's eye—aware that next to him, her father had turned the color of liver. "I will not wed ye, Aonghus Budge—not now, not ever."

"Ye have gone too far this time, wench. Ye insulted our guest and shamed me in front of my hall ... my kin."

Rhona stood before her father, inside his solar. They were alone. He'd summoned her there directly after the feast had ended. A large room with south-facing windows, the solar had a great hearth in one corner with a stag's head mounted above it. Thick furs covered the floor, and richly detailed tapestries depicting hunting scenes hung from the pitted stone walls.

Meeting Malcolm's eye, Rhona tensed. He hadn't raised a hand to her since childhood, yet she feared he might now. His legs were braced, his bulky body hunched, and his hands were fisted by his sides. His face still had a dangerously high color.

"Da ... I—"

"Silence!" He advanced on Rhona, towering over her. Even growing old and fat, he was still an imposing man who dominated any space he occupied. Sometimes Rhona forgot just how tall her father was. But she didn't now.

"I've spoiled ye ... indulged ye," he choked out the words, "and this is how ye repay me. Ye made a fool of me today, Rhona, and I'll not have it."

"But I—"

"Still yer tongue." He grabbed Rhona by the shoulders, pinning her to the spot. "I will not hear another word."

Rhona swallowed and heeded him. Her father was not a man to tangle horns with.

"Aonghus Budge will not have ye now," he growled. "Ye have offended his pride and put my relationship with him at risk."

The news caused a wave of relief to crash over Rhona. She would weather her father's displeasure if it meant she would be free of Chieftain Budge. However, she was careful not to let joy show on her face. Her father would not thank her—not in his current mood

"Aye, ye have spurned yet another suitor," Malcolm continued, "but this will be the last time ye do."

Rhona stared at him, a chill replacing the relief of moments earlier. What did he mean by that?

Malcolm MacLeod pushed his face close to hers. His breath stank of wine, and his grey eyes had turned flinty. "At Mid-Summer this year I will hold games outside this keep," he continued. "Men from all over this isle, and beyond, will be called upon for yer hand." He paused here, perhaps noting his daughter's suddenly strained expression, the horror on her face. Grim victory lit in his eyes as he finished. "Ye shall wed the winner."

Chapter Four

What News of My Wife?

"MY LIFE IS over." The words burst out of Rhona, brittle and choked. She stared out the window at the windswept hills to the south, beyond the gardens.

"Nonsense," came Caitrin's gentle reply. Her gaze was shadowed as she observed Rhona. "Yer life is just beginning. Ye don't know who will win yer hand. He might be a man ye could grow to love."

The two sisters sat opposite each other in what had once been their mother's solar. It was an airy chamber decorated with plaid cushions and bouquets of dried heather. Heavy floral tapestries covered the damp stone walls. Rhona had a basket of wool at her feet that she was supposed to be spinning, while Caitrin worked upon a tiny tunic for the coming bairn.

Rhona tore her eyes from the view and cast her sister a withering look. "Ye sound like Adaira," she replied, not bothering to dilute her scorn. "I don't want to be trapped, dominated … treated like a dog."

Caitrin heaved in a deep breath and leaned back in her chair, wincing slightly as she adjusted her position. Her face appeared strained; the babe did not sit easily in her belly and often seemed to cause her discomfort. "Ye will have to become a wife one day, Rhona," she pointed out after a pause. "There's no use continuing to fight it."

Rhona's mouth thinned. She didn't want to argue with her sister, but she completely disagreed with her. Why should she wed? Men could choose, so why not her?

She favored Caitrin with a narrow look. "Are ye pleased ye wed?"

Her sister tensed, and for a moment, Rhona regretted her bitter words. She knew Caitrin wasn't happy. Often she would see the melancholy in her sister's eyes, that faraway look when she thought no one was looking. She'd wed Baltair, the chief of the MacDonalds of Duntulm, two years earlier—and had rarely smiled since.

"Happy enough," Caitrin replied, her voice dull. She glanced away then. "I chose Baltair ... no one forced me to wed him."

Rhona watched her. Curiosity rose within her. There was a weight of things unsaid in her sister's expression, her soft voice. Rhona realized then that Caitrin had never really confided in her.

"Do ye suffer?" she asked, forgetting her own misery for a moment. "Is Baltair cruel to ye?"

She watched her sister's tension increase. Her lovely face tightened, and her gaze shuttered. "He's my *husband*," she replied, her voice barely above a whisper. "I'm luckier than a lot of women."

Rhona frowned. "That's no answer, Caitrin."

Her sister's blue eyes flashed in a rare show of irritation. "What do ye want me to say?" she challenged. "That he beats me nightly, that he belittles me at every chance? Would that please ye?"

Rhona stared back at her. "No," she replied, her voice subdued. "Of course not."

"Then don't pry ... ye might not like what ye hear."

Caitrin's face twisted suddenly. With a gasp, she dropped her embroidery onto her lap and clutched at her lower belly. A moment later she hissed a curse—one that Rhona had only ever heard her father's men use in the training yard. Certainly not the sort of thing her beautiful sister would utter.

"Caitrin ... what's wrong?" Rhona kicked her basket of wool aside and knelt before her sister, grasping her ice-cold hands.

Caitrin glanced up, face strained, eyes wide. "The bairn ... I think it's time."

Heart pounding, Rhona launched herself to her feet. "Adaira!" she bellowed, knowing that their sister was resting in the bower next door. "Fetch the midwife!"

The birth was a difficult one. Caitrin struggled for the rest of the day and the entire night that followed. Her grunts and cries filtered down through all levels of the keep, and when the midwife told her she should bear the pain more stoically, Caitrin screamed obscenities at her.

Although Rhona wasn't the type of lass to be shocked by cursing, hearing such words uttered by her sister made her wince. It worried her too, for Caitrin seemed in such agony. Sweat poured down her red cheeks. Her eyes were wide and desperate.

During the long night that followed, Rhona and Adaira didn't leave Caitrin's side. Eventually, Adaira succumbed to fatigue, slumping in the narrow wooden chair beside her sister's bed. However, Rhona remained awake. Her eyes burned, her shoulders ached, and yet she stayed at Caitrin's side, gripping her hand tightly when the next onslaught of birthing pains attacked her.

As dawn approached, the gaps between them shortened. Caitrin was almost delirious with pain, her breathing coming in gasps.

"Breathe deeply, Lady Caitrin," the midwife admonished her. "S-l-o-w-l-y."

Caitrin cast her a malevolent look, although she did not curse at her this time. She had long since lost the strength to abuse the poor woman. She was too tired.

"Just a short while longer." Rhona urged as Caitrin's fingers clenched around hers. Her sister squeezed so tightly that Rhona heard the bones in her hands creak. But she didn't cry out. Caitrin needed her to be strong.

"I can't," Caitrin choked out the words, tears streaming down her face. "I'm so tired. I can't take—" Her voice choked off as another wave of pain assailed her.

"Ye will," Rhona replied, fear turning her voice fierce. "Ye must."

Their gazes met and held. At that moment Rhona forgot about her own unhappy situation, about the games that loomed in just a couple of weeks. At that moment, she would have happily agreed to wed the odious Aonghus Budge if it would have kept her sister safe.

"Come, Caitrin," Rhona said, her tone pleading now. "Don't think of the pain, don't think about how tired ye are … just think of the bairn inside ye. It must be born. Once this is over the pain will stop."

Caitrin's fingers clenched around hers. "Stay with me, Rhona," she gasped. Her face was flushed, her mouth tight with pain. "Don't leave me."

"I'll never leave ye," Rhona replied. Her vision blurred, and her chest ached from the love she felt for her sister. "I'm right here at yer side, and I always will be."

A tiny wailing babe was born as the first ribbons of violet and gold decorated the eastern sky. The lusty sound of his cries filled the birthing chamber. His small, red face was scrunched up and angry.

Caitrin sobbed with relief and sank back on the pillows.

"Ye did it." Adaira was weeping as she clutched her sister's hand. "He's so beautiful, Cate. Ye are so clever."

Beautiful. To Rhona, the babe looked anything but. Covered in blood and birthing fluid, he wasn't a comely sight. However, Caitrin did not appear to mind. Her face was a picture of joy as the midwife wrapped the bairn in a soft woolen shawl and handed him to her.

"What will ye name him?" Adaira asked, scrubbing at the tears that still trickled down her cheeks.

"I don't know," Caitrin murmured. "Baltair wanted him named after his father ... Eoghan."

"And where is yer husband?" Rhona huffed, casting a look at the midwife who had sent for him as soon as she'd realized Caitrin was going into labor. The woman, whose face now sagged with exhaustion, returned her look. "He was hunting some distance away, Lady Rhona. He's probably riding here as we speak."

"He shouldn't be away from her ... not when his wife is heavy with child," Rhona pointed out.

She looked away from the midwife, to where Caitrin held the babe in her arms, gazing down at its face with a look of adoration. Caitrin didn't appear to care that Baltair wasn't here.

She hadn't asked after him once during the long labor.

Rhona stepped out into the bailey and stretched her tired back. She really should go to bed, and yet after such a fraught night, she found she'd now reached the point where she was over-tired. She was also ravenously hungry and would soon go down to the kitchens and get cook to fix her something. She'd missed supper the night before and breakfast too.

A blustery bright morning greeted her. The air was sultry, although clouds scudded across the pale blue sky and the wind blew dust devils across the courtyard. Rhona yawned and pushed her hair out of her eyes. The sun felt warm on her skin, and she turned her face up to it.

The bailey was a hive of industry this morning. Men were shoeing horses in the far corner, the tang of hot iron filtering across the yard, while others unloaded barrels off a cart that had just trundled into the keep. A servant was bringing up a pail of water from the well near the Sea-gate.

Meanwhile, two warriors sparred with wooden swords to the left of the steps leading into the keep. Rhona found her gaze drawn to them.

It was Taran and his friend Gordon. Stripped to the waist, the two men moved around each other, attacking and parrying. Curious, Rhona's gaze settled upon Taran's torso. She'd never seen him shirtless before and was surprised to see that his chest and back weren't scarred like his face.

In fact, the opposite was true.

Gordon had a lithe, strong body, but Taran's was broad, sculpted, and quite beautiful. Rhona watched, fascinated. The muscles in his back clenched and flexed as he moved. Although he was a big man, there wasn't an ounce of fat on him either; his bulk was all muscle.

Realizing she was staring, Rhona tore her gaze away. Fatigue had turned her witless this morning.

"Good morning, Lady Rhona," Taran called out. He'd seen her and stepped back from Gordon. He now regarded her with that calm, direct look she'd come to know well. "How are Lady Caitrin and the bairn faring?"

Rhona favored him with a tired smile. She appreciated him asking after Caitrin. "They're both well, thank ye … although my sister is drained."

A frown creased Taran's brow. He opened his mouth to reply but paused as the thunder of hooves interrupted him. Rhona glanced away to the Sea-gate, where a man upon a lathered horse had just ridden in. She drew in a sharp breath, her gaze narrowing.

Baltair MacDonald had finally arrived.

Drawing the beast up short, he leaped off its back and threw the reins to a lad who'd emerged from the stables.

Without a word of thanks, he then turned on his heel and strode toward the keep.

Nearby, Taran and Gordon didn't resume their sword practice. Instead, they tracked the newcomer's progress across the courtyard.

Rhona also watched him approach. Baltair MacDonald was a handsome man, it couldn't be denied.

Tall with long dark hair that flowed over his broad shoulders, he had chiseled features and peat-brown eyes.

Yet the man held an arrogance that grated upon Rhona. He'd always treated her and Adaira as if they were inconsequential. Baltair's attention alighted briefly upon her now, his expression coldly dismissive when he stopped before her. "What news of my wife?"

Rhona regarded him, unsmiling. "She has given ye a son," she replied coolly. "The babe was born but a short while ago."

Something flickered across Baltair MacDonald's face, although it was difficult to ascertain exactly what. Perhaps she had glimpsed joy in those dark eyes. It was so fleeting she might have mistaken it.

Not bothering to thank Rhona for the news, Baltair mounted the steps, brushing past her. "Where is she?"

"In the tower chamber."

She glanced over her shoulder, watching his retreating back, and wondered—not for the first time— why her sister had ever wed such a man.

Chapter Five

Interrupted by the Shrew

"HOW IS YER sister this morning?"

Rhona glanced up from where she was spreading butter on a slice of bannock. Her gaze met her father's. "Much better ... she ate a good supper last night, and her color is much improved."

Malcolm MacLeod nodded, his face relaxing a little, although beside him Una sniffed. "Caitrin is too delicate to bear many children," she said with an expression that Rhona found patronizing. "She takes after her mother."

Rhona tensed at this. She hated it when Una mentioned her mother. Martha MacLeod had died many years ago, yet Una held a strange jealousy toward the chieftain's first wife.

It seemed that Malcolm shared his daughter's view, for he cast Una an irritated look. "Martha bore four bairns without problems," he reminded his wife. "It was not childbirth that ended her ... but a fever."

Una's full mouth pursed at this, and Rhona waited for an acerbic reply. However, none came.

Malcolm reached for his fourth wedge of bannock—a large flat cake made with oatmeal and cooked upon an iron griddle. He then slathered it thickly with butter and heather honey.

"So I hear yer fiery Rhona is to be wed?" An amused male voice interrupted.

Baltair MacDonald sat farther down the table, his hands clasping a cup of fresh goat's milk.

Rhona cast him a swift, dark look, but he merely smirked. From the look on his face, he'd brought the subject up to cause trouble.

"Aye," Malcolm replied with his mouth full. He broke off a piece of bannock and fed it to the wolfhound that sat expectantly at his feet. "I've sent word out—and men from all over the isle, and beyond, have answered."

Rhona's belly cramped at this news, and she swallowed her mouthful of food without enjoyment.

"Even the Frasers?" Baltair asked, a smirk still upon his handsome face. "Surely not?"

MacLeod's face grew thunderous, while Una pursed her lips and cast Baltair a censorious look. Rhona watched a muscle bunch in her father's cheek. Even the mention of the name 'Fraser' was enough to put him in a sour mood. Of late, the Fraser chieftain had been mischief-making: hunting in MacLeod lands, denying travelers passage through his territory, and even refusing to trade with his neighbors.

"No, not them," Malcolm MacLeod growled. "If just one Fraser dares venture here for the games, I'll have him stoned out of Dunvegan."

"I wonder how many warriors will come," Una spoke up, her voice overly bright as she sought to change the subject. "Many have already left to fight at the king's side for the glory of Scotland. There may be few left who are free to travel here to win Rhona's hand."

Malcolm favored his wife with an irritated look. However, her words had managed to distract him from thoughts of his arch-enemy. "The glory of Scotland, indeed," he rumbled. "It's time we took back what is ours. The English think we've gone soft, but we'll show those arrogant bastards."

Baltair snorted in agreement at this, and MacLeod turned his attention to the MacDonald chieftain. "Have ye heard from yer brother? He fights for King David now, does he not?"

"Aye," Baltair grunted. "With the English sailing south to fight the French, he believes our time grows near. David will strike within the next few months."

Malcolm nodded, his brow furrowing. "The timing for the games isn't ideal," he admitted. "But my Rhona's a bonny lass ... I'm sure a good number will turn up on the day. Besides, we only need one winner."

"It was a clever idea," Baltair replied. "If the lass won't choose a husband, take matters into yer own hands." He still wasn't looking Rhona's way, as if she was beneath his notice.

Rhona inhaled deeply, her anger rising. Was it any wonder she wished to remain unwed? There were far too many men upon the isle like Baltair MacDonald—men who believed a woman was of no use at all, except for cooking, sewing, and swiving.

"Rhona may find a good husband this way," Una replied with a cool smile. "Better than she deserves."

"Rhona deserves a man as strong and brave as her," Adaira piped up from where she sat next to Rhona. "At least this way, they get to fight for her hand."

Rhona cast her sister a quelling glance, but Adaira was not looking at her. Instead, she was glaring at Una, her face uncharacteristically fierce. A rush of affection flowed through Rhona.

Her sister looked particularly lovely when riled. Her hazel eyes had almost darkened to green, and her mouth had set in determination.

Una huffed in response although she made no reply.

"And what of ye, Adaira?" Baltair asked. "Surely ye too want to wed?"

Rhona watched the way her brother-in-law gazed at Adaira and felt her hackles rise. Whereas he made a point of ignoring Rhona, he stared boldly at Adaira this morning. His voice, usually rough, was as smooth as cream.

"I will," Adaira replied, suddenly going all meek and flustered under his gaze. She looked down at her half-eaten bannock. "Once Rhona has found a husband."

"The sooner the better," Malcolm cut in, brushing crumbs off his broad chest. "All this talk of suitors and handfastings makes me weary. Sons are far less trouble."

No one at the table replied to that, although Rhona saw her brother, Iain's, chest puff up at the compliment. She also noted that Baltair still watched Adaira, a wolfish gleam in his eyes.

"Have ye heard? Caitrin wasn't the only one to give birth in the keep yesterday," Adaira hurried after Rhona as they left the Great Hall. "Milish has had a litter of pups!"

Despite her now waspish mood, Rhona found herself smiling. "Has she?" Milish was a wolfhound bitch—a matriarch that ruled the pack of dogs her father kept.

"Taran has Milish and the pups in one of the stables," Adaira replied with a grin. "I'll take ye to them."

"Go on then." Rhona's smile widened. "Lead the way."

The young women left the keep and descended the steps into the bailey. Adaira called out cheerfully to servants and guards as she passed by, and they acknowledged her in turn with smiles and waves. It didn't surprise Rhona how popular her sister was—for she had a warm smile and kind word for most folk. However, her sister's open, trusting nature sometimes worried Rhona.

As it had earlier.

The look Baltair had given her sister was alarming; Rhona wondered if she should warn Adaira about him.

Warn her of what?

A bold stare wasn't forbidden—and it seemed that Rhona was the only one at the table who had noticed or cared. Adaira would tell her she was being a goose. Maybe it was best to keep her observations to herself.

They found Milish with her litter in a straw-lined stable. The bitch wore a serene expression as six small bodies wriggled against her teats, their eyes screwed shut.

Rhona knelt down next to the hound, stroking her grizzled muzzle. "Haven't ye done well, lass?"

"Aren't they beautiful?" Adaira's eyes gleamed with tears as she gently picked up one of the pups and cradled it against her breast. "So tiny and defenseless."

"Not for long they won't be." A male voice intruded. Rhona glanced up to see Taran looming in the stable doorway. "Soon they'll be yipping, fighting, and causing no end of trouble. Enjoy the peace while it lasts."

Rhona smiled. She knew Taran's grumblings were just a ruse—for it was he who was in charge of her father's hounds. She'd seen the bond he shared with them.

"Can I have one, Taran?" Adaira asked, turning to him. She still clutched the puppy. It was a fat-bellied creature with tufted grey fur.

The Beast of Dunvegan gave a rare smile. It softened those disfiguring scars and made him appear younger. Rhona realized then that she had no idea how old Taran was. She had thought him at least thirty, yet now realized he was younger than that.

"Ye will need to ask yer father, Lady Adaira," he replied, leaning against the door frame and folding his arms across his chest. "But if he agrees then, aye—ye may have one."

Adaira beamed at him. She then turned and carefully placed the wriggly puppy back with its mother. "I shall ask him now. Then I'll go and tell Caitrin about the puppies."

"Tell Caitrin, I'll be up soon to see her," Rhona said as her sister made for the door, cheeks flushed with excitement.

"Aye," Adaira sang, sliding past Taran and out into the sunlight. "See ye shortly."

Alone with Taran in the stables, Rhona sighed. "Adaira will love ye forever now."

He chuckled, a deep warm sound. "And she didn't before, Lady Rhona?"

Rhona gave him an arch look and rose to her feet, brushing straw off her kirtle. "Adaira thinks well of most folk ... as ye know. Sometimes it worries me."

His expression turned serious, and the Taran she was used to returned. "Why ... has something happened?"

Rhona shook her head, suddenly wishing she'd held her tongue. Taran was as loyal as the hounds he tended. Any threat to Rhona or her sisters and he became fierce.

"No ... it's just that ... sooner or later she'll be wed," Rhona replied. She looked away, her gaze dropping to the feeding puppies. Suddenly, she felt uncomfortable confiding in Taran. "I know she's a woman now, but there's something childlike about Adaira ... I won't be able to protect her anymore."

"Of course ye will."

She glanced up, meeting his gaze.

"Ye have heard about the games?"

He nodded. "Ye are displeased?"

Rhona snorted, not caring that the sound was unladylike. "I'm livid ... but Da doesn't care. I'm just a problem he wants dealt with."

The warrior's face tensed, and she thought for a moment he would reply. However, silence stretched between them, and he broke her gaze. There wasn't really anything he could say, she supposed. Taran was her father's man—and he would never speak against him.

"I'd better go," she said briskly. "Caitrin will be waiting for me."

Taran nodded and stepped back to let her pass. "Good day, Lady Rhona."

Rhona moved past him before stopping. She turned back, her gaze snaring his. "Don't think this is going to turn me into some feeble, sniveling wench," she told him firmly. "I still want to continue our training."

His mouth curved, making his scars alter shape. "Of course, Lady Rhona ... when is our next meeting?"

Rhona smiled back. "Tomorrow at dawn."

Rhona left the stables and stalked back into the keep, taking the stairwell steps two at a time.

She wasn't sure why, but Taran MacKinnon sometimes made her feel uncomfortable. He was a man who said little, yet she often found herself wondering what he really thought. Over the years he'd become a friend of sorts, and yet she knew little about the man beneath the scars and the chainmail.

Was there more to him than the warrior, the loyal servant?

She shook her head, dismissing the thought. What did she care? He was Taran—a man who lived to serve her family, a man who indulged her whims far too often.

It was a steep climb up to her sister's lodgings. Caitrin had given birth in the tower chamber—a large room with a view west over the glittering loch—and she would remain there for another day or two. The birth had weakened her, and she had lost a lot of blood.

As she climbed, Rhona heard a babe's lusty wail. Little Eoghan had a powerful set of lungs.

She had almost reached the landing when she heard voices: a man's low pitch, followed by a woman's soft, pleading tone.

"A bonny creature, ye are. Let's have a look at ye."

"Please ... I need to go."

"Not just yet. What's the hurry?"

"My sister is waiting. I can't—"

"Hush that sweet mouth. I have a better use for it."

Clenching her jaw, Rhona rushed up the last set of steps and launched herself onto the landing. Her gaze swept right, focusing on where Adaira cowered against the wall. Baltair MacDonald had bailed her up, using his arms to bracket her as he leaned in for a kiss.

"What's this?" Rhona hissed. She advanced on them, fists clenched at her sides.

Adaira gave a gasp of relief, ducked under Baltair's arm, and rushed to Rhona. Her face, which had been so alive with joy earlier as she'd held the puppy, now held a traumatized expression. Her eyes glittered with tears.

Baltair straightened up. His look of surprise faded, and he grinned.

"Interrupted by the shrew—how vexing."

"What were ye doing?" Rhona choked out, so angry she could barely get the words out. "Vile dog ... with yer wife and bairn just yards away!"

He arched a dark eyebrow. "Adaira and I were having a private conversation. Ye should mind yer manners, lass—and yer own business."

"This *is* my business. Ye are a guest in this keep. How dare ye corner my sister!"

"Rhona." Adaira plucked at her sleeve, her voice tight with fear. "Maybe we should—"

"Caitrin will know of this," Rhona snarled, cutting Adaira off. "As will our father."

Baltair turned to face her squarely, folding his arms across his chest. He didn't look remotely cowed by the threat. The opposite in fact. "Go on then," he challenged, favoring her with a cold smile. "I dare ye."

Chapter Six

Truth and Deception

RHONA SAT DOWN next to her sister and forced a
smile. "Ye look so much better this morning. It's good to
see some color in yer cheeks."

Caitrin, propped up against a nest of pillows, smiled
back. "I do feel better ... although I'm so tired." She
glanced down at the babe, swaddled in linen, who slept
in her arms. Rhona followed her gaze to the small head
covered in soft black hair before clenching her jaw.

Will he grow up to be like his father?

Caitrin looked up, her gaze meeting Rhona's. Her soft
smile faded. "Is something wrong? Ye are flushed." She
glanced toward the closed door. "I heard raised voices
earlier ... were ye arguing with someone?"

Rhona inhaled deeply. This was her chance. She had
only to say a few words, and Caitrin would know about
Baltair.

*What would have happened if I hadn't interrupted
him?*

The man was a foul letch, preying on Adaira just
yards from where his wife and child lay. He deserved to
be revealed. The whole keep should know what he was—

and yet when Caitrin's soft gaze rested upon her once more, Rhona found the words stuck in her throat.

Caitrin had just endured a difficult birth. Even recovering she appeared frail, exhausted.

The news would destroy her.

Rhona would feel vindicated as she told her sister, spurred on by the memory of Baltair's sneering face as he challenged her. But her victory would be short-lived. She didn't want to make Caitrin suffer.

Rhona slowly loosed the breath she'd been holding. "I was just talking to Baltair and Adaira," she replied, forcing herself not to look away as she spoke. "He wanted ye to come downstairs to the Great Hall for the noon meal, but we both insisted against it. Ye are too weak."

Caitrin sighed, leaning back against the pillows. "Thank ye, Rhona ... men can be insensitive sometimes."

Rhona bit the inside of her cheek to stop herself from replying. Baltair was far worse than that. Although she would spare Caitrin for the moment, she couldn't keep silent about this.

Someone had to know.

She would tell her father.

Malcolm MacLeod frowned at his daughter, his mouth pursing.

Rhona stood before him, as self-confident and haughty as ever. She'd been subdued for a day or two after he'd told her about the games, yet it seemed she'd rallied—especially in defense of her sister.

"Mind yer tongue, lass," he grumbled. "It's not wise to lay such accusations at a chieftain."

Rhona's jaw tensed, her grey eyes growing hard. "Just because he leads the MacDonalds of Duntulm, it doesn't make him beyond reproach. He cornered Adaira, and would have kissed her if I hadn't interrupted."

Malcolm huffed out a breath and put the quill he was holding back into the ink-pot. He was trying to write a letter—one that required a lot of concentration—and wasn't in the mood for this conversation.

"He was probably just being playful ... sometimes men do that, lass."

Rhona's face went taut, her mouth thinning. "He wasn't being playful, Da. What if he gets Adaira alone? What if he—"

"Enough," Malcolm grumbled. For the love of God. What had he ever done to deserve such a difficult daughter? He couldn't wait till she was wedded—a husband would calm her down. "Ye go too far," he continued. "Baltair has not committed any crime against yer sister. Perhaps she encouraged him? Adaira can be a flirt."

"She didn't welcome his attention," Rhona growled back. Her cheeks had gone red, and her hands were fisted at her sides.

"Ye don't know that."

"I saw her face. She was terrified of him."

Malcolm let out a gusty sigh and scratched his beard. "I'm sorry, lass, but this tale must remain between us. I can't risk bad blood with the MacDonalds, not with the Frasers sharpening their swords at our backs." His mood darkened as he spoke these words. Bile stung the back of his throat as the bannocks he'd eaten earlier repeated on him.

His daughter's gaze narrowed. "What have they done now?"

MacLeod glowered at her. "Morgan Fraser is fast becoming a thorn in my arse," he growled. "I've just received a letter from him, which I'm trying to respond to." He gestured to the sheet of parchment before him. "The piece of dung dares challenge me for lands. He's now claiming that Hamra Rinner Vale belongs to him."

His daughter's expression didn't change. She continued to watch him with that bullish look he'd come to know well over the years. "And does it?"

"No!" Spittle flew from his mouth as he boomed out the answer. "The greedy bastard knows we hunt deer on that land. They belong to me, and I'll not give them up."

Malcolm reached for a cup of milk he'd had a servant bring up. Hopefully, it would do the trick and soothe his acid stomach. "We may soon have to face off against the Frasers," he said once he'd taken a gulp, wiping his mouth with the back of his hand. "I'll not start a feud with Baltair MacDonald over something so trivial."

His daughter glared back at him, fury radiating out from her. However, he didn't care that she was angry. He'd been far too lenient with her over the years.

"This incident makes it clear to me that once ye are wed I will need to find Adaira a husband before winter arrives," he informed Rhona. "The lass dances about Dunvegan as flightily as a brownie. She'll ruin herself before long if things continue."

"I told ye before, father," Rhona ground the words out, her voice hoarse with barely suppressed temper. "Adaira was not to blame. Baltair cornered her."

Malcolm reached for his quill once more. He'd had enough of her prattle. "Keep silent about this," he warned her. "If I hear whispers of this story, I shall have ye whipped."

"But, Da—"

"Leave me now, Rhona." He waved her away. "I've a letter to write."

A grey dawn broke over Dunvegan Castle, bringing with it a misty rain. Dressed in plaid braies and a léine belted at the waist, Rhona exited the keep and walked toward the training yard.

Despite the morning's gloom, it wasn't cold. The misty rain kissed her skin, and the air smelt alive and fresh as only dawn air could. Rhona loved this time of day, the early dawn in that short time before the castle awoke. However, this morning she wasn't in the mood to enjoy it.

Her father's dismissive attitude the day before still stung. His complete lack of concern for Adaira's wellbeing enraged Rhona. All he cared about was keeping the peace with the MacDonalds. He hadn't even been able to listen to her properly, his thoughts focused instead on his petty feud with the Frasers.

Unhappiness warred with anger this morning though. She was used to her father's stubbornness. However, being dismissed by him only days after he'd made such a heavy-handed decision about her future, made Rhona feel as if he didn't care for her at all.

He just wanted her wedded and out of the way.

A man stepped out of the dawn's mist ahead—a tall, broad-shouldered figure that she'd know anywhere.

"Good morning, Lady Rhona," Taran greeted her.

"Morning," Rhona answered, her voice as lackluster as her spirits.

Taran's scarred visage tensed as he drew near. "Is something wrong?"

She shook her head. "I slept badly, that's all."

He raised an eyebrow. "We can practice another time if ye are not feeling up to it?"

"I'm well," she snapped, rolling up the sleeves of her léine. Truthfully, she needed something to distract her from her thoughts. The games were just ten days away now—the date loomed before her like an execution.

"Last time ye showed me how to break a man's hold if he grabbed my arm," she said walking past him into the training yard. "This time I want ye to show me what to do if a man catches me from behind."

"Very well," he replied, following her into the yard. "As ye wish."

Rhona stopped in the center of the yard and waited. A moment later she heard the scuff of Taran's boots as he stepped up behind her. Then his arms went around her, clasping her tight.

The contact made Rhona stifle a gasp of shock. She'd never been in such close physical contact with a man. It was a strange, unnerving sensation.

"Can ye break free?" Taran asked. His voice was gruff. He was so close that she felt his breath feather against her ear.

Rhona tried to move but found herself locked, as if in an iron cage. "No."

"If a man grabs ye like this, the first thing ye want to do is try to head-butt him in the face. Now ... throw yerself back against me and try to break my nose with the back of yer head."

Rhona smiled. "Really?"

"Aye ... try it."

Rhona arched against him and threw her head back. However, Taran shifted his head to one side to avoid the blow. "Good," he grunted. "At this point, I might try to lift ye off yer feet. There are two things ye can do to prevent this. The first is to drop as if yer legs can no longer support ye. This will turn ye into a dead weight and make it harder for me to shift ye. Or ye can hook yer foot back behind my ankle and use it to anchor yerself. Try that."

Rhona did as bid, stretching her leg back and entwining it with Taran's. However, his legs were strong, big, and muscular. It was like trying to wrap her ankle around a tree trunk.

"That's right," he replied. "Now, if I try to lift ye, I won't be able to." Taran attempted to pull her off the ground, but Rhona didn't budge. "This will give ye another chance to head-butt me ... or rip off one of my ears if ye get yer arm free."

"What the Devil are ye two up to?"

Malcolm MacLeod's deep voice boomed across the deserted yard, causing both Rhona and Taran to freeze.

Rhona glanced left to see her father bearing down on them. Even the fact he was limping slightly from his gout didn't make him any less intimidating. Two of his wolfhounds skulked at his heels, following their master into the yard.

"Da." Heat rose to Rhona's cheeks. All the times over the years she'd trained with Taran and her father had never known. He wasn't an early riser, especially of late, and Taran had sworn the servants and other warriors to secrecy. Rhona tensed—had someone betrayed them? "Ye are up early?" She tried to ignore the fact her father's eyes were bulging and his bearded face had turned the color of liver.

"I'm taking the dogs out for a hunt," he snarled, stopping before them. "What are ye doing with my daughter, MacKinnon?"

Taran let go of Rhona and stepped away from her. Rhona glanced over at him to find his face unreadable. His gaze was direct as it met her father's. "Lady Rhona bid me teach her the art of hand-to-hand combat and self-defense, Chief," he replied.

"It looked like ye were embracing her to me."

"I was showing her how to get free of a hold."

The clan-chief's attention shifted from Taran, spearing Rhona with a look she knew well. "How long has this been going on?"

Rhona swallowed but held his gaze. "A while."

"I didn't give ye permission to train my daughter, MacKinnon," her father's gaze returned to Taran. "How dare ye go behind my back."

"It's not his fault," Rhona interjected. She didn't want Taran blamed for this—let her father's wrath fall on her. He could be vicious with his warriors if they displeased him; he'd be gentler with her. "I bid him do it … made him swear to tell no one."

Malcolm MacLeod stepped close, and even though she could almost meet his eye, Rhona dropped her gaze. Dread rose within her. Would he beat her for this? She'd defied him deliberately, and she understood his anger.

"There will be no more training," MacLeod said, his voice a low, threatening growl. "Is that clear?"

Rhona nodded, desperation constricting her throat. Her one small freedom—gone.

"I didn't hear ye?" Her father bellowed in her face.

"Chief, I—" Taran began.

MacLeod cut him off. "Not another word from ye."

"Aye, Da," Rhona replied, her gaze still fixed upon the straw-flecked ground between them. "It's clear."

Chapter Seven

Caged

TARAN CLIMBED THE guard tower's circular staircase, returning to his quarters. Unlike many of the young warriors who served MacLeod, Taran didn't sleep in the barracks that took up the lower floor. Instead, his position as one of the chieftain's personal guard had earned him a chamber of his own.

Taran was grateful for that, for, after the scene in the training yard, he was in no mood for company. Reaching the third-floor landing, he strode into his chamber and shoved the door shut behind him. The noise reverberated in the stone tower.

Standing inside his private chamber—a space he'd only just vacated a short while earlier—Taran felt caged. The chamber was small, with damp stone walls and a tiny hearth at one corner, which was unlit this morning, for it was high summer. Clothing hung from hooks on the wall, and a narrow pallet lay under a tiny shuttered window.

Taran raked a hand through his short hair and ground out a low curse.

That was it—the end of his contact with Lady Rhona. He wasn't going to fool himself. He'd receive more than a tongue-lashing when MacLeod returned from taking his dogs out. However, he'd take whatever punishment came.

It had been worth it to be able to spend time with Rhona over the years. Their practice sessions had been irregular at best, yet he'd lived for them. Most of the practice had been with wooden swords, although the past two sessions—when he'd taught her how to defend herself using her hands—would remain forever in his memory.

The close contact with Rhona had been sweet torture. The feel of her body in his arms earlier had made it difficult for him to form a coherent thought. She was oblivious to the effect she had on him, oblivious to the fact he was a man at all. He should hate her for that, but he didn't. He'd never stop wanting her.

Now all of that would end.

Taran inhaled deeply. A boulder sat on his chest; he couldn't breathe. He crossed to the window and yanked open the wooden shutters.

Leaning up against the stone window ledge, Taran glared out at the misty morning. He couldn't believe that the chief had been up so early. Of late, as his gout worsened, he'd become less mobile.

Not this morning though.

Life was about to change, and not for the better. Lady Rhona was about to be taken from him.

Taran gritted his teeth and swung away from the window. *Dolt ... she wasn't yers in the first place.*

He'd been shocked to hear of the games MacLeod was going to hold. The thought of men competing for her hand made Taran feel sick. He'd always known the day of her wedding would come, but he'd imagined Lady Rhona would be allowed to choose her husband, and that it would be a man she loved. That would have made it easier to bear. He'd be miserable all the same, but he'd know that she, at least, was happy.

But the expression on her face the first time he'd seen her after the announcement—Rhona had looked as if she awaited her beheading. Her expression after the confrontation with her father in the training yard had been the same. He'd seen the despair in those storm-grey eyes, the simmering fury she dared not unleash—not in front of her father.

The walls closed in further. If he stayed here, trapped by his own thoughts, he'd go mad. Taran left his chamber, descended the steps, and departed the guard tower, crossing the mist-wreathed bailey. In the Great Hall beyond, there were still a handful of men breaking their fast, Taran's friend Gordon among them.

"There ye are." Gordon flashed him a smile as he sat down. "Ye are just in time. Connel has just finished the last of the bannocks and will scoff the rest of the bread too if ye are not quick."

The warrior in question, a heavy-set young man with a shock of straw-colored hair and a florid face, shot Gordon a dark look. Yet he couldn't answer, for his mouth was full.

Taran nodded and reached for the last chunk of bread. Truthfully, he had little appetite this morning, yet he'd only draw attention to himself if he didn't eat.

"Is something amiss?" Taran glanced up to find Gordon watching him, a shrewd look on his face. "Ye look like ye woke up to find a dog turd in yer boots."

Beside him, Connel Buchanan snorted before reaching for a mug of milk. "Happened to me once," he admitted with a grimace. "One of my father's hounds."

Gordon grinned, his gaze never leaving Taran. "We were just talking about the games," he informed him. "Connel here has thrown in his name."

Taran raised an eyebrow. "Really?"

Connel gave him a disgruntled look. "Why the shock? I've as good a chance as any man."

Gordon smirked. "I'm surprised MacLeod let ye take part. Ye are barely able to grow a beard."

Connel scowled back. "I'm old enough to take a wife." His gaze narrowed as it swept from Gordon to Taran. "Why don't ye two compete for the fair Lady Rhona?"

"My heart is already spoken for, lad," Gordon replied. "Greer won't look kindly upon me competing for the hand of another."

Gordon's reply didn't come as a surprise to Taran. Greer was the comely daughter of Dunvegan's cook. Gordon had pursued the lass tirelessly over the past year and was close to succeeding in winning her over.

Connel's gaze fixed upon Taran. "What about ye, 'Scar-face'?"

Taran didn't appreciate the younger man's tone or the sneer that went with it. But he didn't rise to the bait. He'd been belittled so often about his looks over the years that he didn't take offense. He'd have flattened the nose of nearly every man in this keep if he had. He merely fixed Connel with a cold look. "I think not."

"Why not?" Connel pressed. His gaze was challenging although the sneer faded.

Taran drew in a deep breath. "These games go against Lady Rhona's wishes," he replied. "I'll not be part of them."

Rhona stood on the steps to the bailey and watched Baltair MacDonald prepare to leave Dunvegan. A few feet away Caitrin settled herself upon a nest of cushions on a cart, babe in arms. Lady MacDonald's face pinched as she tried to get comfortable; even so, it would be a bumpy journey to the MacDonald stronghold of Duntulm in the north.

Approaching the wagon, Rhona cast Baltair a dark look. Caitrin wasn't ready to travel—she'd only given birth three days earlier. She'd lost a lot of blood and was still weak. Yet her brother-in-law was impatient to return home.

Baltair wore a sour expression this morning as he tightened his horse's girth. Observing him, Rhona wondered if her father had spoken to Baltair after all. Perhaps that was the cause of his hasty departure. Whatever the reason, it was selfish and careless of him to take Caitrin away from Dunvegan so soon.

An invisible vise gripped Rhona around her chest as she reached out and took Caitrin's hand. Her sister's fingers were thin and cold, but as always, when she looked into Caitrin's sea-blue eyes, Rhona found it difficult to read her mood. She'd previously been so open, so free with her thoughts and feelings. These days her lovely face was a mask.

Anxiety curled in the pit of Rhona's belly. Once Caitrin returned to Duntulm, she would be alone again with Baltair MacDonald.

"Please send word when ye reach Duntulm," Rhona urged, her voice low. "Let me know that ye have arrived safely and that ye are well."

Caitrin favored her with a soft smile before nodding. "I'll write ye a letter after we arrive."

Rhona swallowed an avalanche of things she longed to say. She wanted to urge Caitrin to be honest with her. She wanted to reveal Baltair's true nature publicly, right now. Here, with her father and his retainers looking on.

Malcolm had come out with Una to see his daughter off. Surely, he'd show pity if he saw Caitrin distressed, in fear for her safety. He couldn't be so hard-hearted?

But Rhona knew the truth of it in the depths of her heart. Baltair was Caitrin's lawful husband; she was no longer a MacLeod. She belonged body and soul to another man.

Rhona released her sister's hand and let her own fall to her side. She then curled her fingers into a fist, her nails cutting into her palms. Panic assailed her as she imagined herself in Caitrin's place, forced to obey a man like Baltair MacDonald.

I don't want that. I'll not be owned by a man.

"Travel well, sister." Adaira had appeared at Rhona's shoulder. She reached out and clasped Caitrin's hands with hers. "Come back to see us soon."

"I will," Caitrin assured her. "As soon as I'm strong enough and Eoghan has grown a little, I'll visit."

This comment earned Caitrin a warning glance from her husband. Holding Baltair's gaze, Caitrin's features tightened. She then looked down to where her son nestled in her arms. "I'll come as soon as I'm able," she promised softly.

With a sinking heart, Rhona wondered when she'd actually see her sister again.

"Come, wife." Baltair's voice lashed across the courtyard. "Enough prattling with yer sisters. We've got a full day's journey ahead of us."

Linking her arm through her younger sister's, Rhona guided Adaira back to the foot of the steps, where their father, step-mother, and a few retainers waited. There, they watched Baltair kick his stallion into a brisk trot, leading the way out through the Sea-gate and down the narrow causeway that wound down to the shore.

As the cart bearing Caitrin disappeared from view, Adaira gave Rhona's arm a gentle squeeze.

Rhona reached for her sister's hand and wordlessly squeezed back. She didn't trust herself to speak right now, didn't trust herself not to say things her father would punish her for. He and Una were within earshot.

Heaving a deep breath, Rhona sought to control her urge to rage. Instead, she stared at the point where Caitrin had disappeared.

Caged. She felt trapped by the stone walls of this keep, by the wishes of her overbearing father.

She could now count the days till the games on both hands. Day by day, the cage was growing smaller, the walls closing in.

She couldn't go through with this—could not passively wait for her fate. She wouldn't end up like Caitrin.

Chapter Eight

A Ready Excuse

RHONA KNEW SHE had to act quickly. With the games looming, she had to flee Dunvegan and the Isle of Skye, if she was to have any chance of escaping an unwanted marriage.

She pondered her decision for a full day after Caitrin's departure. Alone in the gardens behind the keep, she circled the beds of roses and the long avenues of lavender and rosemary, oblivious to her surroundings as she planned.

Her mother wasn't from this isle. Martha MacLeod had hailed from the mainland, from Argyle. Rhona's mother had spoken often of her home, of Gylen Castle, where her brother, Rhona's uncle, still lived now. She'd loved Gylen and had wanted to return there, one last time. Cruelly, death had come for her too swiftly.

Rhona would go there.

Her uncle still ruled Gylen, and she had a number of cousins there too. Some of them had visited over the years, and she remembered them as warm, kind folk. Rhona would find a way across the water and head south into Argyle, where she'd throw herself at their sympathies. She could instead find herself a nunnery on the mainland and take the veil, but that plan didn't appeal much. Rhona knew she didn't have the right temperament to become a nun. She was too impatient, too willful. However, if her uncle didn't welcome her, she'd have to resort to that.

The idea didn't thrill her, but at least it would be *her* choice.

The destination decided, Rhona then set about plotting how she would reach it. She would go out on a ride or a hunt and at the first opportunity slip away. Then she would ride south, to the southern village of Kyleakin, the point nearest the mainland. She had coin, a small bag of silver pennies that she had squirreled away over the years. Her father and kin had given her pennies on birthdays or at Yuletide, and whereas Caitrin and Adaira spent theirs on pretty shawls and kirtles at market, Rhona had saved hers.

It was almost as if she'd known this day would come.

She should have enough to buy passage across the water from Kyleakin to the mainland, and for a horse to carry her south after that. The only other things she needed were time, opportunity—and courage.

The thought of fleeing didn't scare her. But the realization that she would have to leave everything she knew and loved, including her sisters, made Rhona feel sick.

Who would protect Adaira with her gone? Caitrin was beyond her help, but Adaira still needed her.

And yet, the truth of it was that she would soon likely be unable to help her younger sister anyway. If she stayed and the games took place, who knew what man would win her hand? She'd heard that many warriors were coming from the mainland. It was highly likely she wouldn't even stay at Dunvegan.

"These are delicious." Rhona took a bite of twice-baked oat-cake and chewed it with gusto before favoring Greer with a smile. "I don't suppose ye could spare some?"

Greer glanced up from where she was rolling out pastry. "Of course, milady. Do ye need anything else?"

Rhona nodded. "Adaira and I are visiting Dunvegan market this morning. We thought to spread out a blanket by the loch's edge and have our noon meal there."

Greer smiled, revealing a deep dimple on one cheek. "I'll fix ye a basket then."

Comely, with thick brown hair she always wore in a long braid down her back, Greer was Rhona's age. Despite their differing rank, the two young women had always shared an easy rapport. Of late, Rhona had seen Greer spending time with Gordon MacPherson, Taran's friend. They'd danced together at Beltane, and Rhona had felt a pang of envy for the lass—not because she wanted Gordon, but because the cook's daughter was free to choose her own future.

"Hurry up then, lass." Greer's mother, Fiona— Dunvegan's cook—clicked her tongue and cast her daughter an impatient look. "Don't keep Lady Rhona waiting."

Greer dusted her hands off on her apron. "What would ye like?"

"Nothing fancy," Rhona replied, feigning casualness. She needed food that would keep well enough for her journey, but which wouldn't raise anyone's suspicions. It was two days since Caitrin's departure; Rhona couldn't risk waiting any longer. "Oat-cakes, a wedge of hard cheese, and some apples will do nicely ... and a skin of water." Rhona tensed then as Greer reached for a large wicker basket. "We're riding to the market ... so a cloth bag will be easier to carry."

The young woman nodded, no sign of suspicion on her face. Rhona was so nervous this morning that she worried others could sense it. Fortunately, unlike Adaira, she was adept at not letting her feelings show on her face for the whole world to see. Even so, involving Greer and Fiona in her plans put her on edge.

Da won't punish them, she assured herself as she watched Greer disappear into the larder to fetch the cheese and apples. *They have no idea what I'm up to.*

What am I doing? Rhona's heart pounded as she let herself into her father's solar. *How will I explain myself if I'm caught in here?*

Rhona didn't have a ready excuse, just a desperation to leave this isle—and to do that, she needed maps of Skye and the mainland.

The morning sun filtered in through the window, illuminating the dust motes that floated down from the ceiling. Servants had been in here and opened the shutters to air the chamber. It was a mild morning, yet they had laid the hearth. Even at the height of summer, this keep remained damp and cold.

Moving to her father's desk, Rhona's gaze searched the piles of parchment and the stacks of books that covered it.

She remembered then that Malcolm MacLeod kept his maps in a clay vase. Turning from the desk, she spied it sitting upon a shelf next to the MacLeod drinking horn. Rhona's heart sank when she saw that the vase was packed with scrolls; she didn't have time to sort through them all.

Fortunately, the map of Skye was the first she picked out. She quickly unscrolled it, her gaze sliding over the familiar lobster-shaped outline of the isle. The map showed the road south from Dunvegan and the various routes she could take to reach Kyleakin. Breathing quickly now, her ears straining for the sound of her father's heavy tread, Rhona rolled up the map and started rifling through the vase for one of the mainland.

Malcolm MacLeod was slow in the mornings. He rose late these days and tended to linger over his bannocks. However, his unexpected appearance at dawn in the training yard warned her not to grow complacent where her father was concerned. He was growing old and fat, but he had a mind like a whetted blade. The man missed little.

It took some searching, but at last, she found a small scroll that showed the western seaboard of the mainland, and Argyle. There, perched on the coast, was Gylen Castle.

Stuffing both scrolls up the sleeve of her kirtle, Rhona strode to the door of the solar and slowly opened it, peering out into the corridor beyond.

All clear.

Stepping out, she glanced left and right before hurrying toward the steps that led to the bower she shared with Adaira. She'd hidden a satchel under the bed with the provisions she'd gotten earlier from the kitchens. The satchel also contained her slingshot. Her father, who had taken her hunting with him when she was a child, had taught her how to use it, although these days she was likely a bit rusty. Hopefully, she'd be able to forage and hunt along the way.

Rhona had nearly reached the stairs when a tall, broad-shouldered figure stepped out of the shadows.

Swallowing a cry of fright, Rhona stopped. "Taran," she gasped, "ye gave me a fright."

"Apologies, Lady Rhona." Taran regarded her a long moment before his brow furrowed. "Ye are flushed. Is something amiss?"

Rhona shook her head and favored him with a bright smile. She'd forgotten that her father's right hand often patrolled the hallways of the keep. "I'm perfectly well, thank ye. I've just come back from a walk in the bailey."

His frown deepened. "But ye have come from the wrong direction," he pointed out.

Braving his ice-blue stare, she raised her chin. At times like these, she forgot that Taran MacKinnon had defied her father in order to train her. 'MacLeod's Hound' indeed. The suspicion in his gaze made her already fast pulse accelerate. "I visited the library too," she informed him, "... not that I need to explain myself to ye."

She was being rude, yet she couldn't let him question her further. She had to get away from Taran before he noted how she clutched the hem of her sleeve in her palm. He would know then that she'd stolen something.

Without another word, she brushed past him and hurried, stiff-backed, up the stairs. Taran let her go, although she felt the weight of his gaze between her shoulder blades until she disappeared from sight.

Chapter Nine

A Visit to Market

RHONA SWUNG UP onto the saddle and readied herself to move out.

Adjusting her skirts, she glanced down at the outfit she'd chosen for today. Preparing for departure had been tricky. It was difficult to bring anything extra with her without raising suspicion. She'd dressed carefully in a brown kirtle that was hard-wearing and good for travel. Underneath her skirts, she wore woolen leggings, essential for the long ride ahead—otherwise, the saddle would chafe her.

Nervousness thrummed through Rhona this morning. She'd hardly been able to sleep over the previous two nights as she planned her escape meticulously, going over each stage of it again and again.

Dunvegan's monthly market couldn't have come at a better time.

Rhona hadn't wanted to involve Adaira in her escape, but in the end, she realized her sister would provide the perfect cover for her. If she rode out on a hunt, her father's men would have to accompany her. It would make it much harder to slip away. Adaira, who would suspect nothing until it was too late, would be easier to fool.

Her sister had needed little convincing to attend the market. Usually, she went on her own as Rhona preferred not to spend her pennies on frivolities. But today, she was delighted to have a companion.

Adaira led her pony, a shaggy bay gelding named Bramble, out of the stables, before she glanced at Rhona. "Why are ye bringing a cloak for?" she asked, her attention shifting to the mantle that was bundled up behind the saddle. "It's a warm morning."

"Ye never know what the weather has in store on this isle," Rhona quipped with a smile. "It may get cold later."

Adaira shrugged. "It's not like ye to care about such things." Her sister then turned back to her pony, tightening its girth.

Rhona let out a slow breath, glad her sister had let the matter drop. She'd hidden the carefully wrapped parcel of food inside the cloak. It was the only way she could carry her supplies without raising suspicion. Like Adaira, she carried a leather satchel across her front. But unlike her sister's satchel, which would be empty save the last of her pennies, Rhona's contained her purse of pennies, her slingshot, and the maps she'd taken from her father's solar.

Finally, Adaira mounted her pony, and they were off. In contrast to Adaira's stocky mount, Rhona rode a fiery chestnut mare, Lasair. The horse's name meant 'Flame', in honor of her mistress's temperament. The stable master had questioned Rhona's choice when she'd picked the mare out three years earlier, but Lasair had proved to be her equal when it came to independence and spirit.

She hadn't taken Lasair out for a few days, and the mare was full of unspent energy this morning, jogging her way out of the Sea-gate and down the winding causeway. Rhona felt the solid weight of the curtain wall rising above her as Lasair pranced and snorted, yet she didn't look back. This was supposed to be an ordinary morning's outing, and she had to behave normally.

Even so, it was hard to contain her excitement and nervousness.

A warm wind gusted in from the south and wispy clouds scattered across a hard blue sky. Adaira was right; it was a lovely morning—too warm for a cloak. It was high summer now, and the slow journey toward the harvest had begun.

The village of Dunvegan sat a short ride from the castle, on the southern edge of the loch, and every month it held a merchant's market. Traders from all corners of the isle converged there just before each full moon, bringing cloth, jewelry, ornaments, pottery, and toiletries to sell.

The road to Dunvegan village was narrow and rutted, hugging the edge of the glittering loch. Sun-browned hills rose either side, bare of vegetation save for the flush of green around the castle. Brambles grew at the road's edge, where berries had just started to form. The warm air was heavy with the brine scent of the loch and the aroma of heather. Rhona breathed the familiar smells in deeply and attempted to settle the fluttering moths in her belly. She was so nervous now that she could feel the steady tattoo of her heart against her breast bone. Her palms, which gripped the reins, were slippery with sweat.

The waiting was torture. She'd be relieved when she was finally on her way—galloping south to freedom.

"I'm glad the sun's out," Adaira sighed. "Last month it rained so heavily they all had to pack up early."

Rhona glanced sideways at her sister. Adaira's long brown hair was loose this morning, and it blew around her face. She wore a wide, excited smile, her hazel eyes scanning the road ahead.

Rhona's chest constricted. How she would miss her sister's smile.

Bramble plodded faithfully. The pony was the quietest of Malcolm MacLeod's stable. Their father had gifted him to Adaira on her thirteenth birthday, and she'd fallen in love with him on sight. Adaira was a keen rider and took Bramble out most days. She often grew restless in winter when bad weather prevented their rides.

Rhona's mare tossed her head, impatient for a run. She then gave a playful buck.

"Lasair's full of herself today," Adaira commented. "Did they give her oats for supper last night?"

"She's just telling me off for not taking her out more often," Rhona replied, urging the mare forward. The truth was that Lasair sensed her rider was on edge this morning. She knew Rhona wanted to flee.

Adaira grinned at that, and the pressure in Rhona's chest increased.

How would her sister fare without her? Would she be angry, feel abandoned?

"Adaira," she said quietly. "Ye must be wary of men ... please promise me ye will."

Adaira's smile slipped. "Stop fussing ... not all men are like Baltair MacDonald."

"Some are worse."

"Stop it, Rhona. Ye are just trying to scare me. None of the warriors in the keep would dare behave in such a way."

Rhona inhaled deeply. Sometimes, her sister's innocence truly worried her. "Many of them watch ye," she replied. "I've seen them in the Great Hall. They know it'll be yer turn to wed soon. Men like Dughall MacLean will approach ye."

Adaira shuddered. "I don't like him."

Relief flowed through Rhona. Finally, some sense. "Aye, and ye are right not to."

Adaira's brow furrowed. "Why? What has he done?"

Rhona met her eye. "A couple of weeks ago he was taking a walk with me in the garden and proposed. When I rejected him, he grew angry and grabbed hold of me."

Adaira gasped.

"Taran stepped in," Rhona continued. "If he hadn't things might have gotten ... difficult."

Adaira's expression softened in relief before her eyes then clouded. "I just want to wed for love," she said quietly. "Why is Da so keen to sell us off like fattened sows?"

"An unwed daughter is a burden," Rhona replied, bitterness lacing her voice. "We are useful only in marriage, for we can unite families or gain land for our clan."

Adaira pondered this a moment before she answered. "Caitrin is unhappy," she said softly.

"Aye." Rhona turned her gaze to the road ahead so Adaira wouldn't see her own despair. "And if we're not careful, we'll suffer the same fate."

Silence fell between them then, the mood turning somber.

Rhona's vision misted. This was potentially the last time she'd ever see her sister. She didn't want Adaira's memory of her to be tainted with sadness. Grief sat like a heavy stone in her belly as the full realization of the situation sank in. Unless Adaira one day visited her upon the mainland, they'd be estranged forever.

Rhona swallowed. *Stop it*, she chastised herself. *Don't think on it ... if ye do, ye won't go.*

A short while later, the sisters rode into Dunvegan village. A sprawl of low-slung stone houses with thatched roofs, the village spread out along the loch side. Softly curved hills stretched south of the village, while Loch Dunvegan stretched north. The prevailing winds on this side of the isle meant that there was little in the way of trees and shrubbery here. Rhona would have little cover as she rode south. She was grateful Lasair was full of energy this morning—she'd need it.

The Stag's Head Inn lay at the heart of the village, with a view out across the loch. Behind it stretched a wide space where the merchants and traders had set up their stalls. Excited voices reached the sisters as they drew up in front of the inn. A large crowd filled the market square. The sight pleased Rhona; it would make slipping away all the easier.

They stabled their horses at the inn. After a morning exploring the market, the plan was that they would enjoy a meal at The Stag's Head before riding home. A meal at the inn was a ritual that Caitrin had once shared with them. The Stag's Head was famed for its mutton stew and oat dumplings.

However, Rhona would not be dining at the inn today.

She followed Adaira as she virtually skipped her way out of the stables and into the market. Her sister squealed in delight as the scent of rose and lavender wafted over them. "The soap man is here!"

Despite her tension and distracted thoughts, Rhona found herself smiling. Usually, they made do with coarse blocks of lye at home. Yet occasionally a soap merchant crossed from the mainland, bearing heavenly scented, colored blocks, as well as perfumed oils and lotions.

Adaira was now heading straight for him.

Rhona followed her to the stall, where Adaira set about sniffing each tablet of soap she picked up. In the end, they were too tempting.

"Good morning Lady Adaira … Lady Rhona." The soap merchant beamed at them. All the vendors here knew MacLeod's daughters on sight; it was impossible for them to be anonymous in this crowd. The clan-chief's daughters were well-loved in the village. Folk didn't hide their delight to see them.

"Good morn, Artair," Adaira greeted the man with a bright smile. "Where are yer wife and daughter today?"

"Visiting my wife's sister," he replied, his broad face flushing with pleasure. "She's having her third bairn."

Rhona found herself smiling, listening as Adaira started chatting to the merchant. She was entirely too familiar with him; Una would have reprimanded her for it. And yet that was what made Adaira so special. Her warmth, her ability to treat everyone—from the high to the low—with genuine attention.

"I'm getting the milk and honey tablet for myself," Adaira announced. She then pointed to the dusky-pink block to her left. "Go on … get yerself some rose soap."

Rhona sighed. "I don't need any scented soap at present."

"Who said anything about ye 'needing' it?" Adaira favored her with a wry look. "Every woman needs a sweet-smelling soap ... isn't that right, Artair?"

"Aye, Lady Adaira," he replied, giving her an indulgent smile. "The rose soap is our best seller."

Rhona huffed. She could see she was outnumbered here. She handed over the penny, took the soap, and slipped the scented block into her satchel. It would be something to remember her sister by.

Grief slammed into her anew.

Don't think about it.

"Good day, Artair," Adaira sang out. She cast another smile in the soap merchant's direction. The man was still beaming at her like a moon-calf.

Oblivious to her sister's turmoil, Adaira linked her arm through Rhona's. "Come, let's take a look at those silks!"

The young women wove their way through the sea of men and women who, like them, browsed the market. The sun warmed their backs, and the aroma of baking bannocks filled the air. An elderly woman was cooking the flat cakes over a griddle and selling them to the hungry crowd. Her name was Eva. No one knew just how old she was, although judging from the web of wrinkles that creased the crone's face, she was easily the oldest person Rhona had ever seen.

"Lady Rhona," the crone called out with a toothless smile. "How about one of Skye's finest oat-cakes?"

Rhona smiled back, before shaking her head. "Maybe later, Eva. I must save my appetite for a bowl of stew at the inn."

Continuing through the crowd, Rhona took in her surroundings. She noted the details she'd often taken for granted: the rosy cheeks of the women, the warm burr of men's voices, and the smiles of the folk who greeted them.

The vise crushed Rhona's ribcage now as the full realization of what she was about to do sank in.

She would leave all of this behind.

The sisters reached the cloth merchant's stall, where a pyramid of brightly colored bolts of fabric rose up before them. Adaira fell upon them, gaze gleaming.

"This green silk is beautiful," Adaira gasped. Rhona tore her gaze away from the milling crowd to see that her sister was holding a bolt of glimmering fabric up to the light. "Look, Rhona ... we could use this for yer wedding gown."

Cold washed over Rhona, obliterating the sadness she was feeling at leaving this place, these people.

Wedding gown.

Just two words, and yet they struck dread into her heart. She had to get away from here before it was too late.

Chapter Ten

Racing South

"ADAIRA ... I NEED the privy," Rhona whispered into her sister's ear. "I should have gone before we left the castle. I'll return to the inn and be back soon."

Adaira glanced up, from where she was admiring a delicate woolen shawl, her gaze distracted. "Of course. I'll still be here ... come find me."

Rhona nodded, forcing a smile. "Don't spend all yer pennies."

Adaira laughed. "I'll try not to. Go on then ... off ye go."

Rhona turned and wove her way back through the milling crowd toward The Stag's Head Inn. Her eyes stung, but she drew in a steadying breath, forcing back the welling tears. It was an effort not to look back, not to take one last look at her sister. Yet she forced herself not to. If Adaira caught her gazing at her, all teary-eyed, she'd know something was amiss.

I could take her with me. The thought niggled at her, not for the first time over the past days, but Rhona dismissed it. What she was doing was dangerous. She'd risk her own neck, and her own reputation, but she wouldn't put Adaira through it. Not only that, but she wasn't sure Adaira would go with her meekly either. Her sister wasn't desperate like Rhona was—not yet anyway.

She continued her path through the crowd. It was difficult not to hurry when every fiber of her being now urged her to run. She needed to be many leagues from here by nightfall.

Rhona focused her thoughts on what lay ahead, not what she was leaving behind. She knew that if she dwelled upon Adaira any longer, she would falter. She needed to remind herself why she was doing this.

The games loomed upon the horizon like an approaching storm. She would not suffer being wed to a man she didn't want. She wouldn't suffer being wed at all.

Rhona set her jaw and marched into the stables behind the inn. Today was the start of a new life, one where she'd carve her own destiny.

Her mare whickered as Rhona approached the stall. Murmuring gently to Lasair, she saddled her before leading her through the yard and out the front to the loch side, avoiding the busy market and her sister.

Beyond she heard the chatter of voices, as the market got busier still. Adaira wouldn't miss her for a while yet, not while a sea of colorful fabrics and baubles tempted her.

Upon the loch shore, Rhona sprang up onto Lasair's back and urged the mare into a brisk trot. They skirted the southern edge of the loch, leaving the village behind, and then Rhona guided her left. They crossed the road before Lasair broke into a bouncy canter.

The first of a series of rolling hills that stretched south rose before her, and the wind fanned her cheeks. A smile split Rhona's face. She crouched low over the saddle and gave the mare her head.

"Foolish wench!" Malcolm MacLeod roared, spittle flying. "Surely ye must have seen which way she went?"

"No, Da." Tears streamed down Adaira's face. She stood before the chieftain in his solar, trembling in the face of his rage. "I'm sorry, but I didn't ... the market was busy and I—"

"Silence!" MacLeod shifted his gaze past his daughter's shaking form, to where Taran stood silently by the door. "Why weren't ye with them, MacKinnon?"

Taran stiffened at the accusation. "The lasses always go to the Dunvegan market without an escort, Chief," he growled back. "Ye agreed to that years ago."

It was a rare day that Taran challenged MacLeod, yet he wasn't about to let himself be blamed for this. The news that Rhona had disappeared felt like a punch to the gut. Taran's hands clenched by his sides. There wasn't any point in laying blame.

MacLeod glared at him, his bearded face thunderous. "Ride after Rhona," he snarled.

"What if someone has taken her?" Adaira gasped, daring to interrupt her father. "She might not have run away. She might be hurt."

Taran's belly clenched at these words, although they had little effect on MacLeod. He continued to hold Taran's gaze. "Then, I'll have the culprit dragged back here and gelded," he growled. "Track her down, MacKinnon, and bring her home."

Taran nodded. "Shall I gather men to ride with me?"

MacLeod shook his head. "There's no time ... and I don't want anyone else to know she's missing. News of this mustn't leave this chamber ... not with the games so close." He shifted a gimlet stare to his daughter. "If anyone asks, Rhona has a fever and is in her bed-chamber. Is that clear?"

Adaira nodded, her tear-streaked face pale and strained.

MacLeod looked at Taran once more. "Find her," he rumbled, "and don't return here until ye do."

Taran gave a brusque nod, turned on his heel, and marched from the solar. Descending the stairwell to the ground level of the keep, he strode out into the bailey and headed for the stables. There, he swiftly saddled Tussock, his rangy bay gelding. The stables were busy this morning, with men, dogs, and horses everywhere. But Taran spoke to no one as he prepared to ride out, his gaze firmly fixed upon his task.

"Where are ye off to?" Connel Buchanan, who'd just returned from a deer hunt bellowed to Taran when he led his horse out into the yard.

"Out on an errand for MacLeod," Taran called back. He took care to keep his tone nonchalant, with the bored edge the other men were used to hearing from him.

Connel's eyes gleamed with curiosity at this. "Why's that?"

Taran ignored him. Connel was as nosy as he was loud; he'd be the last man Taran would confide in. MacLeod had been clear: no one was to know of Rhona's disappearance.

He left the keep at a slow trot, making his way down the narrow winding path from the Sea-gate to the rutted road below. It was only when he was a good distance from the castle that he urged Tussock into a canter. It wouldn't do to be seen racing away from Dunvegan at a flat gallop—it would only set tongues wagging.

Reaching the nearby village, where the market was now finishing up for the day, Taran drew his gelding up and let his gaze sweep from west to east. Adaira had not seen what direction her sister had left in, so it was up to him to track her down.

Firstly he rode into the village, where he discreetly asked some of the folk he encountered if they had seen MacLeod's fire-haired daughter this afternoon. None had. He then went to The Stag's Head. The inn-keeper hadn't seen her, but one of the stable lads had.

"I saw Lady Rhona lead her horse out of here mid-morning," the lad admitted, putting down the pitch-fork he'd been using to muck out one of the stalls. "I didn't see which way she went though."

Taran frowned as he considered the possibilities.

Clearly, Rhona hadn't been abducted. So where had she gone?

Rhona could have gone to Duntulm, but that would be foolish, for her sister couldn't shelter her, and Baltair MacDonald would merely send her home. To his knowledge, Rhona had no other connections upon the isle. Yet, he knew she had kin on the mainland. Lady Martha had hailed from Argyle.

If he'd been Rhona, he'd ride south to Kyleakin and find passage across the water.

It was a bold move, but Rhona wasn't like other maids. She was a strong rider, and with his tuition over the years could handle herself with a knife, sword, and her hands. She was also stout-hearted and not easily daunted. Even so, it wasn't a safe journey for a woman alone. Desperation had made her reckless, foolish.

Taran thanked the lad and swung up onto Tussock's back. Leaving the inn, he urged the horse into a canter, skirted the village, and headed up the first rise south. He'd have to ride hard to catch Rhona up, for she traveled upon a leggy chestnut mare that could outrun most of the horses in MacLeod's stable. Still, what Tussock lacked in speed, he made up for in endurance.

If he kept up an even pace, he'd catch Rhona before she reached the coast.

Lasair raced south, her hooves flying over the dry grass and heather strewn over the ground. The mare had a thirst for adventure and was enjoying being out in open country, galloping free and unchecked.

As the day wore on, the landscape around Rhona changed. Mountains rose against the eastern horizon, bare-backed ridges with thick forest nestled between them where deer roamed. To the south thrust a wall of carven grey peaks: the Black Cuillins. Sloping charcoal sides ran down to the dry hills below, the mountain range's sharp outline etched against the sky. Rhona skirted the base of the mountains, riding southeast now. To the south of these mighty mountains lay the Lochans of the Fair Folk, a collection of pools said to be blessed by the Fae. She'd visited the spot twice, once for a gathering of the MacLeod kin, and the second time for her father's handfasting to Una. They had been wed next to one of the waterfalls.

Rhona would have liked to visit the lochans again, but it would mean a detour, and she had no time for that. Instead, she pressed on southeast, stopping twice briefly during the afternoon to rest and water Lasair.

By the time the light started to fade, Rhona's belly felt hollow with hunger. She'd been so nervous that morning, she'd been unable to stomach more than a mouthful of bannock. The anxiety had fled now she was on her way, and she was ravenous.

Yet she didn't stop. She didn't dare. She needed to get as much distance between her and Dunvegan as possible before nightfall.

Dusk settled, stretching rosy fingers across the western sky. The shadow of the Black Cuillins now behind her, Rhona pressed on. She slowed Lasair to a gentle trot and moved through the gloaming until a cloak of darkness settled over the world, making it impossible to travel any farther.

At that point, she drew Lasair to a halt and made camp for the night. Securing the mare on a long tether to a boulder so that the horse could graze, Rhona settled herself on the ground on the opposite side of the boulder. She leaned against the rock, still warmed from the sun, and unwrapped her precious parcel of food. She was hungry enough to devour the lot, yet she stopped herself after two oat-cakes and an apple. She needed to be careful, although she'd hopefully be able to buy more food at Kyleakin.

Finishing her light supper, Rhona brushed crumbs off her kirtle and gazed up at the night sky where, one by one, the stars were twinkling into existence like tiny jewels against the inky void beyond. She was lucky, for the night was a mild one. She didn't even need to wrap herself up in her cloak, so instead, she bundled it up and used it as a pillow.

Rhona yawned loudly, letting tiredness settle upon her like a warm blanket. For the first time since leaving Dunvegan, she allowed herself to dwell on what she'd left behind. She imagined Adaira's stricken face when she realized what Rhona had done, and their father's rage. She actually shuddered at the thought. Rhona was afraid of her father. He didn't suffer disobedience in his hounds, his men, or his women.

Rhona only hoped that Adaira had escaped his wrath.

She slept lightly that night, dozing only as the hours stretched by. It was an isolated area, far from any villages or farms, and so she passed the night undisturbed. However, as soon as the first blush of the approaching dawn light illuminated the sky, Rhona was up once more. She would not lose the advantage she had gained the day before.

Rhona had left Lasair saddled overnight, with her girth loosened so she'd be comfortable. As such it took only a few moments preparation and the pair of them were cantering south once more into a misty dawn. As she rode, Rhona was surprised to find a smile creeping over her face. She wasn't out of danger yet, and still felt upset at leaving Adaira, but the sense of freedom she felt this morning made her feel as if she'd just been reborn.

This is who I truly am, she thought. *Who I was born to be.*

Chapter Eleven

The Way of the World

ALTHOUGH RHONA PUSHED Lasair as hard as she
dared, they didn't manage to reach Kyleakin by the end
of the day. They were close, she knew it, but the coastal
village was still out of sight as the last of the sun drained
from the sky, casting the world into darkness once more.

Letting out a sharp huff of annoyance, Rhona drew
the mare to a halt in a wooded valley. After riding south
of the Black Cuillins, her journey had taken her sharply
southeast, through the mountainous landscape that had
slowed her journey somewhat. Huge peaks had risen
overhead, making Rhona feel impossibly small. It was a
wild, lonely part of the isle, and Rhona had passed no
one on her travels—something she was grateful for.

At a certain point on her journey, she spied the
peaked roof of a great building in the distance: Kilbride
Abbey, Skye's only convent. Rhona had drawn Lasair up
a moment, her gaze narrowing as she viewed the stone
bulk rising against the western sky. She must be in the
heart of MacKinnon territory now if she could see the
abbey.

Could she save herself a trip to the mainland and find
sanctuary there?

Rhona's mouth twisted. No—the life of a nun wasn't for her. Besides, her father would merely travel to Kilbride and drag her home by the hair.

The only way she'd escape her fate was to leave this isle for good.

Rhona had urged Lasair on once more, turning the mare inland. She'd consulted her father's map of Skye numerous times on the journey and decided that this was a faster route than riding south and skirting the coast. Even so, the hilly terrain slowed Lasair down.

As dusk approached, they left the most rugged land behind them, riding across craggy heather moor interspersed by valleys where hazel, birch, and hawthorn grew in untidy clumps.

There was a burn at the bottom of this valley, where Rhona stopped for the night. Clear water trickled across peaty soil. Rhona knelt at its banks and splashed water on her face before filling her water bladder and drinking deeply. The light had almost drained from the sky now; it was a deep purple against the silhouette of the birch trees surrounding her. The twitter of roosting birds serenaded her, and the silver glow of the waxing moon had appeared in the sky.

Rhona loosed a tired breath. The distance she'd traveled today hadn't seemed great when she looked at her map. She'd been so sure she'd reach Kyleakin by nightfall.

Tonight, she unsaddled Lasair properly and rubbed her down with a twist of grass, for the horse had worked hard over the past two days. Lasair huffed a breath into her hair when she'd done, and Rhona favored her with a weary smile. "Just a wee bit longer, lass ... ye have done well."

Rhona lowered herself onto the ground, a few yards away from where she'd tethered her horse, under the sheltering boughs of a birch. Her backside and thighs ached tonight as she was unused to spending so long in the saddle. This evening a little of the shine had gone out of her adventure. Even so, she had no regrets about leaving; she was just anxious to reach the coast, before her father's men caught up with her.

He would have sent a party to find her and drag her back to Dunvegan—and she knew it was always easier being the hunter rather than the quarry. Some of her father's men were skilled hunters and trackers. She just hoped they didn't travel at night, or she'd never make it to the coast.

Rhona frowned, irritated by the worries that plagued her. Of course they didn't travel at night. They weren't wolves or owls. Just like her, they would need to rest their horses.

Even so, she was on edge this evening. To distract herself from her thoughts, she opened her package of food. Only two oat-cakes and a small wedge of cheese remained. She'd eaten more than she'd planned on the journey and had hoped to be having supper in a tavern in Kyleakin tonight.

Rhona sighed. After a day out riding in the fresh air, she was starving. She didn't want to finish her remaining food, but she knew she would need to. She'd just have to resupply as soon as she reached the coast in the morning, or try her luck with the slingshot if she got desperate.

Leaning back against the rough trunk of the birch, she started to nibble on an oat-cake.

It was then she felt the hair on the back of her arms prickle.

Rhona swallowed her mouthful of food and put the oat-cake down, her heart fluttering against her ribs. She glanced around her, squinting to make out the details of her surroundings in the gloaming. Beside her, Lasair snorted, suddenly restless.

Rhona's pulse quickened further.

Although she couldn't see anyone, her instincts—and her horse—warned her that someone was nearby, watching her from the shadows.

Slowly, Rhona reached into her satchel and withdrew a knife. It had a long sharp blade, a knife that cook used for boning fowl. Rhona had taken it from the kitchens when Greer and Fiona's attention had been elsewhere. She gripped the bone hilt tightly and held the knife close to her waist as she rose to a squat and surveyed her surroundings.

"I know ye are there." Her voice sounded surprisingly fearless, even though her heart now hammered. "Stop lurking in the shadows, and step out where I can see ye."

A long silence followed, and then a few yards away the shadows shifted, and a tall, broad shape stepped out from behind a birch.

Rhona's breathing caught. She knew him.

Even in the half-light, with only his silhouette visible, she recognized Taran MacKinnon's bulk. Few men in Dunvegan had such broad shoulders or walked with such predatory stealth.

"Taran," she choked out his name, rising to her feet. Relief washed over her that it was him and not Dughall MacLean who stalked her. Even so, he was not a welcome sight. "Ye nearly made my heart stop."

"Apologies, Lady Rhona." His voice, gravelly and low, filled the dusk hush. "I didn't mean to scare ye."

Rhona frowned, peering at him. "And where are the others?"

"I'm alone. Yer father sent me to bring ye home."

Alone. The news surprised Rhona as much as it pleased her. "I'm not going back to Dunvegan," she replied firmly. "Tell Da ye couldn't find me."

He loosed a gentle sigh. "I can't do that."

"Why not? Just tell him I traveled too swiftly and crossed to the mainland before ye could catch me."

"He told me not to return until I bring ye with me."

Rhona tensed, her fingers flexing upon the knife's hilt. "I'm never going back there. Turn around and leave. Pretend ye never saw me."

She couldn't see his face, but she saw movement and realized he was shaking his head. "I can't do that."

He advanced toward her then, long strides that ate up the distance between them.

"Stop!" She darted to the side, keeping the knife low and close as he'd once shown her. "Get back from me."

Her heart, which had momentarily settled, now beat a frantic tattoo against her ribs. Panic rose within her, and she decided to take a different approach with him. Taran had always been good to her, indulged her even. Maybe she could sway him.

"Don't return to Dunvegan then," she said, her voice low as she backed slowly away from him. "Cross to the mainland with me. I'm sure my uncle would welcome a warrior like ye at his keep."

"I follow yer father," Taran replied. His tone was flat, completely devoid of emotion. "I'll not betray him. He bid me bring ye home, and I will."

"Get away from me, *Beast*," Rhona snarled. Fear pulsed through her now, not of Taran but of having her freedom torn from her when she'd only just tasted it.

She watched him halt, his body stiffening at the insult. Rhona stilled too. She'd heard others name him such at Dunvegan, but she had never called him 'Beast' before. In other circumstances, she'd have felt sorry for it. Yet not now, not when he stood between her and a new life.

She took another, quick, step back from him then, desperate to widen the distance between them. A heartbeat later, her foot caught on a root, and she stumbled. With a cry, Rhona fell backward.

He was on her in an instant.

She never knew such a big man could move so fast.

Rhona tried to fight him off, pushing back against the heavy body that slammed into her, but he was too strong, too fast. Desperate, she drove her knee up, aiming for his cods. During their training, Taran had told her numerous times to strike a man there if attacked. But she couldn't lift her knee as he now leaned his weight over her body, crushing her into the dirt. His hands fastened like iron shackles around her wrists, pinning them to the ground.

"Bastard!" She spat the insult at him. "Let me go!"

"Do ye promise to behave yerself if I do?" His voice was low, and—did she imagine it—tinged with wry amusement.

Fury surged within Rhona, but she swallowed it. "I promise ... just get off me. Ye are crushing my ribs."

He moved then, rolling off Rhona and rising to his feet with a speed that unnerved her. She'd forgotten that Taran MacKinnon could move with frightening swiftness. She should have remembered that, for she'd sparred with him often enough over the years.

A heartbeat later, Taran reached down, took Rhona by the arm, and pulled her to her feet. She was not a frail or tiny woman, and yet he lifted her as if she weighed nothing.

The moment Rhona was on her feet she reacted. As he'd taught her, just days earlier, she twisted, shoved herself against him, and threw her head back. She wanted to head-butt him, break his nose. But, once again, Taran thwarted her.

He grabbed hold of her wrists and yanked them behind her, pressing them into the small of her back.

"That was a half-arsed attempt, Lady Rhona. I hope if someone really intends to do ye harm, ye would do better than that." He then started fastening a cord around her wrists. "Ye have to be ready to hurt yer attacker," he chided. "That move wouldn't have fought off even old Niall, the rat-catcher."

Rhona let forth a string of gutter curses—words she'd personally never uttered to anyone before. None were insults befitting a high-born young lady. "Ye have no right to tie me up like a hog," she gasped at the end of the rant.

"Ye made me a promise," Taran replied, completely unruffled by her venom, "and ye broke it. I'll not trust yer word again."

Rhona fell silent, shocked that a warrior who had indulged her, even gone against her father's wishes in order to train her, was so unyielding now. She realized then that he wouldn't be moved. No amount of yelling, cursing, or threatening would change his mind.

I'm going home.

Tears welled in Rhona's eyes. She couldn't bear it. He was taking her back to Dunvegan.

"Ye don't understand, Taran." She choked out the words, letting her despair show. "I want to choose my own husband. Who knows what man will win the games? I could end up wedded to a brute."

"I'm sorry for ye, Lady Rhona." Taran took her by the arm and guided her back to the tree where she'd been sheltering before his arrival. There he gently pushed her down into a sitting position. "But ye cannot run away like this. It won't change anything. Ye will only make MacLeod angry."

Rhona's mouth twisted. "And what would ye have me do instead?"

Taran didn't answer that. Instead, he moved over to a nearby tree and settled down. Although she couldn't see his face, Rhona could just make out the gleam of his eyes as he watched her.

Silence stretched between them for a while, broken only by the hoot of a distant owl, before Taran spoke again. "It's not an easy fate," he began quietly, "to be a clan-chief's daughter. Did ye ever consider taking the veil? You could go to Kilbride?"

Rhona huffed. "How long do ye think I'd last before the abbess cast me out? A day?"

Taran answered with a soft snort. "A week ... at least."

Chapter Twelve

Nothing Good

AS SOON AS the first rays of sun spilled over the edge of the mountains to the east, Taran packed up camp, and they made for home.

In daylight, Taran MacKinnon's face was as inscrutable as his voice had been in darkness. If anything, the long night had given Taran a hard edge. He was taciturn as he prepared the horses, his scarred face cold. He said little to Rhona, other than issue instructions, and she answered him with sullen grunts. Rhona hadn't slept overnight. She couldn't—not when she'd just had her freedom stolen from her. Instead, her thoughts circled incessantly as she dwelt on her fate.

Taran set off northwest upon his stocky bay gelding, Tussock, leading Lasair on a tether. Rhona's hands were bound before her as she rode. A cloak of despair settled over her; they were headed back the way she'd come.

All that risk, all that urgency. For nothing.

A warm, overcast day greeted them, with no refreshing breeze to fan their faces as they rode. The horses sweated, their long tails switching at the clouds of midges that plagued them. The mugginess grew as the morning drew out, and by the time they stopped at noon, sweat drenched Rhona's back. The midges had tormented her all morning, and with her hands bound she hadn't been able to swat them away from her face. She felt as if she'd breathed them in, as if they'd burrowed up her nostrils and into her hair.

As they traveled, a large red mountain rose to the northwest, its outline hazy, for the landmark was still some way off. That was Beinn na Caillich, or 'The Hill of the Hag' as many knew it. Dread twisted in Rhona's belly at the sight of the mountain. They'd traveled farther than she'd realized this morning. This time tomorrow she'd be back in Dunvegan.

At noon they stopped for a short spell. Taran tried to feed her some bread and cheese, for Rhona couldn't feed herself with her hands tied. However, she refused the food. She'd been hungry after her frugal supper the night before, but her belly had closed today. The sight of food made her feel ill. Dread robbed her of appetite.

Taran didn't force the issue or comment. Instead, he rose to his feet, brushed crumbs off his braies, and fixed a cool gaze upon Rhona. "Come, lass … it's time to move on."

Rhona scowled at him, not bothering to move. She felt as if she'd only just sat down. She was weary, body and soul.

"Lady Rhona." Taran hunkered down before her. "I know this isn't pleasant for ye … if I could change things I would."

She met his eye. "I thought we were friends, Taran," she replied softly. "Why would ye do this to me?"

His gaze guttered, a shadow moving in its depths. "This isn't my decision."

Rhona clenched her jaw. She was growing tired of the excuse he kept repeating whenever she challenged him. "Now I know why folk call ye 'MacLeod's Hound'," she growled out. "Ye are as loyal as a dog. Ye have no will of yer own."

He drew back from her at that, a shield raising between them. Taran then rose to his feet, pulling Rhona with him. "Ye waste yer breath insulting me, Lady

Rhona," he rumbled. "I've been called far worse than that over the years."

Rhona and Taran spent the rest of the day traveling in silence.

The afternoon pressed on, as humid and smothering as the morning had been. Clouds of midges plagued them the whole way. Rhona blinked and sneezed from the insects.

Taran drew up for the day at the foot of the Black Cuillins, just a few furlongs from where Rhona had camped on her journey south. He brought down a grouse with his slingshot and roasted it over a small fire while, around them, the light slowly faded. Night fell very late this time of year, and the twilights seemed endless. Mercifully, as the air cooled, the midges disappeared. Even so, Rhona's skin itched at the memory of them. How she wished to bathe in a cool creek or loch and wash away the sweat and dirt of the day.

Seated by the fire, her wrists still bound, Rhona watched Taran turn the grouse on a spit. She inhaled the aroma of wafting gamey meat mixed with the pungent scent of burning peat. Her belly growled, aching with hunger. Despite that her insides felt knotted at the thought of returning to Dunvegan, she had to admit that she was hungry.

Hearing the rumbling of her belly, Taran glanced up. "It's almost ready."

Rhona looked away, avoiding his gaze. Self-pity enveloped her. She wasn't one to let despair beat her. But this evening she could see nothing but a bleak future before her.

When the grouse was ready, Taran pulled the steaming meat off the bones and placed a large portion of it on an oiled cloth. He then put it on the ground beside Rhona and untied her wrists.

Her belly betrayed her, growling loudly once more. She wasn't used to missing meals, even if this was the first time all day she'd felt hungry.

Rhona started to pick at her grouse, while Taran returned to his side of the fire and began his supper. As she ate, Rhona found her gaze kept returning to Taran.

The glow of the fire pit between them highlighted the disfiguring scars on the warrior's face. They were old, yet deep—scars that had left thick silver ridges after the healing. His face was grim as he ate. As always, he wore that heavy mail shirt—he hadn't even shed it during the worst of the day's heat. The firelight glinted off the silver rings, illuminating the harsh planes of his face. Unlike a lot of her father's men, he cut his hair very short. It was a style that only added to the austerity of his look.

Glancing up from his meal, Taran's gaze snared hers. "Do I hold a fascination for ye, Lady Rhona?"

Rhona swallowed a mouthful of grouse, heat flaring in her cheeks at being caught staring.

Silence stretched between them before she finally answered. "I'm sorry, Taran," she began hesitantly. Her cheeks warmed further; apologizing didn't come easy to Rhona MacLeod. "About what I said earlier ... I know ye swore an oath when ye arrived at Dunvegan. Ye are bound to my father."

Taran's expression softened a little. "Aye, but that doesn't mean I'm happy about all of this. I hate to see ye suffer."

Rhona inclined her head. "Why did ye come after me alone?"

He pulled a face. "Yer father's orders. He doesn't want anyone to know ye tried to run off."

Rhona huffed a rueful laugh. "He won't be able to hide it."

"He bid Adaira tell everyone ye were taken ill in yer chamber and were not to be disturbed," he replied. "I'm sure there will be tongues wagging upon our return, but since some of the warriors have already arrived to prepare for the games, he wants to keep this quiet."

Taran's words made fear knot itself in the pit of Rhona's belly. Her father would be wrathful; she needed to ready herself for it.

Her supper suddenly felt oily in her belly, and she swallowed the bile that now stung her throat. Across the fire, Taran's grey-blue gaze remained upon her, steady and direct. He too knew what awaited her in Dunvegan.

The rain pattered down, stippling the surface of the loch, when they reached Dunvegan at last. The summer shower had freshened the air and brought out all the smells: the salt of the loch, the sweetness of grass, and the rich scent of warm earth. Thunder rumbled in the distance as slate-grey clouds rolled in from the west.

Lasair side-stepped, snorting nervously at the sound of the approaching storm. Rhona reached forward and soothed her with a stroke to the neck. Shortly before arriving at Dunvegan village, Taran removed the restraints from her wrists. It would look suspicious if he brought her home a captive.

Following the loch-side road north, the two riders didn't speak. Rhona spared a glance in Taran's direction, noting the sternness of his expression as he stared straight ahead. It was the look of a determined man, one who'd almost completed the task his chief had given him.

They rode up the steep causeway, passing through the Sea-gate and into the bailey. Folk turned to watch them, and Rhona stiffened. It seemed her disappearance wasn't the well-kept secret her father had hoped. It would make his mood all the sourer upon their reunion.

Inside the courtyard, they drew more stares. Unfortunately, Dughall MacLean was one of the warriors to spot them first. He'd been shoeing a horse but straightened up when the two riders clattered into the yard.

"What's this?" he said with a smirk, his gaze raking over Rhona. "Not laid-up with the grippe, after all, are ye?"

"Leave it, MacLean," Taran rumbled, drawing up his horse and swinging down from the saddle.

Dughall's smirk faded, although his eyes remained sharp. "Led ye on a merry dance, did she?"

Despite that Rhona braced herself for the blow, the impact of her father's palm hitting her across the face nearly knocked her off her feet.

"Disobedient, headstrong bitch," Malcolm MacLeod snarled, drawing his arm back once more. "Ye have defied me for the last time."

The second blow threw Rhona back against the wall. Her skull cracked against stone, and her vision swam. Sagging against the cold stone, Rhona raised a hand to her face. Her fingers came away bloody, and she realized her bottom lip was bleeding; one of her father's rings had cut her.

"I gave ye everything, but ye appreciated nothing. Ye humiliate me ... ye shame yerself." His voice was choked, and glancing up, Rhona saw he was standing motionless facing her, his big fists clenching and unclenching. Fear arrowed through her, making it difficult to breathe.

He looked as if he wanted to kill her.

"I'm sorry, Da," she whispered. And she was. Suddenly, all the fight had gone out of her. His rage was a terrible thing to behold, and she only wished to hide from it.

MacLeod glared at her, his eyes narrow, glittering slits. His face had turned the color of raw meat, and a nerve ticked in his cheek.

"Not sorry enough," he growled. "I'm done with ye." He turned his head toward the closed door to the solar. "MacKinnon!"

The door flew open, and Taran strode inside. He abruptly halted, his face pale and taut. He stared at where Rhona leaned against the wall, still cradling her injured mouth. Their gazes met, and she saw his ice-blue eyes turn flinty.

"Take this wench up to the tower room and lock her in. She'll not leave it till the day of the games—is that clear?"

Taran hesitated, a muscle bunching in his jaw. Then he nodded.

"Get on with it then," the clan-chief growled. "I've nothing more to say to her."

Tears welled in Rhona's eyes at the venom in her father's voice. His loathing of her was worse than his rage. She'd have preferred his fists to this cruel dismissal.

"Da ... I—"

"Take her away, MacKinnon. Before I lose what's left of my self-control."

Malcolm MacLeod turned away then and crossed to the window. The shutters were open, although rain was driving inside, wetting the stone sill. Taran stepped close to Rhona, his fingers closing around her upper arm.

"Come," he murmured.

Rhona let Taran lead her out of the solar. Her legs were shaking so much she barely made it. In the hall outside, she wrenched free of his restraining hand and flattened herself against the wall. Her vision swam, and a sob rose up within her. However, she kept it sealed inside, her hand pressing against her injured mouth.

"Lady Rhona," Taran rasped her name. He stepped close, his gaze clouded with worry. "Are ye hurt?"

When she didn't answer, he reached up, his fingers encircling her wrist. Then he gently pulled her hand from her mouth. "Ye are bleeding."

"Aye." The word gusted out of her. The cut to her lip was nothing compared to the rent inside her. "He hates me now, Taran ... I saw it in his eyes."

"No, lass," Taran replied softly. "Ye are his flesh and blood. When his anger cools, he'll remember that."

Rhona shook her head. "No, he won't. I know that look in his eye. It's the same one he gets when he speaks of Morgan Fraser. Ye should have let me leave Skye, Taran. Nothing good can come of this now."

Chapter Thirteen

Locked Away

TARAN SLAMMED HIS fist into the stable wall. Wood splintered, and the horse in the nearby stall snorted. The beast then kicked out with a shod hoof at the partition between them.

Rage pulsed inside Taran as he stood there, ignoring the pain in his clenched knuckles. He'd drawn blood, but he didn't care. He punched the wall again, his fist breaking through into the layer of mud and straw that formed the exterior wall to the stables.

This was a mess, and it was his doing.

The rage twisted into self-loathing. Rhona was right. He was MacLeod's dog. He deserved every bit of her derision and more. The despair, the fear, he'd seen in her eyes when he'd entered the solar still haunted him. She'd said nothing on the journey up to the tower room, and she'd turned her back on him when he'd left, locking the heavy door behind him. He'd stayed in the hall beyond though, for a long while after, unable to leave her. Only when he'd caught the sounds of muffled sobs had he turned and fled to the stables, to vent his rage.

"There ye are." A voice intruded, and Taran turned to find Gordon standing a few feet behind him. His friend's brow was furrowed.

"What?" he rasped, wishing Gordon would leave. He was in no mood for company right now.

Gordon's gaze flicked from Taran to the hole in the wall behind him. "So, it's true then ... Lady Rhona ran off?"

"Aye," Taran growled. "MacLeod bid me fetch her, and so I did."

"She's been punished?"

Taran nodded. "Locked in the tower room until the games."

Gordon heaved a sigh and moved into the stall where Taran stood. "I feared it would come to this. The lass has always been too wild."

Taran raked a hand through his hair, his gaze fixing upon the beams above him as he attempted to master his temper. "Aye, yet it seems a harsh price to pay. She begged me to let her go, Gordon ... but I didn't."

Gordon snorted. "And just as well. MacLeod would flay ye alive."

At that moment Taran didn't care. "I'm a coward."

He lowered his gaze to find Gordon standing before him, frowning. "We both know ye are not. Ye are loyal to the chief."

"Aye, and I was always proud of it ... but not anymore."

Gordon inclined his head, his expression sharpening. "If I didn't know better, I'd think ye in love with Lady Rhona."

The dark look Taran gave him in answer made Gordon draw back. A moment later he laughed. "My mistake." He reached forward, clasping Taran by the shoulder. "Come on. Let's get a cup of ale and a hot meal in the Great Hall ... ye look like ye need both."

"I'm not hungry."

"Ye will be when ye see what Fiona's prepared for today's nooning meal: venison pie."

Taran couldn't have cared less, yet Gordon's earlier comment about him being in love with Rhona had made him wary. The last thing he wanted was folk thinking that. He couldn't bear their smirks, their whispered comments.

The Beast of Dunvegan is in love.

Gordon wouldn't mock him, but he was one of the few Taran trusted. He needed to regain control. He needed to put the shield back in place and get a leash on his temper. It wouldn't serve him now.

Taran followed Gordon out of the stall, massaging his stinging knuckles as he went. Leaving the stables, the two men crossed the rain-lashed yard. Thunder crashed overhead, and dark purple and black clouds loomed. Shaking off the rain from their clothing, the warriors left the storm behind and entered the cavernous space of the Great Hall. Owing to the weather, folk had come early to the nooning meal. The tables were nearly full, and the toothsome aroma of pie filled the air. At the far end, upon the raised dais, MacLeod and his kin had taken their seats at the chieftain's table.

Rhona was, unsurprisingly, absent. Confined to the tower room, she would no longer join the rest of the keep for meals here.

Gordon and Taran took their seats at the end of one of the long scrubbed wooden tables. It wasn't the place Taran would have chosen to sit, especially not in his current mood, for Connel and Dughall sat opposite. He didn't like the way they both smirked at him.

A servant placed two large pies before Taran and Gordon, while another slammed down frothing tankards of ale. Gordon dug in to his meal, ripping through the buttery pastry shell to the dark meat stew underneath. However, the sight of the food made Taran's belly clench. He was too wound up to be hungry. Instead, he took a long draft of ale.

Around him, men fell upon their pies, the clatter of spoons and the thud of tankards blending with the rumble of their voices. Taran forced himself to start eating, aware that not to do so would raise eyebrows. But each mouthful tasted like ash.

"Why the scowl, Scar-face?" Connel's voice drew Taran out of his brooding. He glanced up to find the straw-haired youth grinning at him. "I hear ye are a hero. Tracked Lady Rhona down and dragged her home. Well done."

Taran didn't answer. Instead, he lifted his tankard to his lips and took a large gulp.

"Aye ... although I find it odd he sent ye out on yer own," Dughall spoke up. The warrior had finished his pie and was watching Taran with a hooded gaze. "How can we be sure the lady's virtue is intact?"

Connel cast Dughall a wry look. "Fear not ... ye can count on The Beast's honor. He'd cut off his own rod rather than sully a highborn woman with it."

Taran clenched his jaw. He then helped himself to another tankard of ale from a passing servant. Once again, he remained silent. Connel and Dughall were baiting him. They wanted to anger him.

Next to him, Gordon gave a snort of derision. "At least he's got a rod," he said to Connel. "That slug in *yer* braies can't be named such."

Gordon's comment caused barks of laughter to erupt around them. But Connel didn't look amused. He favored Gordon with a sour look and was about to respond when Dughall interrupted him.

"I hope ye are right, Buchanan." Dughall's gaze didn't leave Taran as he spoke, the threatening edge to his voice hard to miss. "When I win her hand at the games, I want my lady wife to be a virgin when I take her."

Connel snorted. "Ye are competing against me so I wouldn't be so full of yerself."

Dughall's lip curled, and he gave Connel a look that told him exactly what he thought of that assertion. His attention then returned to Taran. "Fifty warriors have pledged to compete at the games," he said. "Lady Rhona is a prize it seems."

Taran glared back at him before he finally answered. "Aye, she is."

"I can't believe ye ran away. Ye could have taken me with ye!"

Rhona turned from the window to meet her sister's angry glare. She'd been waiting for this confrontation, although with less dread than the one with her father.

"It's just as well that I didn't," she replied. Her cut lip stung as she spoke. "Since ye would be in trouble now too."

Adaira scowled, a rare expression for such a sweet-tempered lass. Her hazel eyes sparkled with unshed tears. "I was so worried." Her voice wobbled slightly. "I thought someone had carried ye off ... had done ye harm."

Rhona stared back at her. She hadn't thought Adaira would come to that conclusion. Her throat constricted, and she swallowed. "I'm sorry. I didn't want to leave without saying anything, but I had to."

Adaira scrubbed at the tears that had escaped and were now cascading down her cheeks. "Da is in a terrible rage."

Rhona suppressed a shudder. "I know."

Adaira's gaze dropped to her sister's swollen lip. "He hit ye?"

Rhona nodded before turning away. She didn't want to talk about it.

The shutters to the tower room were open, revealing a cool afternoon. The sky was still grey, but the storm had spent itself before moving east. The air that drifted in was fresh and clean.

Rhona took the scene in numbly. None of this seemed real. Two days ago she'd been free, riding with the wind in her face toward a future of her own making. Now she was to be confined to this chamber till the games. She could already feel the walls closing in on her.

The soft pad of slippered feet warned her of Adaira's approach. A moment later she felt an arm loop around her waist. Adaira hugged her tight, the strength of her embrace warning Rhona of the emotions her sister held on a tight leash.

"The world is so unfair," her sister whispered. The broken sound of her voice made Rhona's vision blur. "I can't stand to see ye unhappy."

Rhona's mouth twisted at the irony of it. She could stand anything except seeing either of her sisters hurt. The bond between them had always been strong, enough to weather anything—even this.

"Whatever happens, don't let them break ye," Adaira continued, her voice turning vehement. "It's bad enough that Caitrin is like a ghost these days. I don't want to lose ye too. If ye had succeeded in running away, we never would have seen each other again. Was freedom worth that much?"

A tear trickled down Rhona's face. Reaching up, she knuckled it away. She knew Adaira didn't understand why she'd had to flee. "It ripped a hole in my heart," she answered softly, "but aye, it would have been worth it."

Silence stretched between them. The sisters stayed where they were, Adaira clinging to Rhona like a barnacle. Rhona let her, for her sister's embrace brought her comfort.

"What will ye do now?" Adaira asked finally.

"I don't know ... nothing it seems."

"Ye could try to sneak away again ... take me with ye this time. There's that passageway in the dungeon we discovered years ago. We could leave that way."

Rhona shook her head. She'd already considered the hidden passage as a means of escape and dismissed it in favor of taking a horse south to Kyleakin. Rhona, Caitrin, and Adaira had stumbled upon the passageway one summer while exploring the dungeon. Folk at Dunvegan had long talked about the existence of a hidden passageway somewhere in the keep. Once they discovered it, the sisters made a pact to keep its location secret.

Tears flowed, hot and silent, down Rhona's cheeks. "Da will post guards outside my door at night. Even if we got past them, they'd run us down like deer. We wouldn't get far."

"But I want to help."

Rhona took Adaira's hand and squeezed. She didn't deserve such a sweet-natured sister. She'd acted selfishly, and yet Adaira still loved her, still wanted to help her. "Ye are helping," Rhona replied softly. "More than ye realize."

Chapter Fourteen

The Day of the Games

THE DAY OF the games dawned warm and sunny. The weather didn't care if Rhona was miserable, that she'd dreaded each sunset that brought her closer to her fate. The time had sped by—and Rhona awoke to honeyed sunlight filtering through the shutters into her chamber.

A short while later, Liosa brought a platter of food up to her. The hand-maid found Rhona swathed in a thick robe, perched on the sill of the open window, knees pulled up under her chin.

"Morning." Liosa favored her with a smile and carried the tray over to the table that sat in the center of the chamber. "Lady Adaira didn't think ye would be hungry, but Fiona insisted."

Rhona's gaze glanced off the fresh bannock, butter, and honey, and the mug of milk that accompanied it. Her belly lurched. "Adaira's right," she replied. "I can't eat."

Rhona remained seated on the window sill while Liosa padded about the room, readying the clothes Rhona would wear for today. They'd already picked out her outfit: an emerald-green kirtle over a dove-grey léine. The kirtle, edged with gold thread, had a low rounded neck and long bell-like sleeves. It was the costliest item of clothing that Rhona owned, and had she not felt so miserable, she'd have enjoyed wearing it.

As it was, she felt like hurling it from the window.

Rhona dressed in silence, while Liosa said little—unusual, for the hand-maid was usually full of observations in the morning. Neither of them spoke as Rhona fastened the laces of her kirtle down the front of her bodice.

Outside, the excited chatter of women in the bailey below filtered up. The folk of Dunvegan had been looking forward to this day for weeks; everyone loved games, for it broke up the routine of everyday life and gave servants a break from their chores.

"I've never seen the keep so busy," Liosa said finally. "Men from as far away as Caithness and Lothian have come to compete."

Rhona drew in a deep breath at this news. "How long will the games last?" she asked. In her misery, she hadn't considered the details of what her father was planning.

"Two days. It'll start with a day and a half of strength tests, and then the finalists will wrestle each other for yer hand."

Rhona inhaled once more, trying to ignore the anxiety that twisted inside her belly like a trapped eel. She smoothed her sweaty palms upon the silky material of her kirtle and squared her shoulders. She'd be damned if she'd let anyone see her despair.

"Come on then," she said, turning to Liosa and meeting her eye. "Let's get this over with."

A summer's breeze laced with the scent of crushed grass feathered against Rhona's cheeks. She sat upon the stands before the competition field and waited for the first of the strength games: the tossing of the caber.

Erected out of slabs of pine, the stands rose three tiers high. Much preparation had gone into this day. The MacLeod plaid—a crosshatch of yellow, black, and grey, threaded with red—fluttered from the ring that encircled the competition field.

Excited spectators chattered around Rhona, while crowds of village folk gathered around the perimeter of the field. She sat in-between her father and Adaira, hands folded upon her lap. Since leaving the tower room, no one besides Adaira had spoken to her. Caitrin hadn't come to the games, as her infant son had a fever, although Baltair was here. He sat farther along the bench, laughing over something with the man seated next to him.

Baltair had not greeted Rhona, or even acknowledged her—not something that bothered Rhona. But it stung that her father ignored her. Even Una stared right through her.

It was all part of her punishment. Rhona's fingernails bit into her palms. How she wished she was far from here.

Men, clad only in plaid braies, their naked chests gleaming in the morning sun, walked out onto the field. Rhona's throat closed at the sight of them.

So many ... at least fifty.

Most of the faces she didn't recognize, however, some she did. A blond, grinning young warrior called Connel, and Dughall MacLean. Of course—she'd known he'd compete.

The latter stood at the front of the group, dark blue eyes riveted upon the stands—upon her. Rhona ignored him. *Let him stare,* she thought. *If he wins the games, I'll scratch his eyes out on our wedding night.*

But Connel and Dughall weren't the only faces she recognized in the crowd. Rhona's breathing stilled when she saw a big, broad-shouldered figure with short dark-blond hair and a scarred face standing at the back of the group.

Taran MacKinnon.

Confusion swept over Rhona, muddling her thoughts for a few moments. Connel and Dughall she understood, for both of them had made their interest in her clear.

But Taran?

Betrayal followed swiftly on the heels of confusion. She'd been furious with Taran for dragging her back to Dunvegan, yet she'd believed he'd had some sympathy for her plight. What was he doing competing for her hand?

Rhona clenched her jaw till it ached. She glared at Taran, willing him to meet her gaze, yet he did not. Instead, his ice-blue stare seemed unfocused, as if he was deep in thought.

Beside her, Malcolm MacLeod rose to his feet. The chatter in the stands quietened, and the crowd of warriors waiting below shifted their gazes to the clan-chief.

"Welcome." Her father's voice carried across the field. "For some of ye, Dunvegan is yer home, while for others ye have traveled far to reach us. I greet ye all and thank ye for doing us this honor."

A few of the warriors below cheered at this, while others beamed up at MacLeod. Malcolm then turned to where Rhona sat silently next to him. "Daughter, stand up."

Rhona complied, hands still clasped before her. Dozens of hungry male gazes raked over her. She felt as if they were stripping her clothing from her. Rhona raised her chin, barely suffering the indignity.

"Aye." Her father's voice held a smug note as he continued. "Lady Rhona MacLeod is a fiery beauty. She'll make one of ye a fine bride and bear ye plenty of sons ... but ye will have to fight for her. The motto of this family is 'Hold Fast'. The MacLeods face down our enemies without fear, and we charge toward our destinies. I encourage all of ye to do the same."

A cheer went up, and when it died away, all gazes fixed upon Malcolm MacLeod, awaiting his next words. Tension rose around them, and Rhona saw the excitement in the contestants' eyes, their eager smiles. The sight just made Rhona feel ill.

Her father's command, when it came, fell like an executioner's axe, splitting the silence. "Let the games begin."

The morning was torture. Rhona sat there, silent and tense, watching as one-by-one, the warriors competed at tossing the caber. They heaved a long log off the ground and balanced it vertically, staggering forward before tossing it. The log spun, turning end over end before striking the earth with a dull thud.

Three men succeeded in tossing it farther than the others. Two of them were warriors from the mainland, both sons of clan-chiefs, while the third was Taran MacKinnon.

Rhona watched him toss the caber into the air. She'd seen Taran shirtless before and remembered his sculpted torso.

She wasn't the only one to notice. Two women seated beneath Rhona started to whisper and giggle.

"He may be an ugly brute, but he's got the body of a god," one of them tittered.

"Aye," her companion replied with a smirk. "I'd wager the rest of him is just as big and strong."

Rhona's face flushed at their bawdy language. She glowered down at the women, hating their smugness. It wasn't their fate that was to be decided here.

The Braemar Stone and hammer throw contests came next. Dughall did well in the former. Rhona watched him take his position. He took the large, heavy stone in his hand, and cradled it in the crook of his neck. Dughall's body tensed, his gaze focused on the strip of grass before him. A moment later he tossed the stone from standing, hurling it away from him. A cheer went up in the stands. He'd bested all the warriors who'd gone before him.

Rhona didn't join them.

Grinning, Dughall glanced up into the stands, his attention focusing on Rhona.

"Dughall MacLean looks confident today," Una murmured to her husband.

"Aye," Malcolm grunted, unimpressed. "He's cocky, but let's see if he lasts the distance."

"I can't believe Taran is competing," Adaira whispered to Rhona, her gaze wide as she watched the warrior stride up to take his turn at hurling the Braemar Stone. "I didn't think he was interested in taking a wife."

Rhona frowned, although she had to admit her sister was right. In all the years Taran had served her father, he'd been a lone wolf. Unlike some of the other warriors, who flirted with the servants inside the keep and stole glances at MacLeod's three daughters, he'd seemed oblivious to women.

Of course, that was ridiculous. He was an adult man; he would have needs like any other.

"I don't know what his game is," Rhona muttered, wincing as another bout of cheering rocked the stands— Taran had thrown well. "I can't believe he'd betray me like this."

Adaira turned to her, eyes as big as moons, as something occurred to her. "Do ye think he's in love with ye?"

"What?" Rhona almost snarled the question. Sometimes her sister could be as silly as a goose.

Unfazed, Adaira continued. "Don't look so shocked. It makes sense. Maybe that's why he's never taken a wife."

"Nonsense," Rhona snapped, turning her attention back to the competition. "It makes no sense at all."

By the time the first day of the games was over, Rhona had a terrible headache. Her mother had suffered from such pains, but until today Rhona had not. Her temples pulsed with red-hot agony, and the gilded late afternoon light hurt her eyes as she climbed onto the wagon that would take her back to Dunvegan Keep.

The pain made it difficult to concentrate, to focus. It felt as if an iron band had fastened around her skull and was slowly tightening. The intensity of the pain made Rhona feel giddy and nauseated.

For the first time since returning to Dunvegan, she longed for her cool, dark tower room, where she could shut out the daylight and the world.

The spectators moved on, their voices drifting through the warm air as they returned to their homes, their chores, and preparation for supper. Meanwhile, the contestants filed back to the keep, ready for an evening of drinking, feasting, and entertainment. Rhona had heard that a bard had come with the men from Lothian and would entertain the revelers.

Rhona was relieved she wasn't invited.

Instead, she fled up the steps to her tower room, her head throbbing with every step. Adaira joined her for a spell, and Liosa brought up a tray of supper, before Rhona sent them both away.

"I'll see ye first thing tomorrow morning," she assured her sister, who looked at her with a worried frown and hurt in her eyes. "For now I just need to sleep."

After Adaira and Liosa had gone, Rhona splashed cool water on her face, closed the shutters tight, and stretched out upon her bed. Agony constricted her skull with each breath, and she closed her eyes.

The noise from the rest of the keep, although muffled by thick stone, still reached her: the raucous laughter of men and the shrill, excited voices of women.

Everyone had enjoyed the first day of the games. All except Rhona.

With a groan, she turned over and pressed her aching forehead into the cool pillow. She only wished the pain would carry her away, pull her into oblivion, so that she would not have to suffer another day of this humiliation.

Chapter Fifteen

Decide My Fate

"READY FOR THIS, *Scar-face*?"

Connel Buchanan challenged Taran across the training ring. Two days outside under the hot sun hadn't agreed with Connel's pale skin. His grinning face was pink and shiny, his straw-colored hair tied back at the nape of his neck.

"Aye, I'm ready," Taran replied, not returning the grin. It was getting late in the day and he, like all the others who'd won the strength tests and progressed to the wrestling, was starting to tire. Connel was too, Taran noted. The redness in his cheeks wasn't just due to the sun, and sweat beaded his heavy brow.

The watching crowd had swelled as the day progressed, spectators now jostling around the edge of the wrestling ring. Taran hadn't looked up at the stands for most of the day. Yet he knew Rhona would be there, pale-faced and hollow-eyed next to her father.

"Wrestlers—take yer positions," Aonghus Budge called out from where he stood, legs akimbo at the edge of the ring. Although recently widowed, the clan-chief of the Budges of Islay was too unfit and portly to compete in the games. He'd brought a couple of warriors with him, but neither had gotten further than the strength contests the day before. As such, MacLeod had chosen Budge to oversee the wrestling matches.

Connel and Taran readied themselves. They gripped each other around the waist and the back. Taran rested his chin on Connel's shoulder and readied himself for the bout, gripping his opponent firmly. Connel did the same.

"Hold!" Aonghus's voice boomed across the ring.

The two men slammed into each other with brute force. The aim was simple: Taran had to either get Connel to break his hold or touch the ground with any part of his body save his feet. The best of five bouts won.

Connel was a stocky, heavily-built young man; a physique that had advantaged him during the strength games. However, he wasn't as strong as Taran. His bare feet scrabbled on the grass, his toes digging in, as Taran drove him back.

The contest didn't last long. Connel went down on one knee during the first bout, lost his hold in the second, and collapsed on one side in the third. Chieftain Budge grabbed Taran by the hand and pulled their arms aloft. "The winner!"

Cheers thundered across the field.

Breathing heavily, Taran went over to the ringside, where Gordon waited. His friend passed him a mug of ale. "Here ... ye look like ye could do with this. Although Connel needs it more by the looks of things."

Taran glanced over at where Connel stormed out of the ring, with face like thunder, and huffed out a breath. "Sore loser."

He lifted the mug to his lips and took a deep draft. The surrounding cheering died away, a murmur of anticipation taking its place. The whole day had been leading up to this moment.

The last two competitors left standing. The deciding wrestling match.

Taran's opponent stood on the far side of the ring, watching him.

Dughall MacLean was staring him down, challenging him to meet his glare, but Taran ignored the warrior for the moment.

Let him wait.

"Dughall's good," Gordon advised Taran. "He'll try to take ye down with his feet. Make sure ye are ready for him."

Taran nodded. "Aye ... I've been watching him wrestle," he replied. "I know his tricks."

He glanced north then, for the first time looking to the stands. This was to be the final contest of the games, the one that decided everything. He'd been avoiding looking in Rhona's direction, but he needed to now.

Seated between her father and Adaira, Rhona wore a low-necked green kirtle over a grey léine, clothing that hugged her statuesque form. Her long dark-red hair was loose, spilling over her shoulders, framing a face that had never been more beautiful. Even pale and tense, her full lips compressed, she captivated him.

Her grey eyes met his gaze and held for a long-drawn-out moment. Her skin tightened over her high cheekbones. He didn't need to exchange words with Rhona to know she was furious.

She looked at Taran as if she wanted to grab a pike and gut him.

He didn't blame her, but he didn't regret this either.

He'd been unable to sleep for the first two nights after their arrival back in Dunvegan. He'd wrestled with his conscience, his duty, and his desire—and in the end, his desire had won.

All his life he'd stood aside and let others claim what they wanted. For once he'd make a stand for himself. If he lost to Dughall MacLean, he would be bitter, but at least he would know he'd tried.

Either way, Rhona would hate him. But at least with him, she'd never be mistreated.

"Wrestlers," Aonghus Budge boomed once more, impatience in his voice. "Take yer positions."

Taran tore his gaze from Rhona and passed the empty mug back to Gordon. The warrior met his eye and winked. "I'd wish ye luck, but I know ye have no need of it ... ye never have. Ye have always won out of sheer force of will, and this time will be no different."

Taran's mouth curved into a wry smile. He appreciated Gordon's confidence in him. They'd soon find out if it was warranted.

Rhona twisted her fingers together until the joints hurt.

She was living a dark and terrible dream. Two men—both of whom she knew and neither of whom she wanted—were about to compete for her hand.

Taran MacKinnon and Dughall MacLean.

Either way, she was doomed.

Bile rose, stinging the back of Rhona's throat. Fate was cruel indeed. It was punishing her for her headstrong ways. Of all the warriors who'd competed here over the past days, it had come down to these two.

Hysteria bubbled up within her as she watched the two men grapple with each other, taking up positions.

"Hold!" Aonghus Budge barked.

The warriors slammed together, circling, their bare toes digging into the trampled grass as each tried to over-power the other. The roar of the surrounding crowd was so loud that it broke like thunder over the stand.

Rhona stopped breathing. She watched Dughall hook his left leg around Taran's right. The two men danced right and then left, crablike, and then Taran toppled sideways.

The crowd bayed, and Aonghus Budge grinned. He took hold of Dughall's hand and held it aloft. "The first bout goes to ... Dughall MacLean!"

Rhona swallowed. She felt as if she was going to be sick. Dughall couldn't win this. Fate could not be so cruel.

"This is yer fault, lass." Rhona glanced right to find her father studying her. Malcolm MacLeod's face was unreadable, his gaze shuttered. "Ye had the choice of many men ... but now ye really will end up with one ye don't want."

Rhona stared back at him. Part of her wanted to plead with him, wanted to break down in tears and beg him to stop these games. Yet she knew it would gain her nothing. All she had left was her pride; she wouldn't destroy the only thing that was keeping her rooted to her seat.

Her father blinked and then turned his face away, focusing on the match below.

"Hold!"

Taran and Dughall grappled once more. This bout was fast, edged in violence. The two men spun around each other, clinging in a death-grip. Dughall's leg struck out once more, but Taran danced out of his way. Taran was the bigger and heavier built man of the two, yet Rhona had seen that agility and flexibility almost counted more in a sport like this.

Her chest began to ache as Dughall brought Taran down once more, with a flip that sent his opponent crashing down onto his back.

Rhona muttered a curse under her breath, tore her gaze from the wrestling, and stared down at her hands. This really was happening.

"Do ye want Taran to win?" Adaira asked, her voice barely audible over the roar of the excited crowd. "Ye would prefer him over Dughall?"

Rhona's gaze snapped to where her sister watched her. Adaira's pretty face was pale, her eyes seeming unnaturally big this afternoon.

"I don't want either of them to win," she choked out the words.

"But ye just cursed."

"That's because soon the games will be over ... the next bout will decide my fate."

Rhona swung her attention back to the wrestling as the third bout commenced. She hadn't told her sister the truth. She had no desire to be Taran's wife, but she'd choose him over Dughall. Taran was no comely young warrior, but she'd spent enough time in his company to know he wasn't cruel. He wasn't a bully like Dughall.

Sweat glistened off Taran's bare back as the wrestling resumed. His scarred face screwed up in concentration as he fought for dominance. The expression made him look even more frightening than usual. In contrast, a grimace twisted Dughall's handsome face, turning him ugly. He twisted and shoved against his opponent.

Dughall's leg struck out, just as Taran's foot kicked forward and hooked behind Dughall's calf.

Letting out a roar, Dughall lost his balance and lunged sideways.

Cheering erupted as he slammed into the ground.

Wiping the sweat off his forehead with the back of his arm, Taran straightened up. A heartbeat later, Chieftain Budge grabbed his hand and yanked it aloft. "The third bout goes to Taran MacKinnon!"

Rhona watched Dughall spit on the ground and snarl something at Taran. It was too far away for her to make out the words, yet the insult seemed to have little effect on Taran. He merely gave Dughall a cold look while he shrugged out the muscles in his shoulders and waited for Budge to call them forward once more.

The fourth bout seemed to go on for an age. The warriors grappled, their grunts rising into the charged air. Dughall tried to hook his leg around Taran's numerous times, but at each attempt his opponent blocked him.

The bout ended when Taran spun them both around and kicked out at Dughall's ankle. The latter jumped back, lost his balance, and went down on one knee.

Two to two—the contestants were now on equal footing.

"God's bones," Adaira muttered next to Rhona. "I can't bear it."

Rhona clenched her jaw, grinding her teeth. The tension had turned her into a wreck. Sweat coursed down her back and between her breasts, and her heart pounded as if it had been her down there wrestling.

"The final and deciding bout." Aonghus Budge strode into the center of the ring, hands aloft. His ruddy face glowed as his gaze swept the crowd. "Who will win the hand of the lovely Lady Rhona? Contestants ... step forward."

Dughall and Taran did as bid. They stepped up either side of Budge, each taking the chieftain's opposite hand as he raised their arms high. Aonghus grinned at them, his attention shifting from Taran to Dughall. "Make this one count, lads." His voice rang out across the field. "Which one of ye will be lucky enough to tame that wild mare?"

This comment brought laughter and sniggers from the stands and the gathered crowd below. Rhona sucked in an angry breath, noting that although Dughall had grinned at the comment, Taran did not.

The warriors took their positions.

"Hold!"

And so it began.

The cheering was deafening. Around Rhona folk clambered to their feet, bellowing insults or encouragement. In order to see what was going on below, she was forced to stand up. However, her legs nearly gave way under her when she did so. Adaira grabbed her, looping her arm through Rhona's.

"Courage, sister," she murmured. "It's almost over."

Around and around they went, first one way, and then the other. Fast as an eel, Dughall struck, again and again, trying to hook his leg around one of Taran's huge calves. And after half a dozen tries, he managed.

Only this time it didn't end as it usually did.

Taran used his strength to his advantage, heaving Dughall against him. It was a parody of a lover's embrace—and would have looked foolish if there hadn't been so much at stake. They tottered forward a few paces, Dughall struggling and snarling in Taran's arms, and then backward.

A heartbeat later, Taran twisted around and launched the full weight of his body forward, unbalancing them both. Limbs still tangled, the two contestants crashed to the ground like two mighty trees, Dughall crushed beneath Taran.

Chapter Sixteen

Behold

TARAN ROSE TO his feet. He barely noticed the roaring and cheering crowd. Dughall still lay sprawled on the ground, chest heaving. The fall had winded him.

"We have a winner!" Aonghus was suddenly at Taran's side, gripping his hand and holding it high. Did he imagine it, or was there a vindictive gleam in the man's eyes? "Taran MacKinnon has won the Dunvegan Games, and in doing so he has won the hand of Rhona, daughter of Malcolm MacLeod."

The cheering continued, crashing across the arena like waves upon a shingle beach. Dughall rolled onto his side, his gaze seizing Taran's. "Ye fought dirty, Beast."

Taran favored the warrior with a dismissive look. "Aye, but then so did ye."

He looked away from Dughall, ignoring the hate on the man's face, and shifted his attention to the stands. The crowd was in a frenzy; folk applauded and whistled.

Yet amongst it all, Rhona remained as still as a statue carved from granite.

Taran's chest constricted. Her skin was ashen. He hadn't expected to see joy on her face at his victory, in fact, he hadn't let himself think about victory at all. He'd never thought he'd even get this far. Some of the warriors he'd competed against over the past two days had been formidable. And yet here he was.

And there Rhona was, looking as if her life was about to end.

Gordon appeared at his side then and slapped him on the shoulder. His friend was smiling. "Well done. He was a slippery bastard, but I knew ye would get the better of him."

Taran huffed. Exhaustion dragged down at him. His body ached. "Did ye? I wasn't so sure for a while there."

Their gazes held, and Gordon's smile wavered. "Are ye sure this is what ye want?" he asked, his voice almost drowned out by the cheering.

It was Taran's turn to smile, although the expression wasn't a humorous one. "It's too late for regrets," he replied. "I wouldn't have competed if I hadn't wanted to wed Lady Rhona."

Gordon watched him, understanding lighting in his eyes. "Ye kept that secret hidden well," he murmured. "Ye had me convinced of the contrary when I dared suggest ye loved her."

Taran waved him away, breaking eye contact. He didn't want to talk about his feelings for Rhona, or why he'd never confided in Gordon. Truthfully, he was beginning to wonder if he was the world's biggest fool. He'd just won the hand of a woman who would most likely hate him.

Eventually, the surrounding crowd quietened and a tense hush settled over the hillside. A cool breeze fanned in from the loch, feathering across Taran's heated skin as he watched the clan-chief of the MacLeods rise to his feet.

"Come forward, Taran MacKinnon." Malcolm MacLeod's voice boomed down from the stands. There was a harsh edge to it, and Taran realized that despite the chief's calm demeanor, MacLeod was angry.

At him—for winning his daughter's hand.

Taran left Gordon's side and did as his chieftain bid. He walked forward to the edge of the arena, his gaze meeting MacLeod's.

"Congratulations." There was no warmth there. Taran had served MacLeod since his sixteenth winter. His loyalty to the chief was unquestionable. Hence the name 'MacLeod's Hound' that those who'd been jealous of his status at Dunvegan Castle had given him. However, Taran had the sense that all of that was about to change. He'd stepped out of line, reached too far above himself. The clan-chief hadn't stopped him from competing— perhaps believing Taran would never reach the finals— but looking at the man's face now, Taran knew the truth of it.

MacLeod would never trust him again.

"Ye have won my daughter's hand," Malcolm MacLeod continued before inclining his head. "Stand up, Rhona ... so yer intended can look upon ye properly."

Beside MacLeod, Rhona obeyed. Her eyes glittered, and her jaw clenched. Even from yards away, Taran could see the tension quivering in her body. She looked like a deer set to flee.

"Behold the victor." Malcolm MacLeod's lip curled as he spoke. "A fine warrior, indeed. The Beast of Dunvegan has won his beauty."

This comment brought whispers, giggles, and smirks from the watching crowd.

Taran grew still. Never had MacLeod used that name with him. It was a taunt he expected from the likes of Dughall or Connel—not his chief. Malcolm's use of it now only made his resentment of Taran plainer.

Rhona's throat bobbed as she swallowed. But she didn't speak—nor was she expected to.

MacLeod's slate-grey eyes, so like his daughter's, speared Taran. "A warrior who has demonstrated such prowess, such skill, should receive his reward sooner rather than later." His voice dropped to a drawl. "Since we have so many visitors here, we shall not disappoint them ... the pair of ye shall be wed at sundown this evening, and Dunvegan will celebrate yer union with a great feast."

These words brought gasps from the surrounding crowd. Behind Taran, he heard Dughall spit a curse.

Rhona's eyes flew open wide, and she took a step toward MacLeod. She murmured something to her father, her expression panicked.

"Nonsense, lass," MacLeod cut his daughter off, his voice ringing across the stands. "Ye have plenty of fine clothes—choose one of them. Leave the rest of the preparations to the servants." His gaze shifted back to Taran. "Go bathe and make yerself presentable MacKinnon ... for yer bride awaits."

Rhona picked her way down the spiral stone stairwell. In her left hand she held her skirts aloft, while with her right, she steadied her passage. She'd barely eaten all day and was starting to feel light-headed.

"Rhona ..." Adaira's concerned voice sounded behind her. "Are ye well?"

"No," Rhona snapped. She'd never been further from well in her life. It felt as if all of this were happening to someone else, as if she watched from afar.

Adaira didn't reply. Rhona's tone had obviously warned her off.

Silently, the two sisters descended the tower and made their way along a vaulted hallway to the Great Hall. The twang of a harp and the rumble of excited voices reached them as they approached.

Rhona's stomach lurched, and her step faltered. She halted, frozen like a mouse under the glare of a swooping owl.

Adaira stopped next to her. "Rhona?"

Smoothing her sweating palms on the silken material of her kirtle, Rhona sucked in a deep breath, and then another. She'd never fainted—she wasn't that kind of woman. Yet at that moment, her limbs trembled under her, and her body felt as if it might crumble. She realized then that she was afraid, deathly afraid.

She dared not look at Adaira, for the pity she knew she'd see in her sister's eyes would be her undoing. Instead, she stared forward at where those open doors yawned like some dark maw before her.

"I'm not sure I can do this," she whispered.

A cool, slender hand touched hers. Adaira's fingers closed around hers, reassuringly strong and steady. "I wish I could spirit ye away from here," she murmured. "I understand now why ye fled."

Rhona squeezed her sister's hand back. "Ye are not still angry with me ... for leaving ye here?" It was good to focus on something else, something other than what lay before her.

"No ... not anymore." A beat of silence passed, before Adaira continued, her voice hardening. "Da shouldn't have forced ye into this."

Rhona shut her eyes and struggled to master her emotions. She needed to remain in control, put on a mask for all those curious stares that would stab her the moment she stepped into the Great Hall. She wouldn't put on a show for them. They'd had enough entertainment for one day.

"No," she said softly. "It's not right, but I can't change it now. I tried to run and failed ... there's nowhere to go now but forward. I must face this." And with that, Rhona inhaled deeply and released her sister's hand.

Opening her eyes, she walked the final few yards to the Great Hall.

Taran was the first to notice his bride-to-be enter the hall. Dressed in flowing pale blue, her thick red mane— threaded with white daisies—piled up on her head, Rhona looked like a queen as she glided toward him.

Head held high, she glanced neither right nor left. However, she wasn't looking at him either; her gaze seemed fixed upon the wall behind him where axes, swords, and shields hung upon rough stone.

The crowd had parted to admit her, all gazes riveted upon Malcolm MacLeod's second daughter—the one who had refused to wed.

The one who was about to marry the ugliest man in the keep.

Taran saw their smirks and heard their sniggers, the whispered words between the ladies' hands as their gazes darted from Rhona to Taran. He knew what they were saying, what amused them so.

Clenching his jaw, Taran shifted his attention back to Rhona. He didn't care what they said about him—he'd developed a tough hide over the years—but he did care that Rhona was now the subject of ridicule. By winning the games, he'd humiliated her.

But it was too late to be sorry for it now.

The priest stood behind him, and MacLeod and his wife watched from the side of the dais that Rhona now approached.

Even if he'd wanted to, Taran couldn't stop this.

Rhona forced herself to stop staring at the great shield, which had once belonged to her grandfather, upon the wall. With great reluctance, she lowered her gaze and let it rest upon Taran.

She'd never seen him dressed this way.

Taran wore braies of plaid, bearing the green and red cross-hatching of his clan, the MacKinnons. Supple boots of dark leather covered his lower legs. Across his broad shoulders and muscular torso, he wore a crisp white léine. His rugged jaw was freshly shaven, his short dark-blond hair still slightly damp from bathing.

Rhona stiffened as she studied him. His ice-blue eyes were steady as he watched her approach; nothing on his scarred, forbidding face gave his thoughts away.

Why are ye doing this?

She wanted to rage at him, yet her anger would have to wait till later.

The priest, a slight young man with thinning dark hair and sharp blue eyes, stepped forward. Rhona stopped next to Taran before the dais, and both of them faced the priest. "Please join hands."

Rhona swallowed before reaching out with her left hand. A heartbeat later, Taran took it, his big hand enveloping hers. His touch though was gentle, his skin warm and dry. He didn't seem to be nervous, not like her.

The priest stepped down to meet them. In his hands, he held a length of MacLeod plaid: yellow, black, and grey, threaded with red.

Slowly, he bound it around their joined hands, and then he began to speak. The man had a quiet, yet powerful voice that carried over the hushed crowd. "Behold the bride and groom ... who will be joined today in the sight of God in holy matrimony."

The priest continued, reciting the words Rhona had heard many times, for she'd attended a number of handfastings over the years. But Rhona barely listened today.

She could hear little over the thundering of her own heart.

Chapter Seventeen

The Bedding Ceremony

"TO THE BRIDE and groom!"

Malcolm MacLeod stood at the head of the chieftain's table, drinking horn aloft. His gaze scanned the room as if he dared anyone to contradict him.

None would.

Seated next to her new husband, Rhona watched her father. Handfastings were supposed to be joyous occasions, yet there was no happiness on MacLeod's face this evening. His eyes gleamed, and his bearded jaw was tight.

"To the bride and groom." Voices echoed high into the rafters of the Great Hall, and although Rhona dared not look at the faces of those surrounding her, she could hear mockery there. All of them had expected her to wed the son of another clan-chief, not MacLeod's Hound.

Rhona kept her gaze fastened upon the large, empty wooden platter before her. She would share the coming feast with Taran off it. The aroma of roast venison and mutton wafted through the hall. She wasn't sure how she was going to manage a mouthful without gagging.

Her father sank his bulk back down into the carven chair at the head of the table, and the rest of the hall followed suit. Conversation erupted as guests fell upon the feast.

Rhona swallowed as she watched Taran carve slices of venison and mutton, help himself to turnips mashed with butter and milk, and spoon a good helping of braised onions onto their platter. He then reached for a basket of bread studded with walnuts and held it out to her.

For the first time since the ceremony, Rhona raised her gaze to look at him. And in the midst of the feasters, the pair stared at each other for a heartbeat. It was a silent, guarded look. Taran's face was serious, although his eyes were shadowed. As she watched him, her husband's throat bobbed, before he wet his lips.

He *was* nervous. The realization came as a surprise. The man had appeared hewn from stone until now.

"Bread?" he asked when the silence between them drew taut.

Rhona nodded. She had not smiled once since entering this hall. The way she felt right now, she wondered if she'd ever feel light of heart again. Unspeaking, she took a bread roll and turned her gaze from him.

"Bramble wine for the bride?" A servant appeared at Rhona's elbow.

"Aye." Rhona grabbed the heavy goblet before her and held it aloft. She usually preferred ale to wine and drank sparingly. Tonight was different. Maybe some wine would take the edge off her misery, would make the rest of this ordeal easier to bear.

The servant filled her goblet, and Taran's, before moving on.

Ignoring the man beside her, even if she was acutely aware of his presence, Rhona lifted the goblet to her lips and took a large gulp, welcoming the warmth of the wine as it slid down her throat.

Please Lord make this night pass swiftly, she silently prayed.

However, as the sound of laughter and the lilt of a harp echoed off the stone walls, she realized that this was about to be the longest evening of her life.

"Rhona."

Taran's voice roused Rhona from her thoughts. Taking another sip—of her third goblet of wine—she reluctantly shifted her gaze to him. She found Taran watching her steadily.

"Ye can call me 'wife' now, ye know?" she challenged him. The words slurred in her mouth, warning her that the wine had gone straight to her head. She'd hardly touched the platter of food before her. It was still piled high with food, for Taran appeared to have little appetite either.

His mouth quirked. "I'll need time to get used to that."

She eyed him coldly. Around them, the hall thundered with raucous voices and laughter. It was so loud now that it drowned out the music. Still, the harpist played on at the end of the dais, where the chieftain's table sat.

No one could hear the conversation between the newlyweds, although—across the table—Rhona could sense Adaira watching her. The poor girl was seated in-between Aonghus Budge and Baltair MacDonald. Although Baltair ignored Adaira, Chieftain Budge hadn't. If Rhona hadn't felt so sorry for herself, she would have pitied Adaira this evening. Her sister had worn a hunted expression ever since taking her seat for the feast.

"I'm sorry." Taran's voice was gruff, as if he'd had to tear the words from his throat. "I know this isn't what ye want."

"Then why did ye go through with it?"

Taran didn't answer, although he continued to hold her gaze.

Rhona stared back. The wine had made her bold. She didn't usually stare like this, nor so brazenly hold a man's eye. Cressets burned on the wall behind them, illuminating the lines of Taran's face. He often looked as if he needed a shave, his rugged jaw shadowed, but he'd scraped the stubble off for his handfasting. His smooth jaw drew the eye to the two long scars that marred his face. The one that slashed vertically, from his brow and down his left cheek, was the scar that stood out the most.

She wondered how he'd gotten that awful wound and still kept his eye.

Rhona took another sip of wine, her gaze never wavering from him. "How did ye get those scars?"

The moment the question was out of her mouth, Rhona wanted to call it back. There were some things you just didn't ask someone, no matter how much wine you'd imbibed. Taran's gaze guttered, and he drew back from her as if she'd just spat at him. "It doesn't matter," he replied, his voice terse.

Then he turned his attention from her and reached for his own goblet of wine. Raising it to his lips, he took a long draft. His face had drained of color.

Rhona turned her attention back to her untouched meal. She wanted to apologize, and yet the words stuck in her craw. Why should she? He was the one who'd trapped her. She wanted to break his nose, and yet something inside her twisted at the sight of his ashen face.

"It's time for the bedding ceremony!"

The words Rhona had been dreading all evening reached her through the din of laughter and singing. The feast had long since ended, and the tables had been pushed back so that the revelers could dance.

Rhona and Taran hadn't joined them. Instead, they'd sat in stony silence while the rest of the hall celebrated. Eventually, red-faced and bleary-eyed, Malcolm MacLeod had lurched to his feet and held his drinking horn aloft to make his announcement.

Ice washed over Rhona, despite that the air was close and warm inside the hall. She kept her gaze fixed forward, not daring to look Taran's way. She didn't want to see his reaction.

"Come on then!" Aonghus Budge, even redder in the face than MacLeod, raised his goblet. "Get them up to bed."

Ribald laughter echoed around the hall, and some of the men shouted out coarse comments. Then, a group broke away from the dancing and moved toward the dais.

Rhona dropped her gaze to her hands. Her heart was pounding so hard she thought it might leap from her chest. She glimpsed movement from the corner of her eye and saw that Taran had risen to his feet.

"Don't look so worried, MacKinnon," one of the warriors jeered. "We'll be gentle with ye."

"Aye ... we'll carry yer pretty bride to bed," added another.

Taran let out a soft growl in return. "I don't need yer help. I'll carry her upstairs myself."

This comment brought forth hoots.

"Go on then," someone shouted out from the crowd.

"Rhona," Taran said gently. "Stand up."

Face flushing, Rhona rose to her feet. Her face glowed like a lump of peat. The humiliation wasn't to be borne. She didn't look toward her father or her sister. Instead, she turned to Taran. "Don't touch me," she growled.

Laughter rocked the hall. Taran's face tensed. Then he took a step toward her so that they were nearly touching. "Sorry, lass," he murmured, "but this has to happen."

A heartbeat later, he scooped her up into his arms and stepped away from the table. For a moment, Rhona was too stunned to react. But when the shock passed, she began to struggle. "Let me down."

Taran's arms fastened around her, pinning her against him. He skirted the table and stepped down from the dais. The crowd parted to let him through.

"That's the way to handle her, lad," Chieftain Budge called out. The laughter that followed this comment made a red haze of fury settle over Rhona. It pulsed inside her.

"Bastard," she addressed Taran through gritted teeth. "Put me down."

"I wouldn't," one of the men laughed. "A woman that skittish will run off."

"Make sure ye bed her, MacKinnon," Malcolm MacLeod called out from the dais behind them. "I'll have the sheets checked in the morning—and if they're clean, I'll have both of ye whipped."

Cheers reverberated around the room, and Rhona stopped struggling. Horrified by her father's callous words, she huddled against Taran's broad chest.

She couldn't believe her father had just said that.

Taran ignored them all, MacLeod included, and strode through the midst of the crowd. A group of men followed, heckling them, up to the tower room, where the servants had prepared the chamber for the newlyweds.

The priest was waiting for them. He stood next to the big bed that had been sprinkled with sprays of heather and rose petals.

Rhona knew why he was here—to bless the bed and witness the arrival of the couple. The crowd of drunken warriors, Connel Buchanan among them, jostled into the chamber behind Taran and Rhona.

The priest appeared unfazed by the escort. Instead, he turned to the bed and, dipping a hand into the pot he carried, sprinkled holy water over the coverlet. "Let us bless this bed, Lord so that this couple may remain firm in yer peace and persevere in yer will. May they have a strong union and be blessed with children, and finally arrive at the kingdom of heaven through Christ Our Lord ... amen."

As soon as the priest stepped back from the bed, Connel pushed his way forward. There was a glint in his eye that Rhona didn't like; the young man was well into his cups and wore a mean, bitter expression. "Into bed with ye then. I'll help the bride off with her clothes."

Taran lowered Rhona to the ground and turned, moving so that he barred Connel's way. "Get out."

The words fell heavily in the chamber.

"Ye heard the man," the priest said, as he headed toward the door. "Let the newlyweds have some privacy."

"I don't think so." Connel folded his arms across his chest and stared Taran down. "I think we'll stay and watch."

Taran aped the gesture, his feet shifting into a fighting stance. Rhona couldn't see his face but could feel his rising anger.

"I won't ask ye again," Taran growled. "Leave us."

"Make me," Connel sneered back.

Taran lunged with the same speed he had on the evening he'd caught Rhona. It shocked her now, as it had then, that a big man could move that fast.

A heavy fist slammed into Connel's nose, and the warrior sprawled back into the crowd of men standing behind him. He would have collapsed onto the ground if the other warriors hadn't caught him.

Blood streamed from Connel's nose. He cursed, sagging against the men who held him.

Taran flexed the hand he'd just punched Connel with. His gaze swept the group before him. "Get out … and take him with ye."

There were a few dark looks, curses, and muttered threats, yet no one else challenged Taran. Instead, they kept hold of Connel, who was frantically trying to stem the flow of blood from his nose, and left the chamber.

Taran followed them before he threw the heavy oaken door shut in their wake. The boom of the thudding door shook the room. Not taking any chances that the bedding party might return, Taran turned the iron key.

He and Rhona were now locked inside.

Chapter Eighteen

I Won't Lie With Ye

"I WON'T LIE with ye." Rhona faced Taran as he turned from locking the door. "Ye will have to force yerself on me."

Taran didn't reply. He merely favored her with a weary look and crossed the room to the sideboard, where the servants had left a ewer of spiced bramble wine and two goblets for them. Wordlessly, Taran poured them both a drink.

Watching him, Rhona could see the tension in his shoulders, the grimness of his jaw. It dawned on her then that he'd been dreading this moment as much as she had.

"I'm not going to rape ye, Rhona," he said, his voice low. There was a note of fatigue to his tone that hadn't been there earlier. He carried the goblets across to Rhona and handed her one.

She took it without a word of thanks, her fingers clenching around the stem. "So, what happens now then?"

His gaze met hers. "I don't know."

Rhona moved away from him, shifting over to the window. Liosa hadn't closed the shutters, for it was a warm evening. A sultry breeze whispered into the chamber, feathering across Rhona's face. She lowered herself onto the padded window seat and took a sip of wine.

Spiced with pepper and cinnamon, costly ingredients that she only usually tasted at Yuletide, the rich red wine was delicious. She really shouldn't drink anymore, for her senses had already been numbed by the wine at the feast. However, the nerves that danced in her belly needed settling. She was trapped in this room with her husband—a man who was supposed to bed her or they'd both be whipped in the morning.

Silence stretched out between them. Eventually, it was Taran who broke it. "I wish it didn't have to be this way. I didn't think yer father would make us wed so soon. I thought ye would be given time ... to warm to me."

Rhona turned to him, scowling. "I used to trust ye, Taran. I'll never do so again."

Taran actually flinched at that, his gaze shadowing. His throat bobbed. "And I hope ye will grow to trust me again."

She shook her head, her mouth twisting. "I hate ye."

Silence fell between them once more, and then he loosed a deep sigh. Crossing to the hearth, which sat unlit on this mild night, he leaned against the mantelpiece, still cradling his untouched goblet of wine. "I've made a mess of things."

"Aye, ye have." Rhona looked away from him, staring out into the dark night. There was no moon out tonight; the sky was pitch-black. She could hear the faint noise of the revelers, who were still dancing, drinking, and singing in the Great Hall below.

The sound made the center of her chest ache as if a heavy hand pressed down upon her breast bone. Her eyes burned, and she blinked, pushing back the tears that threatened. She wouldn't cry. Not here, not now.

Never had she felt so alone.

"It was my father," Taran said. His voice was barely above a whisper, yet in the silent tower room, she heard the words clearly.

"Excuse me?" She tore her gaze from the night and forced herself to look at him.

He met her eye. "Ye asked how I got the scars. It was my father."

Rhona went still for a moment, taking in the two dark slashes disfiguring his face. Then, she drew in a deep, shaky breath. "I shouldn't have asked ye that," she said, the words clumsy. "It was cruel."

"Ye are my wife." His voice was flat, emotionless. "Ye should know about my past." A beat of silence passed between them before he continued. "It happened a long while ago. Da was mad … a man torn between periods of morose moods and murderous temper. He terrorized my mother and thrashed me daily. Everyone knew what was happening, but none stopped it … not until the day he beat my mother to death. I tried to prevent him, and he slashed my face with a boning knife." Taran reached up, tracking the vertical scar with his fingertip. "He would have killed me too if our neighbors hadn't finally intervened."

Rhona stared, a sickly feeling welling inside her. "What happened after that?"

Taran's severe face turned even grimmer. "The MacKinnon clan-chief executed him … took his head off with an axe."

Rhona swallowed. She had no answer for that. Any response would sound glib.

She watched Taran in silence, really looked at him. For the first time ever, she saw beyond his role. To her, he'd only ever been her father's loyal warrior: the man who trained her in secret and the guard who shadowed her father. She'd never given a thought to his past, to his family.

"Do ye have any siblings?" she finally asked, her voice subdued.

He shook his head. "I had a younger sister ... but she died when she was three. Da's madness grew worse from that date."

Despite the warm evening, a shiver went through Rhona. She looked away from him, her gaze focusing on the darkness beyond the room.

He was right, this situation was a mess—and yet it wasn't just of his making, but hers too. She'd been too proud, too arrogant. She'd virtually goaded her father into hosting these games.

"Do ye remember the warrior from Atholl who visited us last winter?" she finally asked.

"Aye," he replied quietly. "The chieftain's son."

Rhona stared out into the night. "He was handsome and kind ... and I was rude to him."

Taran huffed out a breath. "I remember that."

Rhona tensed. "I humiliated him in front of the Great Hall, spurned him when he asked me to dance." She broke off here, wincing at the memory. "He left before dawn the following morning ... Da didn't speak to me for days afterward."

Taran didn't reply.

Rhona heaved in a deep breath and turned from the window. "Why would ye wish to wed such a shrew?"

He held her gaze, the moment drawing out between them. When he finally answered, his voice held a rasp. "Do ye really have no idea?"

Rhona shook her head in answer. She remembered what Adaira had said to her during the games then, and her body went cold.

Taran pushed himself off the mantelpiece and moved toward her. Rhona stared at him, frozen in place.

"I never wanted to feel this way," he continued. "But from the first time ye spoke to me—just after yer sixteenth winter—looked me in the eye, and asked me to teach ye how to wield a sword, I was lost."

Rhona clasped her fingers together, squeezing hard. "I had no idea..."

He came to a halt, around three feet from where she sat. His mouth twisted. "I'm good at hiding how I feel ...

it's how I've survived." He raked a hand through his hair, a gesture she'd never seen him do before. "I never intended to tell ye. Loving ye from afar was safe, easy. I'd resigned myself to the fact ye would wed someone else."

Loving ye from afar. The words made Rhona's breathing still.

"What changed?" She folded her arms across her chest, a protective gesture that created a barrier between them. "Ye didn't have to enter the games."

"Madness of a kind seized me," he admitted with a bitter smile. "I couldn't bear the thought of the likes of Dughall having ye. I told myself that if ye wedded me, ye would be protected at least. I might be foul to look upon, but I'd never raise a hand to ye. I'd never treat ye ill."

Rhona's chest squeezed hard. "Ye aren't *foul* to look upon."

His face twisted. "There's a good reason why folk call me 'The Beast of Dunvegan'."

"And they shouldn't." The words tumbled out of her. "It's not true."

"The fact remains, I'm no woman's choice of husband."

Rhona didn't deny it; she couldn't bring herself to lie to him. She'd never been the type to flatter or soften things. Even so, for the first time, she felt the loneliness and pain of this man's life. Scarred, shunned, isolated— no wonder he so loyally served her father. He had nothing else.

She glanced away, blinking rapidly. Tears threatened once more, and yet they weren't for her own predicament this time. The wine was turning her weepy.

"I lied before," she said softly. "I don't hate ye ... I just feel trapped. Da has just managed to achieve what he's always wanted—to lock me away."

A hush settled over the chamber, and they both let it draw out. Rhona was aware of Taran's nearness, his gaze upon her. Yet neither of them felt the need to speak for the moment. After the conversation that had just passed between them, Rhona was reeling. She wondered if he felt the same.

"So, what are we going to do about tonight?" she asked finally, addressing the problem that loomed over them like a great shadow.

"Yer father wasn't lying earlier," he replied. "He's angry with us both. Ye for defying him … me for daring to compete for ye. He'd happily wield the switch himself."

Rhona drew herself up, turning back to Taran. "He wouldn't beat me."

Taran raised an eyebrow. "He raised a hand to ye after ye escaped," he reminded her. "Do ye wish to test him?"

Rhona's pulse quickened. She wanted to deny it, yet she remembered how he'd struck her after her failed escape. She saw too the truth of the situation on Taran's face. She could bear the pain of being whipped, but the humiliation of it—for her father usually administered his floggings in front of an audience—would be difficult to recover from. She'd never be able to hold her head high inside this keep again.

And yet the thought of consummating this marriage, with this big, intimidating man before her, terrified her.

Rhona raised her goblet to her lips and took a large gulp of wine. She couldn't do it.

"Ye look terrified," Taran observed, his voice rueful. "Am I really such an ogre?"

Rhona gave a nervous laugh and took another sip of wine. "No, but I'm a maid … and this situation is …"

"Difficult."

She snorted. "Ye are the master of understatement tonight."

His mouth curved into a rare smile. "What if we made a game of it?"

Rhona stilled, gaze narrowing. "What?"

His smile faded, and his ice-blue eyes grew intense. "If we are to lie together tonight, we need to take things slowly, to ease into it."

Silence fell between them. Rhona's heart started to hammer. She didn't like the direction this conversation was leading them in. She was entering never-explored territory.

After a few moments, Taran continued. "Let us play a game of riddles. Ye ask me one. If I answer it incorrectly, I must take off an item of clothing."

Rhona inhaled sharply. "And what if ye get it right?"

"Then *ye* must remove a garment of my choosing."

Rhona's mouth had gone dry, her breathing shallow. "I don't like the sound of this game."

He raised an eyebrow. "Do ye have a better one in mind?"

"Knucklebones."

He snorted. "I'd beat ye."

"I wouldn't be so sure ... I'm a fiend at knucklebones."

"Let's play riddles ... a game that requires us to think," he replied. "Knucklebones is boring."

The directness of his gaze made Rhona's body grow warm, and her stomach dipped and pitched as if she perched upon a high swing. Such a game was too intimate, too risky—and yet an unexpected thrill of excitement went through her.

She raised her chin to meet his gaze. Drawing her shoulders back, Rhona inhaled deeply. "Very well. Who goes first?"

Chapter Nineteen

Riddles

SHE DIDN'T LIKE this game. It moved too quickly.

They'd only been playing it a short while and already they were both down to their last items of clothing. Rhona wore nothing but her long léine. Taran on the other hand was naked save for his braies.

The lamplight played across the muscular lines of his bare chest. Rhona remembered what those ladies in the stands had said about his body during the games, and felt heat rise, flowering across her chest and up her neck. They'd been crude, but they'd both been right—Taran MacKinnon's naked body was magnificent to gaze upon.

"I don't like riddles," she protested as she took off the necklace she'd worn for the handfasting. Gold and amber, it had once belonged to her mother. Her hands were trembling slightly, and it took her an age to unclasp the necklace. "It isn't fair anyway—men have more items of clothing to take off."

"No, we don't."

"But ye were always going to win."

Taran favored her with a small smile, although his gaze remained serious. "Or could it be that yer riddles are too easy?"

She glowered at him. "Or yers too hard?" She'd actually asked him the hardest riddles she could come up with, and yet he seemed to know them all.

"Come on," he replied. "It's yer turn."

Rhona huffed a breath and sat down upon the window seat. The warm night air tickled the naked backs of her arms. She felt exposed sitting here, wearing only her léine. The material was thin and clung to her form; she was thankful that Taran didn't let his gaze stray from her face as he waited for her riddle.

"All right then," she grumbled. "How about this one? What is the sister of the sun, though made for the night? The fire causes her tears to fall, and when she is near dying they cut off her head."

Taran frowned at that, scratching his chin as he pondered it. He sat upon a stool opposite her. Rhona watched him, holding her breath as she waited for him to come up with the answer. Taran seemed stumped.

"It's a candle?" he asked finally.

Rhona's heart leaped. *God's nails ... I've lost.* "Aye," she croaked. "That's right."

Silence drew out between them as she summoned the nerve to rise to her feet. They both knew what she had to do; there was no need for Taran to command it. "What happens," she croaked as she reached for the hem of her shift, "when we're both naked."

His gaze grew limpid, even as it never left her face. "We go to bed."

The promise in those words made her knees wobble beneath her. She truly was in the midst of a situation beyond her control, swept along by a tide she had long stopped fighting. The wine had taken the edge off, but even so, she was scared.

Holding her breath, Rhona grabbed her shift's hem and pulled it up over her head in one swift movement. There was no point in drawing out the embarrassment. Best to get it over with.

A heartbeat later, she stood there, naked before him.

Taran's gaze did leave her face then. It swept down over the length of her body and then up so that he met her gaze once more. She watched his lips part, his pupils dilate. Rhona's legs trembled underneath her in response.

He gave her a long look. "I suppose this means it's my turn."

Panic rose in Rhona's chest. She wanted him to remain clothed; the longer this game went on, the longer she'd have to avoid the inevitable. She reached for her goblet of wine but found it empty. *Satan's cods.* She needed more wine if she was to endure this.

"Are ye ready?" he asked.

Rhona swallowed before wetting her lips. She had no more clothing to remove, and if she answered one more of his riddles correctly, he'd be completely naked. Men didn't wear anything under their braies.

Reluctantly, she nodded.

"Truly no one is outstanding without me, nor fortunate," he began. "I embrace all those whose hearts ask for me. He who goes without me goes about in the company of death, and he who bears me will remain lucky forever. But I stand lower than earth and higher than heaven."

Inhaling deeply, Rhona paused. Curse him, but she knew the answer to this one. However, she needed to pretend otherwise. "Happiness?" she asked after a moment.

His brow furrowed. "The answer was 'humility' ... but I think ye knew that."

Rhona tensed. "No, I didn't."

He cocked his head. "No cheating."

"I'm not!" Rhona glared back at him. She fought the urge to cover herself up, to cross her arms over her bared breasts.

"Ready for another riddle then?" His voice had a husky edge to it now.

Rhona inhaled deeply, steadying herself. "Go on."

"I have one, and ye have one," he began slowly. "So do the woods, fields, streams and seas, fish, beasts, crops, and everything else in this revolving world."

Rhona drew in a measured breath. "That's a tricky one," she admitted after a moment. Good—she didn't know this riddle; she could answer honestly. Rhona plucked the first idea that swam into her thoughts. "Is it 'a shadow'?"

A beat of silence passed before Taran smiled. "Aye, that's right."

Rhona's breathing hitched. *God's bones ... no.*

Wordlessly, Taran rose to his feet and began to unlace his braies. Rhona watched him, her pulse skittering, her breathing suddenly ragged. She regretted ever agreeing to this wretched game. This was going too far. The chamber suddenly felt tiny, airless.

Taran's braies dropped to the stone floor, and he stepped out of them.

Rhona kept her gaze resolutely fixed upon his face. She wouldn't look down; she didn't want to see his rod. She wanted to bolt from this room and run howling into the night, naked or not. And yet she did nothing of the kind. She remained frozen to the spot as Taran approached her.

In just three paces he was standing before her, so close there was barely any space between them. She inhaled the warm male scent of his skin, aware of the heat that emanated from his body. She was a tall woman, but she felt small next to him.

"Rhona." He said her name in a caress, and despite herself, she shivered. Rhona averted her gaze, fixing it upon his shoulder. She couldn't bear to look him in the eye; it was too intense, too intimate. A moment later he lifted a hand and trailed his fingertips down her jawline to the slight cleft in her chin. "Ye are the loveliest sight I've ever looked upon. A man could die from wanting ye."

She sucked in a breath at these words, at the simmering need in them. She wasn't ready for this, didn't know how to respond or what to do, and yet a strange heat flared in her lower body at his words. There was a raw edge to him, to his words, that ensnared her.

His hand tracked lower, his fingertips tracing the column of her neck down to her collar bone, before trailing a lazy path between her breasts. His touch swept over the curve of her left breast, the backs of his hand grazing her nipple.

Rhona's breathing caught.

Taran moved then, dipping his head and lowering himself before her. He took her breast into his mouth.

Rhona gasped. Her hands went to his shoulders with the intention of pushing him away, but as he began to suckle, drawing her in, her fingers dug into his flesh and held on.

She didn't shove him from her. Instead, she held on for dear life as ripples of pleasure arched out from the tip of her left breast. A moment later he released her nipple and shifted to its twin. He was gentle at first, and then the pressure increased.

Rhona stifled a groan and swayed on her feet. She felt as if her legs might give way under her at any moment. His mouth was working magic on her; she had no idea she could feel this way. The way he suckled her made another sensation rise within her, an aching hunger. She didn't understand it, and the feeling scared her. What could she possibly be hungry for?

Taran tore his mouth from her breast and straightened up. He gazed down at her, his expression fierce. "It's time ... are ye ready?"

Rhona nodded, trying to quell the trembling in her limbs. "What must I do?"

"Lie down on the bed."

The command sent a tremor through her. She edged around him, moving toward the bed in tentative steps.

Fear and an odd excitement pulsed within her. How was it possible to be afraid, and yet yearn for something? It felt as if she had strayed into a strange dream. What was she doing alone in this chamber, stark naked, with Taran MacKinnon?

We are man and wife, she reminded herself, *and this is our wedding night.*

Keeping her gaze upon his face, she lay down upon the coverlet, amongst the sprays of heather and rose petals. The sweet, woody scent enveloped her.

Taran towered above Rhona, and for a long moment, he merely observed her, his gaze drinking her in.

Rhona attempted to steady her breathing. Her body flushed as his gaze slid down the length of her, branding her. Her skin tingled, and her breasts ached.

Without meaning to, she let her own gaze shift from his face, down the hard, muscular planes of his chest, to his groin.

She stifled a gasp. He was fully aroused and very big. The hard column of his erection reared up against his belly. Rhona swallowed. Dampness flooded between her thighs at the sight of it, even as her pulse started to thunder.

Caitrin had told her that her first time with Baltair had been traumatic. Would Taran hurt her?

Chapter Twenty

Nothing to Prove

TARAN LOWERED HIMSELF onto the bed, and she felt it give under his weight. On his knees, he moved between her thighs, parting them.

Mortification flooded through Rhona. He had spread her thighs wide, exposing her to him. There was nowhere to hide. No one had ever looked upon her there. She watched him gaze down at her, saw the flush that suddenly stained his cheekbones. His chest was now rising and falling fast; she felt the tremble in his body.

Looming over her, Taran placed the head of his shaft against the entrance to her womb and began to gently rub himself against her. Rhona gasped at the sensation, at the slick heat of their flesh meeting.

A throb began deep in her belly.

He continued to move against her, shifting his hips in slow, sinuous circles.

Groaning, Rhona threw back her head against the coverlet and rode the waves of pleasure. Unbidden, her thighs parted wider, and she hooked one leg around his hips, drawing him against her. She was no longer afraid. She now ached to have him inside her. She didn't care if it hurt; she felt as if she could die from wanting.

"Rhona," he gasped her name. "I want to take this slow ... I don't want to hurt ye."

She whimpered in response and met his gaze. She wasn't sure how much more of this she could take before she started begging.

They stared at each other for a long moment, and then Taran breathed a curse. Reaching down, he grasped her hips, lifting her up to meet him. And then, slowly, he slid into her.

It didn't hurt at first, just a full sensation as she stretched to accommodate him. But then, a sharp, stinging pain caught her by surprise. Rhona gasped, her body growing taut. Her eyes widened, and she grasped hold of Taran's wrists, stilling him.

He gazed down at her. "That's it, lass," he murmured. "The worst is over ... it shouldn't hurt anymore."

And with that, he lowered himself further. Rhona felt the full length of him penetrate her. A wonderful aching sensation filled her womb.

"Oh," she gasped, releasing his wrists.

"That's right," he rasped. There was an edge to his voice as if he was barely clinging onto control. "Give yerself to it."

Rhona obeyed him. She closed her eyes and let her head roll back once more. Caitrin hadn't told her that it could feel like this, no one had.

However, her eyes snapped open, her head lifting, when Taran started to move inside her. Pleasure coiled deep within her womb, tightening, building. The intensity of it frightened her. "Taran," she gasped. "I can't ..."

Taran murmured her name, hushing her. He took hold of her left knee, for her right leg was still wrapped around his hips, and lifted it high. He then drove into her. He took her in slow thrusts, his gaze never leaving hers.

Rhona heard a woman's cry echo through the chamber—it must have been her own, although she had never before made such a sound. It was a wild, keening cry. Her body trembled, need thrumming through her.

And yet there was more, so much more, she could sense it as the aching pleasure deep within coiled tighter still.

She was reaching toward it, brushing the edge of it, when Taran's body arched above her.

She stared up at him, fascinated, watching him go rigid. The sinews on his neck stood out as he threw his head back and choked back a cry. Even now, even at this moment, the man still fought for control.

Then she felt the heat of him release inside her, and Taran's body shuddered.

Rhona awoke slowly, blinking in the warmth of the sun that filtered in through the open window.

She had slept deeply, her limbs loose and rested. However, her mouth and throat felt parched, and her head ached.

Too much wine.

Stifling a groan, Rhona pushed herself up onto one elbow. Her gaze settled upon the naked man who lay sprawled upon the bed next to her. For a moment, she just let her eyes feast upon him.

How had she ever thought Taran MacKinnon ugly?

His face, relaxed in sleep, was much softer than when he was awake. Even the scars seemed less evident. His mouth, which often appeared a hard slash, was sensual this morning, his usually furrowed brow smooth. She realized then how much of the cares of the world he carried with him.

Her gaze slid down to his body, and memories of the night before flooded back. Heat crept up Rhona's neck as she remembered what they'd done, how she'd arched under him and cried out. He'd taken her once more before exhaustion pulled them both down into its clutches. That coupling had been even better than the first. He'd brought her to the brink, and then taken her over the edge with him.

Rhona's cheeks flushed hot as she recalled how she'd gasped his name, had pleaded with him for more. She ran a hand over her face, stifling a groan of mortification. How would she ever look him in the eye again?

Taran stirred, his eyes flickering open. "Morning," he rasped. "Lord ... my mouth feels like a piece of leather."

"Too much wine will do that to ye," she replied huskily. "I'll get us some water." Rhona slid off the bed, pulled on a robe, and padded over to the sideboard, where a ewer of water and two cups sat. Filling them, she returned to the bed.

Taran had pulled up the sheet to cover his naked loins when she handed him the cup. Rhona's chest constricted; she didn't know whether to be disappointed or relieved by his modesty.

She perched on the edge of the bed and drank the water. An awkward silence fell between them. Eventually, Taran broke it. "Are ye well, Rhona?"

She glanced up, meeting his gaze. "Aye."

"Last night ... I ... we ..." His voice trailed off. The look on his face was so pained she almost pitied him.

"Don't worry," she replied. "Ye didn't force me, Taran. I lay with ye willingly." The relief in his gaze made her smile. "What? Did ye think I'd rage at ye?"

His mouth curved. "I didn't think that far ahead. I got carried away last night."

Rhona took another sip of water and observed him over the rim of her cup. It was odd how shy she was of him this morning. It made her realize that although they were wed, and had lain together as man and wife, they weren't comfortable around each other. Until yesterday their ranks had imposed a certain type of relationship upon them, a distance.

Taran drained his cup before running a hand down his face. "What time is it?"

Rhona glanced toward the window, at where the sun pooled upon the flagstone floor. Outside, she could hear goats bleating and the laughter of children. "Almost noon, I'd say."

He stiffened, gaze widening. "I've never slept so late."

She favored him with an arch look. "Since it's the morning after our wedding, I think my father will forgive ye."

Unfortunately, the mention of Malcolm MacLeod had an instant effect on them both, like a cloud blocking the sun. Taran scowled, and Rhona's mood soured.

Her father might end up overlooking her past defiance now that she was a wife, but she would never forgive him for humiliating her. Nor would she ever forget his parting words as Taran had carried her from the Great Hall.

I'll have the sheets checked in the morning—and if they're clean, I'll have both of ye whipped.

Rhona frowned, her gaze shifting to the crumpled coverlet. There was a small dark stain upon it. Her fingers tightened around the cup. "Ye are not the 'Beast of Dunvegan', Taran," she said, her voice low and fierce. "My father is."

She felt the bed shift. A moment later Taran was sitting next to her, his thigh pressing against hers. He was so close she could see the blond stubble on his jaw. His nearness unnerved her. Rhona gripped her cup tightly, staring down at it. She felt so strange this morning, full of conflicting emotions.

It was as if she'd been asleep her whole life and had just awoken. Everything seemed different.

Taran hooked a finger under her chin, raising it gently so that their gazes met. The tenderness in his grey-blue eyes made her breath catch.

"I never would have wished for any of this, Rhona," he said softly, "and yet I can't bring myself to regret it. If I die tomorrow, I'll go to my cairn a happy man."

She managed a half-smile. "Ye speak hastily ... I don't think I'll make a good wife. Ye may regret this yet."

His mouth quirked. He let go of her chin and brought his hand up, stroking her cheek. "Can we start again?" he asked.

"What do ye mean?" His touch made her breathing quicken. She was aware of how close he was sitting, the heat of his naked body.

"Would ye let me woo ye?"

Rhona inclined her head, pushing aside the need that was curling like wood smoke in her belly. She would have smiled if his face hadn't been so serious. "But we're already wed?"

"Aye, but not in the best circumstances. I want a chance to prove myself to ye."

Their gazes held. The earnestness in his eyes made Rhona's throat constrict. It was a strange sensation, one she had never felt before. Did she deserve a man like this? She hadn't treated Taran well at all, and yet it was him who wanted to be worthy of her.

She reached up and cupped her hand over his, pressing it against her cheek. "Ye can woo me if ye like," she murmured, "although ye have nothing to prove."

Chapter Twenty-one

Friendly Advice

RHONA FOUND ADAIRA in the gardens behind the castle. Her sister was collecting flowers, placing them carefully in the wicker basket she carried slung over one arm. It was a humid afternoon, with not even a sea breeze to cool the air. As such, Adaira wore a light linen kirtle. Her thick brown hair was piled up on her head, although tendrils had escaped, curling at the nape.

Adaira didn't see her sister approach. Instead, she swiped at a fly that dove at her face, before muttering a curse as she caught her thumb on a rose thorn.

"I hope I didn't teach ye that word," Rhona teased. "Una would faint to hear it."

Adaira swiveled around, a smile stretching across her face. "I was wondering when ye would surface."

Rhona gave a soft laugh. "Too much wine, I'm afraid."

She saw concern shadow her sister's eyes and held up a placating hand. "Worry not, I am well. The marriage is consummated. Da has no cause to flog us."

Her sister's shoulders relaxed at this news. "I've been so worried."

Rhona smiled. She appreciated her sister's concern; it felt as if she was the only one in the keep who actually cared about her welfare. "Continue with yer collecting," she said, stepping close and peering into Adaira's basket. "We can talk while ye work."

"I was going to make rosewater," Adaira said, moving along the avenue of roses. "Would ye like some?"

"Aye, ye know I love the scent of roses."

Adaira stopped and carefully snipped off three pink roses from a bush. She then cast Rhona a veiled look. "So ... what was it like?"

"What?" Rhona replied, pretending she didn't know what Adaira was asking. She knew only too well, for she herself had been filled with curiosity after Caitrin had wed.

"The bedding," Adaira said, a groove forming between her eyebrows. "Is it as awful as Caitrin said?"

Rhona paused, wondering how best to answer her sister. Her experience last night had been a revelation. "I thought it would be an ordeal," she admitted quietly. "I was terrified."

Adaira's blue eyes grew wide, and she straightened up, her slender body growing tense. "So, Caitrin was right?"

Rhona shook her head. "She would have spoken the truth about her own experience ... but mine was different." She broke off here, suddenly embarrassed. "Taran wasn't what I expected."

She didn't think her sister's hazel eyes could get any bigger, but they did then. "Did ye *enjoy* it?"

Rhona cleared her throat before managing a nod.

Adaira's cheeks flushed. "So ... are ye in love with him?"

"What?" Rhona gave a laugh. Adaira could be such a goose. Her head was full of silly ideas. "How could I be?"

Her sister looked crestfallen. "I just thought ... after last night ..."

"Just one night? Love takes time."

Adaira nodded. She then moved on to the next rose bush and started snipping. "It's all backward, isn't it?" she said after a pause. "Ye are supposed to fall in love *before* ye wed."

"Aye," Rhona agreed. "But there are many unions where there is never any love. I'm grateful Taran won the games and not Dughall MacLean."

Adaira shuddered. "That man makes my skin crawl ... although not as much as Baltair MacDonald does."

Rhona frowned. "Has he been bothering ye again?"

"Not since ye interrupted us," Adaira replied. "I think ye offended his pride. He makes a point of looking through me these days ... and I'm grateful for it."

"And I'm relieved ... I wish our sister wasn't wed to the brute."

Adaira glanced up, her gaze shadowed. "She's so unhappy, Rhona. I don't want to wish anyone dead, but I sometimes find myself hoping he chokes on a fishbone. That way Caitrin could come back and live with us."

Rhona sighed. She too had fantasized about Baltair MacDonald meeting his end, although her imaginings had been a lot bloodier than her gentle sister's. "Maybe he will," she replied, before favoring Adaira with a wicked smile. "Or someone will poison his wine."

Gordon was shoeing a horse when Taran found him.

The warrior plunged the glowing iron horseshoe into a pail of cold water after shaping it, and steam billowed. A few feet away the waiting horse snorted and stamped its unshod foot.

Sensing someone's approach, Gordon glanced up. "Good afternoon," he greeted Taran with a grin. "Ye look a bit worse for wear."

Taran grimaced. "Aye, a handfasting will do that to a man."

Gordon straightened up and wiped his sweaty forehead with the back of his arm. "I've never attended a celebration like it." Gordon eyed him, his expression speculative. "The bride didn't scratch yer eyes out, I see?"

Taran's mouth curved. His friend's curiosity was palpable. "No, she didn't."

Gordon put aside the horseshoe, his work forgotten. "And are ye preparing yerselves for a whipping?"

"There'll be no need for that."

Gordon inclined his head before giving a low whistle, his mouth twitching. "Ye rogue. I didn't think she'd let ye anywhere near her."

Taran huffed. "I'll try not to take offense at that."

Gordon scratched his stubbled jaw. "So, all is well between ye?"

"For the moment," Taran replied. He paused here, considering the question he'd sought his friend out to ask. He wasn't sure how to present it, so he decided to be blunt. "Gordon ... how did ye manage to woo Greer?"

Gordon raised an eyebrow. "Who says I've succeeded?"

"Ye are set to wed her at Samhuinn. The girl adores ye."

The warrior cleared his throat and glanced away. Taran's candor had thrown Gordon off guard; he actually looked embarrassed. "I'm not sure what I did to deserve her," he said finally. "Why do ye wish to know?"

"I must woo Rhona."

"But ye are already wed to her."

"It matters not. I want my wife to love me."

Gordon's gaze widened. "Of course," he murmured. "I'd forgotten that ye have been long carrying a torch for her."

"Aye." Taran dragged in a deep breath. The night before seemed like a dream, but everything had moved so fast. He wanted to take things back to how they should have been. "Do ye have any advice?"

A wolfish smile spread across Gordon's face. "Aye, throw the lass down on the bed every night and plow her till she begs for mercy. She'll soon not be able to live without ye."

Taran raised an eyebrow. "Is that it?"

"Aye." Gordon puffed out his chest. "It works for me."

Taran snorted, casting his friend a rueful look. He was still no wiser about how to approach his wife, to win her heart. "Remind me not to ask ye for advice in future."

Supper in the Great Hall was a tense affair that evening. Taran and Rhona joined the chief, his wife, Adaira, and Aonghus Budge at the long table upon the dais. Many of the warriors who had attended the games had left for home, emptying out the keep. Baltair MacDonald had departed for Duntulm as well.

The Great Hall seemed silent after the revelry of the night before.

Rhona broke a piece of crust off the hare pie and chewed it slowly. Beside her, Taran ate with a similar lack of enthusiasm. The mood at the table had robbed them both of appetite.

Malcolm MacLeod sat hunched over his meal. He devoured it with grim determination as if his supper were a foe to be vanquished. He had not spoken a word to either his daughter or his son-in-law since they'd joined him at the table. Beside Malcolm, Una nibbled at her meal, a pinched expression upon her pretty face.

Aonghus Budge broke the weighty silence. He leered across the table at Taran and raised his goblet to him. "Good to hear yer new wife did her bidding last night."

Taran didn't answer. Rhona felt him grow still next to her; the thigh that rested against hers under the table tensed.

Oblivious, Chieftain Budge blundered on. "Although with a face like that, I suppose ye have always had to force yerself on women, eh laddie?"

Una tittered, and Malcolm gave a snort that might have been a laugh.

Rhona inhaled sharply, noting that Taran's fingers had clenched around the bone hilt of the knife he'd been using to cut himself a wedge of cheese.

"He's not the husband I'd have chosen for her, Budge," MacLeod growled. He looked up from his pie, his iron-grey gaze baleful as it swiveled to Taran. "But in the end, Rhona got what she deserved."

"They're well suited then," Aonghus Budge replied.

Rhona raised her goblet to her lips and took a measured sip of wine. After the previous night's overindulgence, she was wary of drinking too much. Across the table, she met Adaira's eye. Her sister wore a pained expression.

Chieftain Budge helped himself to another wedge of pie before he glanced at Adaira. Like the night before, she'd been seated next to him. "I see ye are very different to yer willful sister, Lady Adaira. Mild-mannered and biddable."

Adaira raised her gaze and gave him a startled look. She opened her mouth to reply, but her father cut her off. "Aye, she's a good lass ... a credit to her sire. A daughter who has always known her place."

Rhona watched her sister's slender jaw tense. Irritation flared in her hazel eyes. "I admire my sister," Adaira said, her voice so low it was barely above a whisper. However, it carried down the table. "I wish I had her spirit."

Rhona cast Adaira a grateful smile.

But her sister's comment hadn't pleased their father. "Save yer admiration for those who warrant it," Malcolm replied with a scowl.

Chapter Twenty-two

True Secrets

"I CAN'T BEAR it." Rhona finished unbraiding her hair and turned away from the window. Outside the long twilight was drawing out. The sky to the west had turned dusky, promising another warm day to come. It had been the hottest summer Rhona could ever remember. "How long will he continue to insult us?"

"For as long as it suits him," Taran replied. Like her, he was readying himself for bed. He had just unlaced his heavy mail shirt and was shrugging it off. "Best to ignore it. He'll get bored eventually."

Rhona met his eye. "I wish we could go away from here."

Taran's gaze clouded. "And I wish I had a broch we could live in ... unfortunately though, my father was the youngest of five brothers."

"But we could go to live amongst yer kin at Dunan?"

Taran huffed. "I left my birthplace for a reason. The MacKinnon clan-chief makes yer father look like a lamb."

Rhona heaved a sigh. "So, we're trapped here then." She stepped behind the screen in the corner of the chamber and began to undress. Despite the intimacy they'd already shared, she felt shy around her husband. She wasn't used to sharing her space with a man; all her life she'd only ever slept in the same chamber as her sisters. The newness of it put her on edge.

Disrobing, she donned a long linen léine. She emerged from behind the screen to find Taran had stripped down to plaid hose and a sleeveless tunic. He then climbed into bed.

Rhona hesitated. "Do ye not sleep naked?"

The look he gave her was almost pained. "Aye … usually."

"So why don't ye undress?"

His gaze met hers across the chamber. Excitement fluttered under Rhona's ribcage. The day had seemed long, and although all of this was new to her, she'd found herself looking forward to seeing Taran naked again.

His throat bobbed. "I bedded ye last night because it was necessary," he replied quietly, "to save us both a beating. But things are different now. I told ye this morning I wanted to woo ye … and so I shall."

Rhona swallowed. "Didn't ye enjoy it?"

His face tightened. "Aye, very much." His voice had a rasp to it now. "I just want us to get to know each other properly before I bed ye again."

Rhona inclined her head, her gaze narrowing. She had never heard of the like: what husband acted this way?

Taran moved over and patted the mattress next to him. "Come to bed, Rhona. Let us talk."

Body tense, she padded over to the bed and climbed in next to him. "What about?" She knew he was just trying to be kind, respectful. Yet a part of her was disappointed. Last night he'd given her a taste of something she now found herself hungry for.

They lay down next to each other, shoulders touching. "Tell me a secret," he said after a moment, "something no one else but ye knows."

Rhona glanced over at his profile. "Something I haven't even told my sisters?"

He met her eye, smiling. "Aye … a true secret."

Rhona heaved in a deep breath and thought hard. There were a number of things she'd kept to herself over the years. She wasn't sure which secret to share.

"I saw one of the Fair Folk once," she said finally.

He rolled over onto his side toward her, propping himself up on an elbow. "Ye did?"

She wondered if he believed her. The Fair Folk, or the Aos Sí as they were also known, were a part of this isle's folklore. Fairy mounds and stone circles littered the island's green hills. Folk were wary of them.

"I was around eight," Rhona replied. "And out exploring the shore with my sisters. We were collecting shells before the twin fairy mounds north of the keep."

Taran nodded. "I know the place."

"We had lingered too late, and dusk came upon us," Rhona continued. "We were just about to turn for home when I saw a woman standing before the mounds. She was clad in flowing white, her hair long and dark. She had the face of an angel. I've never seen anyone so beautiful."

"Did yer sisters see her too?"

Rhona shook her head. "They'd already turned back." She paused as the memory of that strange day returned to her. The scent of brine from the loch, the mist that curled like crone's hair around the woman's skirts. "We looked at each other, and then she smiled. It was a lovely expression, full of gentleness and warmth ... and then she beckoned to me."

"She wanted ye to follow her?"

Rhona glanced back at him and saw that his brow had furrowed. "Aye ... and I would have too if Da's voice hadn't reached me. He'd come out looking for us, ye see. He bellowed my name and broke the spell. I glanced over my shoulder at where my sisters were running toward him, and when I looked back the woman was gone."

"Ye had a narrow escape," Taran said gently. "She would have taken ye."

Rhona nodded. "I knew it too afterward ... that's why I never said anything to my sisters, or to Da." She swiveled around to face him properly. "Yer turn. Tell me a secret."

Taran met her eye. "I'm afraid of rats."

Rhona drew back, incredulous. "Is that it?"

"I'm terrified of the bastards, Rhona. Just the sight of one sends me into a cold sweat."

She favored him with an arch look. "Ye are teasing."

He shook his head. "I wish I was."

She huffed. Taran MacKinnon was the biggest and fiercest of her father's warriors. She couldn't imagine him afraid of anything. Certainly not rodents. "No one likes rats," she said after a moment, "but what do ye find so repellent about them?"

"Their long naked tails," he said with a twist of his face that wasn't feigned. "Their scrabbling feet, beady eyes, and twitching noses. When I was a bairn, Ma used to check my bed every night to make sure there weren't any rats hiding under the sheets ... until Da stopped her. He said she was coddling me too much."

"And no one knows of this fear?"

His gaze seared hers. "Only ye." The way he said the words made Rhona's pulse quicken. She knew so little about her husband.

All that was about to change.

"Keep yer elbows bent and close to yer body," Taran commanded, "and keep yer sword raised at all times."

Rhona snorted, circling him, the hilt of her wooden practice sword gripped tight in both hands. "I know all this."

"Ye are rusty, lass," Taran replied, brow furrowing. "It bears repeating."

Rhona raised an eyebrow. The pair of them faced each other in the practice yard. Now that they were wed, her father could no longer forbid Taran from training her. Three days had passed since their handfasting, and Rhona was eager to restart her lessons with Taran. Dressed in leggings, a loose léine belted at the waist, high boots, and with the wind tugging at her braided hair, she felt ridiculously happy this morning.

Taran attacked unexpectedly, with a speed she'd come to anticipate. The blade of his practice-sword cut through the cool morning air.

Rhona stepped back and brought her blade up to block the attack. She then twisted free and danced sideways, grinning. "Ye are fast, husband ... but not fast enough."

"And ye are full of yerself, wife," he growled back, his gaze twinkling. "Too much so."

He attacked again.

Rhona parried this time, pushing his sword out of the way with her own, before she attacked him.

A smile split Taran's face. He was enjoying this—as much as she was.

Clack. Clack. Clack.

The ring of their colliding blades echoed out over the yard. Rhona was vaguely aware of a crowd gathering around the edge. Greer, the cook's daughter was among them. Like many in the keep, Greer would have heard the rumor that Rhona had long trained in secret; she could feel the curiosity in Greer's stare now as she watched her.

However, Rhona didn't take her eyes off Taran.

When he attacked her again, she counter cut him— stepping back and then swinging her blade around to strike his arm. The wooden blade struck Taran's forearm. He let out a hiss and shifted back, out of reach.

Grinning, Rhona went after him. She stabbed her blade toward his torso, going for his belly.

Taran stepped to the side, his blade sweeping around. Too late, Rhona realized she'd left her flank exposed. An instant later the wooden blade slammed against her ribs.

Rhona lurched to the side, going down on her knees as the breath gusted out of her.

"Only stab when yer opponent is incredibly vulnerable," Taran warned her. "Ye just left yerself wide open to an attack."

Rhona gritted her teeth and climbed to her feet. "I knew that."

Taran huffed. "As I said ... ye are rusty."

"She's a woman," a belligerent voice intruded. "She doesn't know what she's doing."

Rubbing her aching ribs, Rhona glanced over her shoulder at where Dughall MacLean stood at the edge of the practice yard. Connel Buchanan stood next to him. The smirks on both their faces made her hackles rise.

"My wife handles a blade as well as ye, MacLean," Taran replied. His tone was mild, although when she glanced back at him, Rhona saw a warning in his eyes.

Dughall snorted. "Maybe ye should lend her to me awhile then ... let me see for myself." His lip curled. "And then after I've bested her, I've got another sword she can attend."

This comment made Connel snigger, although none of the surrounding crowd appeared to share the young man's mirth.

Taran's gaze narrowed. Tension suddenly crackled in the air.

One look at Dughall's face told Rhona that he nursed a great bitterness toward her husband. A muscle ticked in his cheek, and his large hands fisted by his sides.

Taran cast aside his wooden practice sword and approached Dughall in long strides. Rhona tensed. This was what Dughall wanted. He was deliberately goading Taran, hoping he'd make him lose his temper.

However, Taran MacKinnon wasn't easily drawn into a fight. He'd spent his life weathering taunts and insults. Instead, he pushed his face close to Dughall's, and the two men eye-balled each other for a long moment.

When Taran spoke, his voice was deathly cold. "Never."

Chapter Twenty-three

Lammas Morn

"ARE YE SURE about this, Taran?" Rhona cast a wary glance up at the sky as she followed her husband down to the loch's edge. "It looks like it might rain."

Taran cast her a look over his shoulder and smiled. "Just a few clouds ... nothing to worry about."

Rhona pursed her lips. "If ye say so."

Reaching the pebbly edge of Loch Dunvegan, Rhona's gaze alighted upon the small boat awaiting them. She cast Taran a questioning look. "Is this yer surprise?"

Taran smiled once more, an expression that made Rhona's breathing hitch. He looked like a different man when his gaze softened with humor and a smile stretched across his face. It made him look younger. "Aye, the first of them."

Excitement danced in her belly as she gazed at him. Three weeks had passed since their handfasting. But still, Taran hadn't touched her. He'd not even tried to kiss her.

She ached for him to do both.

Rhona adjusted the woolen shawl around her shoulders. A cool breeze breathed in off the loch. The summer was waning, and today was the feast of Lammas, celebrating the first wheat harvest of the year.

Adaira had gone off to visit the bustling Lammas market taking place in Dunvegan village this morning. Local women would decorate the altar of Dunvegan kirk with sheaves of corn, flowers, and breads made from the first reaping of wheat, barley, oats, and rye. Later on, folk would feast on breads, cakes, and ale in the village market square.

Rhona stepped into the boat and settled herself down, adjusting her skirts around her while Taran pushed the craft out onto the water. Climbing in, he then began to row the boat away from the shore.

Despite the dubious sky, Rhona found herself enjoying the outing. She twisted, her gaze taking in the majesty of Dunvegan Castle behind her. Surrounded by green, its great curtain wall and battlements rose high above the loch.

"I've never seen the keep from this angle before," she murmured. "It's beautiful."

"Aye," Taran replied, a smile in his voice. "I thought ye would like it."

Rhona turned back to him, and their gazes met. "I do, thank ye."

Taran looked away first, glancing over his shoulder. He rowed the boat out into the midst of the long loch.

Despite that they'd grown easy in each other's company of late, there was an odd tension this morning. She sensed that he was nervous, that he wished to impress her.

"This isn't another attempt to woo me, is it?" she asked finally, favoring him with a gentle smile. The last weeks had been a succession of romantic gestures. Just yesterday he'd brought her a red rose from the gardens. He'd actually blushed when he handed it to her.

Taran's mouth quirked. "Can't a man take his lovely wife out for a boat ride on Lammas morn?"

Rhona's smile widened although she said nothing. She did appreciate the effort he'd made over the past weeks, but it really wasn't necessary. Heat rose in her cheeks when she thought of what she really wanted: the pair of them naked in bed, leisurely exploring each other's bodies.

Swallowing, Rhona shifted her attention from her husband's broad shoulders to the dark rippling water. Despite that it was late summer, the loch would be breathtakingly cold; it never warmed, not even during the hottest weather.

When they reached the center of the lake, Taran stopped rowing. The boat drifted gently, and Rhona found her gaze drawn back to his.

"I'd like to sing ye a song," he murmured. "Would ye like that?"

Rhona inclined her head. "Ye can sing, Taran?"

He gave her an embarrassed look. "Well enough."

"Then I'd love to hear it."

Taran nodded, his throat bobbing. He glanced away, drew in a slow breath, and then began to sing. He had a gentle tenor, a low, lilting voice that made the fine hair on the back of Rhona's arms prickle.

Breathless, she listened as the words filtered out across the loch.

"Ae fond kiss, and then we sever;
Ae fareweel, alas, for ever!
Deep in heart-wrung tears I'll pledge thee,
Warring sighs and groans I'll wage thee!
Who shall say that Fortune grieves him
While the star of hope she leaves him?
Me, nae cheerfu' twinkle lights me,
Dark despair around benights me."

When Taran's voice died away, Rhona drew in a soft breath. "That was beautiful ... but so sad."

"Ma taught me it years ago," Taran replied with a lopsided smile. "It was her favorite song. It wasn't supposed to depress ye though."

"It didn't ... do ye know any others?" Truly, she could listen to his voice all day.

He favored her with an apologetic look. "Only drinking songs ... none of them fit for a lady's ears."

Rhona laughed then, tilting her face up to the sky. The wet splash of raindrops on her cheeks made her gasp. She noted then that the rain clouds she'd spotted earlier were now directly overhead.

She met Taran's gaze once more and gave him a rueful look. "I told ye."

The words were barely out when the drizzle increased to a light patter.

"It's just a summer shower," Taran replied with a shrug.

As if to prove him wrong, the heavens then opened.

Great icy sheets of water washed over Dunvegan Loch, stippling the surface of the water and completely soaking Taran and Rhona.

Muttering a curse, Rhona crouched under the onslaught. Rain sluiced down her face, blinding her. It soaked her clothing and trickled between her breasts.

She glowered at Taran. He sat, water streaming off him. His short blond hair was plastered to his skull, although his eyes glinted. Unlike Rhona, the squall didn't seem to bother him.

"A summer shower?" she growled.

"Worry not, lass," he replied, his mouth curving. "It will pass soon enough."

Rhona reached down and wrung out her sodden skirts.

Taran had been right, the storm had ended as quickly as it had begun—only, it was so heavy Rhona felt as if she'd been doused by buckets of icy water. Back on shore, she realized she was soaked right through to her léine. She removed her woolen shawl and wrung that out too, amazed by the volume of water it yielded.

"Apologies, Rhona." Taran stepped up next to her after pulling the boat onto the shore. "That didn't go as I'd hoped."

Rhona huffed. "Ye should know ye can't trust the weather."

Her gaze left his face then, traveling down his body.

Unlike most days Taran didn't wear his heavy mail shirt this morning, only a loose léine which was now plastered to his body. Rhona stared at his chest, at where his flat nipples were visible through the thin cloth. Her fingers itched to reach for him.

Catching herself, Rhona jerked her gaze away. She had to stop staring at him like some lusty tavern wench.

"Ye said the boat ride was the first of yer surprises," she said, trying to ignore the fact that she suddenly felt breathless. "What's the next one?"

He stepped forward and reached up, brushing a wet curl of hair off her cheek. "Ye aren't annoyed with me then?"

The feel of his fingers against Rhona's skin made hunger curl deep within her. Taran seemed oblivious to the effect even his merest touch had on her.

"Of course not," she husked. "Ye can't control the weather."

He reached for her hand, his fingers entwining through hers. "Come on then, follow me."

Taran led Rhona to the edge of a copse of trees that looked over the water.

He loosed a relieved breath when he spied the wicker basket he'd left there earlier. Tucked under the boughs of a sheltering willow, the basket had escaped the worst of the rain. The blanket he'd left folded up on top was only slightly damp.

Retrieving the basket, he set it down by the water's edge and spread out the blanket for them to sit upon.

Rhona sat down, arranging her wet skirts around her. The sight was distracting, for she'd lifted the hem of her léine and kirtle, revealing pale, shapely ankles and calves. The rain had wet the fabric through, and her clothing clung to her midriff and full breasts in a way that made it difficult for him to keep his gaze averted.

He needed this to go better than the boat ride had. He was starting to feel somewhat of a failure when it came to wooing a woman. He wondered if Rhona thought him a fool.

"A cup of ale for ye, Rhona?" he asked, withdrawing a clay stoppered bottle from the basket.

A warm smile spread across her face. "Aye, what's this, Taran?"

Watching her, Taran found it hard to breathe. How he longed to reach for her, to pull her into his arms. And yet he didn't. Instead, he returned her smile. "I thought I'd have our own Lammas feast prepared. Greer packed the basket for me. There's Lammas bread, butter, boiled eggs, and some oat-cakes sweetened with honey."

"Sounds delicious." Rhona reached into the basket and withdrew the loaf of Lammas bread, a plaited braid made with the first of this harvest's wheat. "It's still warm," she exclaimed.

Taran poured them a cup of ale each while Rhona broke off two pieces of bread and spread on some butter. She then peeled them both an egg each.

"This was a bonny idea," she murmured, holding her cup up to him. "The keep is so busy these days ... it's good to spend some time alone together."

Her words warmed him, far more than his first draft of ale did. "The morning isn't a complete disaster then?"

She grinned at him, turning her face up to where the sun now shone its friendly face down upon them, drying their clothing. "No ... ye have redeemed yerself."

They ate in silence. Taran enjoyed Rhona's easy company. She wasn't a woman who felt the need to fill a pause with chatter. Instead, they ate and drank, and listened to the soft lap of the water on the shore. Occasionally, Taran caught the faint burst of laughter or voices from Dunvegan village. Even though they were some distance away, the sound carried across the water.

Once they'd finished their meal, Taran poured the last drops of drink into their cups, and they sat, shoulder to shoulder, upon the blanket lingering over their ale.

"I like it here," Rhona murmured. Her voice was slightly drowsy. "I could stay upon this blanket for the rest of the day."

"Then we shall," he replied. Tentatively, he looped an arm around her shoulders, drawing her against him. He ached to do more, and yet he didn't.

Taran had counted each day of the three long weeks that had passed since their handfasting. Every night in that bed with Rhona sleeping within reaching distance had been torture. And yet this was his own doing; he saw from her eyes that she wanted him. Over the past weeks, they'd gotten to know each other, had deepened the easy relationship that had already existed between them into something far stronger.

Taran knew it was time for him to take their relationship forward.

And yet now that he'd reached the crossroads, he found he couldn't.

Chapter Twenty-four

Hold-Fast

RHONA WATCHED HER husband dress, admiring the way the muscles in his back and shoulders rippled as he reached for his léine.

She stifled a sigh. She'd enjoyed Lammas the day before, and the effort Taran had made for her. Only, she'd expected him to at least kiss her—and he hadn't.

Taran pulled on his tunic and turned to her. Their gazes met, and Rhona felt that familiar pull. A knot of excitement pooled in the pit of her belly. She didn't notice his scars at all these days; instead, his eyes mesmerized her, as did his lips. She often caught herself staring at his mouth, imagining what he'd be like to kiss.

She was staring now, but she didn't care. Her body felt restless, her breasts uncomfortably sensitive. Initially, Rhona had been flattered by his insistence on wooing her, but these days his reticence was beginning to frustrate her.

"Will ye join us for the hunt today?" Taran asked with a smile as he fastened his belt. "Yer father's got a hankering for roast boar."

"Aye," Rhona replied, her mood lifting. It had been a while since she'd been out on a hunt. Lasair loved a good run. A hunt would help vent Rhona's frustration.

Taran reached for his mail shirt. "Well, ye had better get dressed then. We ride out within the hour."

Rhona threw back the covers and leaped out of bed. "Why didn't ye say something earlier?"

He favored her with a playful smile, his gaze twinkling. "I didn't think ye would be keen."

A short while later, Rhona was seated upon her chestnut mare, nibbling at a piece of bannock while Taran tightened Tussock's girth beside her. The gelding snorted and pawed at the ground, eager to be off.

A sea of horses, men, and dogs surrounded them. The rumble of male voices and the excited yipping of the hounds filled the misty morning air. Rhona smiled, her senses sharpening. It had been too long since she'd ridden out on a hunt.

They left Dunvegan in a clatter of hooves and barking dogs. Fog, as thick as clotted cream, drifted in off the loch, turning the morning cool. It would burn off soon enough, but for the moment Rhona was relieved she'd donned her woolen cloak before setting out.

Leaving the keep behind, they rode east over bare hills. The shadow of great mountains rose ahead, marching closer as they left the shroud of coastal fog behind. Rhona rode at Taran's side and found herself stealing glances at him. She'd gotten used to having him close to her over the last weeks, and yet at the same time she was growing ever tenser in his company.

What does he want from me?

Taran glanced her way, spearing her with his ice-blue gaze. "What is it, love?"

Pleasure feathered down Rhona's neck at the low timbre of his voice. *Love.* Did he really mean it?

"Nothing," she murmured, tearing her gaze from his and fixing it in the direction of travel. "I'm just enjoying riding out with ye ... that's all."

She felt his gaze remain on her, the intensity of it causing heat to flush across her chest. Did he have any idea of the effect his proximity had on her?

"And I, with ye," he replied, with a teasing smile. "I'm glad we've been able to make a new start, Rhona."

Her gaze snapped back to him. They'd done that, but she wanted more. She had no idea how to voice her feelings.

The hunting party continued east and entered a valley between two mountains. A dark pine forest carpeted the ground of the steep vale. Rhona inhaled the scent of pine resin and enjoyed the cool kiss of the woodland air on her skin. This valley was one of her father's favorite hunting grounds for deer and boar.

It didn't take them long to flush out a boar—a small female that the dogs cornered without much trouble. The warriors then closed in bearing boar spears, weakening the animal, before Dughall MacLean finished it off with a stab to the heart.

Congratulating themselves on their easy kill, the men hoisted the carcass onto the back of a horse and continued on their way.

They had ridden deep into the valley, the trees rising high overhead, when a dark shape hurtled out of the forest before them.

It was a large male boar with a wiry black coat and long gleaming tusks. The beast ran at the dogs squealing with rage, while warriors stabbed at it, slowing its path.

Connel Buchanan and Gordon MacPherson were among them. Grinning, Connel circled the boar and drove his spear into its side. Rhona drew up Lasair, her gaze riveted on the scene up ahead. Boar were dangerous, clever, and stout-hearted. Even surrounded, as this one was, it wouldn't surrender without a fight.

The men and dogs tightened the net. One of the hounds went down, howling, as a sharp tusk found its mark. Yet, the boar was starting to tire. Grunting, it staggered around the clearing, blood running down its flanks.

With a whoop, Connel leaped down from his horse to make the final kill.

"Careful Buchanan," Malcolm MacLeod roared. "This boar's a wily one."

"Hold-fast, chief!" Connel shouted back. Shouts of encouragement went up around him. 'Hold-fast' was MacLeod's rallying cry, one he'd used ever since he'd killed a rampaging bull years earlier. He'd been a much younger man then, when, armed only with a dirk, he'd slain the beast and broken off one of its horns as a trophy. It was now the clan-chief's favorite drinking horn.

Connel hoisted his spear high. The boar spear had a crosspiece on the shaft, which would halt the beast. Otherwise, the boar was capable, even when speared, of charging the hunter and killing him.

Lasair snorted, tossing her head nervously and backing up. The scent of blood, violence, and the boar's odor, unnerved the mare. Rhona didn't blame her; a boar hunt was violent and not for the faint of heart.

Although she'd never liked Connel Buchanan much, she had to admit he showed courage facing off against the enraged quarry. She glanced right at Taran; he'd drawn Tussock up next to her, his gaze fixed upon the snorting, grunting boar. She was glad he'd stayed at her side.

"Finish it, Buchanan," Dughall MacLean shouted. "Stick it in the throat."

Connel ignored the warrior. Instead, he danced around the boar, toying with it.

Rhona's brow furrowed.

"What's the fool doing?" Taran muttered from next to her.

She was wondering the same thing.

Connel struck the boar in the hindquarters. With a squeal, it turned and lumbered toward him. Still grinning, the warrior leaped aside and stabbed it in the flank.

"Just end this, Buchanan," MacLeod called out. "Stop showing off."

But Connel didn't heed the chief. He continued to dance around the maddened boar, sticking it and prodding it until the creature huffed and wheezed.

"Stop him," Rhona muttered. She enjoyed a good hunt, but she didn't like to see senseless cruelty. The boar was in pain and confused. She wished her father would step in.

Tussock shifted, as Taran urged him forward. "Connel." His voice lashed across the glade. "Finish it." Yet the warrior didn't heed him either.

Connel danced around the boar once more, sticking it again in the flank. With a shriek of rage, the creature turned on him. Heedless of pain, of the spear now stuck in its side, it lunged. The warrior staggered back, his grin slipping—and tripped.

In an instant, the boar was on him. It gored him repeatedly, in a frenzy of fury and pain. Connel Buchanan's screams echoed through the trees.

Moments later, Gordon brought it down with a spear to the back of the head.

Taran leaped down from Tussock and rushed to Gordon's side. Dughall joined them, and together, the three men heaved the dead boar off Connel.

"Rhona!" Taran called out. "We need yer help."

Swinging down from Lasair's back, she went to them. Rhona was no healer, yet she was the only woman in the party—the only one who had been taught to tend wounds.

She knelt at Connel's side, bile rising in her throat.

One glance and she knew it was bad. The léine and plaid braies Connel wore were now crimson; the tusk had sliced through leather and linen like a knife through curd. Blood pumped out of wounds to his stomach, groin, and upper thigh.

Rhona swallowed. The tusks had pierced an artery. Connel was bleeding out over the ground.

With trembling hands, she ripped the hem from her léine and started to bind it around the wound to Connel's thigh. It was hopeless, but she had to do something.

Face pale, blue eyes wide, the young man stared up at her. He wore a startled expression as if he couldn't believe this was happening to him.

A twig snapped behind them, and Rhona glanced over her shoulder to see that her father had dismounted and now stood behind them. His bearded face was thunderous as he stared down at Connel.

"Chief," the warrior rasped, staring up at him. "Ye were right … he was a wily bastard."

"Aye, lad," MacLeod replied, his expression softening. "He was." His gaze shifted down to the young man's injuries.

Rhona tore her gaze from her father and looked back, at where her hands pressed into the wound she'd just bound. Red stained her hands. She couldn't staunch the bleeding.

"Close yer eyes, lad," the chief rumbled, his voice softer than Rhona had heard it in a long while. He knelt at the warrior's side, taking hold of Connel's hand. The sight made Rhona's throat constrict. Her father could be fierce, brutal even, yet he inspired loyalty in the men who followed him for a reason. "Rest now."

The man did as bid, his eyelids flickering. His face was the color of milk. Long moments passed, and around them, the forest glade went silent. The men bowed their heads as Connel Buchanan died.

Rhona splashed water on her face and inhaled the scent of rose. The perfume soothed her, dulling the sharp edges of the day she'd just passed.

A senseless, reckless death.

It was difficult to mourn the passing of a callow youth she'd never liked, yet the violence of Connel Buchanan's demise would haunt her dreams in the days to come. Rhona shook her head to clear the memory of the blood and gore. She picked up a square of linen, drying her face.

She emerged from behind the screen to find her husband already abed.

Taran lay on his back staring up at the ceiling, his hands clasped behind his head. A deep groove cut between his eyebrows, giving him a fierce look.

"Ye are angry," she observed, approaching the bed.

"Aye," he ground out. He didn't look her way but continued to stare up at the rafters. "The dolt had his whole life before him."

Rhona gusted out a sigh and sat down upon the bed. "Ma used to say that reckless young men are always the first to die."

He inclined his head to her then, a humorless smile curving his mouth. "She was right."

Rhona met his gaze. "But ye are not reckless, are ye Taran MacKinnon ... quite the opposite I'd say."

He huffed. "What's that supposed to mean?"

"Exactly what I said. Ye are a brave man ... but a thinking one." She frowned then as the memory of how Connel had baited that boar needled her. "Ye would never treat an animal that way either."

His mouth thinned. "Had he lived, I'd have broken his nose for that."

Rhona loosed a sigh. She pulled back the covers and slid into bed. Tiredness pulled down at her, and she sank willingly into the softness. She was aware of the heat of Taran's body just a couple of feet from hers. After what they'd both witnessed, she longed to reach for him, yet she suddenly felt shy.

She wasn't sure of him anymore. Here she was, right next to him, but he merely watched her with that intense look that made her breathing quicken, her pulse race. He could pull her into his arms, could kiss her—yet he did nothing. Did he prefer this arrangement—sleeping in the same bed but never touching?

Perhaps he did.

A long moment passed, and then Taran reached out a hand, stroking her gently on the cheek. "Goodnight, m'eudail," he murmured. *My darling.*

"Goodnight," Rhona whispered back, aching for his hand to linger.

However, he withdrew it and rolled away from her, leaving Rhona with nothing but a view of his broad back.

Chapter Twenty-five

Prove My Worth

"I TAKE THE Vale of Hamra Rinner as my own. From this day forth the land belongs to clan Fraser. Any MacLeod who sets foot upon it will be trespassing. His life will be forfeit."

Malcolm MacLeod slammed his fist down on the table. The noise echoed through the Great Hall. "Thieving, bloody bastards." His bellow shook the rafters. "I'll slay them all ... every last stinking Fraser!"

Taran, who'd been spreading honey onto a wedge of bannock, froze. It was just after dawn, and he and Rhona had risen early to join the chief and his wife as they broke their fast. A week had passed since that fateful boar hunt. Aonghus Budge was visiting Dunvegan yet again, and MacLeod had planned to take him hawking this morning. Taran would ride out with them.

"My love." Una put down a cup of milk she'd been sipping, her gaze widening. "Calm yerself."

"Villain!" Malcolm ignored his wife and heaved his bulk up from the table, scattering bannocks as he did so. In his right hand, he gripped a sheet of parchment. "Morgan Fraser has gone too far!"

At the sound of her former husband's name, the chieftain's wife paled. Watching her, Taran wondered if she'd ever loved the Fraser chieftain. She'd needed little persuasion to run off with Malcolm MacLeod. The union mustn't have been a happy one.

"How dare Fraser take the Vale of Hamra Rinner as his own."

Aonghus Budge swallowed a mouthful of food, his watery blue eyes hardening. "Aye, those are yer lands, MacLeod."

"We've hunted stags in that valley for generations," Malcolm snarled. "I'll not have a Fraser tell me we can't."

A rumble of outrage followed this announcement, rippling over the Great Hall like thunder. Taran glanced over at Rhona to find her staring at her father, brow furrowed.

"Ye can't let him get away with it, Da." Iain MacLeod spoke up. The lad's sharp-featured face was taut, his grey eyes flinty.

"I don't intend to, laddie," Malcolm MacLeod growled back. He drew himself up to his full height. Even corpulent and red-faced, he was still a formidable man to look upon. "Finally, the MacLeods and Frasers will meet in battle. We shall stain that valley crimson with Fraser blood." His gaze swept to Iain. "Ride to Duntulm," he barked. "Tell Baltair MacDonald to ride to us with as many warriors as he can spare."

Aonghus Budge rose quickly to his feet, hands clenched by his sides. "The Budges of Islay are with ye too, Malcolm."

MacLeod nodded to his friend. "Thank ye, Aonghus," he rasped. His hand crushed the parchment. "I'll answer Fraser now. We shall meet those dogs in battle at noon, two days from now."

Next to Taran, Rhona leaned forward. "Da ... I will join ye. I can fight."

"No." The word was out of Taran's mouth before he could stop it.

The table went still. Rhona inclined her head toward him, her eyes narrowed. "Excuse me?"

"If my daughter wants to fight, she can," MacLeod replied, favoring Taran with a sneer. "Ye went behind my back to teach her how to wield a sword after all."

Taran stiffened. He didn't like the goading tone to Malcolm's voice, the challenge he'd just laid down. Ignoring the chief, he met Rhona's gaze. "It's too dangerous," he said. "Ye have never seen combat, Rhona."

His wife drew herself up, jaw tightening. "I can handle myself."

He admired her courage, he really did. Yet her confidence was misplaced. She could wield a sword, but she'd lived a sheltered existence within the walls of this keep. How would she react when a battle-crazed warrior rushed her with his sword drawn? She'd handled Connel's death well, but she had no idea what war was like, and her father knew it.

"The answer's still no," he replied, his tone hardening. "I'll not put ye at risk."

Rhona's lips parted as she prepared to answer. But her father's snort forestalled her.

"Far be it for me to stand between a man and his wife," he drawled. He favored Rhona with a smirk. "Ye will have to obey MacKinnon now, daughter."

"Why did ye bother teaching me how to fight?"

Rhona faced Taran, hands on hips. She'd followed him outside into the stables, waiting till they were alone. He turned, his face adopting a forbidding expression she knew well; it was the Taran MacKinnon who served her father, the man who wore his scars like a shield.

"Because ye commanded me to," he replied.

Rhona scowled. "Ye could have refused me. Ye could have gone to my father."

He folded his brawny arms across his broad chest. "Ye know why I didn't."

Anger rose within Rhona in a hot tide. She felt humiliated, patronized. She'd hated how her father, brother, and Aonghus Budge had all smirked at her in the Great Hall. Taran should have supported her, instead, he'd cut her down in front of them all. "So, ye think I'm not capable of fighting in battle, is that it?"

He huffed out an exasperated breath. "I'm just trying to protect ye."

"I don't need yer protection," she shot back, furious now. "I'm a warrior's daughter. I asked ye to train me so that I could fight alongside my menfolk one day. Da will let me ... why won't ye?"

Taran's ice-blue gaze hardened. "He agreed merely to have his revenge upon me."

"What? That's ridiculous."

He took a step toward her. "Is it? He's furious I won yer hand. He didn't want ye wed to the likes of me ... to the 'Beast of Dunvegan'. He'll see both of us punished for it."

Rhona glared at him. She wanted to deny his words, insult him for them, yet in her gut she knew he spoke the truth. The look on her father's face inside the Great Hall had been clear. He had no respect for her, but if she wanted to ride into battle with him and his men, he'd allow it. Especially if it hurt Taran.

Shoulders rounding, she let the anger drain out of her. Hurt replaced it. Her gaze dropped to the straw-strewn floor as she struggled to control her emotions. "I'm not useless," she whispered. "I'm not a decorative ornament born to wear pretty gowns, press flowers, and embroider cushions. I wish I'd been born a man ... ye would all respect me then."

Silence fell between them. She heard the scuff of Taran's boots as he moved closer to her. A heartbeat later, a strong finger gently hooked under her chin and lifted it.

Their gazes met, and Rhona was relieved to see that the shield he'd raised earlier had lowered. "I'm glad ye were born a woman," he murmured, smiling. "And a fierce one at that."

"What does it matter how fierce I am?" she replied. She heard the bitterness in her voice but didn't care. "I'll never get a chance to prove my worth."

"Ye don't need to," he replied, his gaze soft. "Not to me."

"Do ye really want to fight?"

Adaira glanced up from where she was playing with the puppy on the floor of the women's solar. The pup had grown considerably in the past few weeks and had taken to nipping Adaira's hands with its new, needle-like teeth. Adaira bore red welts over her hands and forearms, yet she didn't appear to mind.

Rhona huffed a breath, lowering the embroidery she'd been trying to focus on. "Aye."

Adaira watched her, fascinated. "I wish more women were bold like ye." A grin spread across her face. "Then we'd rule over men rather than them over us."

Rhona snorted. "That's fanciful thinking. Ye saw Da and Taran this morning ... I don't decide my fate. They do."

The pup gave a mock growl and started pulling at the hem of Adaira's kirtle. Rhona arched her eyebrow. "Best ye don't let Una see him do that ... she'll have Dùnglas skinned."

Adaira gave a gasp, scooping the wriggling pup up into her arms. "Nasty Una ... we'll not let her touch ye!" She cuddled him against her breast, her attention returning to Rhona once more.

Rhona glanced back down at her embroidery. She didn't like it when Adaira favored her with one of her 'searching' gazes. It was all too easy to forget that Adaira saw far more than she let on.

"Is all well between ye and Taran?" Adaira asked after a pause.

Rhona's needle slipped, stabbing her in the finger. She loosed a curse and lifted her injured hand to her mouth. "What kind of question is that?"

Adaira's hazel eyes narrowed as she set Dùnglas down on the ground once more. The pup pounced on a ball of wool Adaira had given him to play with. However, this time the young woman didn't shift her gaze to her puppy. Instead, she continued to watch Rhona. "A direct one," she replied, her mouth curving. "And clearly a question ye don't want to answer."

"I don't know why ye would ask it," Rhona replied. She heard the sour note in her voice and suppressed a wince.

Adaira inclined her head. "Ye both looked happy after the handfasting ... but of late something has changed. When I see ye together, there's ... a distance."

Rhona swallowed the lump that had risen, unbidden, in her throat. Aye, Adaira was too perceptive by half. She hoped no one else had noticed the tension between her and Taran. That was the problem with living in a keep the size of Dunvegan. There were too many curious eyes upon her, too many flapping ears and gossiping tongues. Her relationship with Taran was under constant scrutiny.

"He's a good man," she murmured finally, dropping her gaze from her sister's. "Better than I deserve."

Adaira snorted at the comment but didn't answer, waiting for Rhona to continue.

Staring down at where a drop of blood had beaded once more on her finger, Rhona inhaled sharply. "I'm so confused, Adaira ... I don't know what to do." She glanced up and met her sister's eye. "On the night of our handfasting, Taran admitted that he'd been in love with me for years. That's why he'd defied Da and let me train with him ... of course, I'd been oblivious."

Adaira frowned but again held her tongue.

"I never saw him as a man until that night," Rhona continued. Her chest constricted as she spoke, yet she forced herself to press on. Perhaps sharing her feelings with her sister would help. "We lay together that night ... but he's not touched me since."

The furrow on her sister's brow deepened. "Really? Why not?"

"He says he wants to 'woo' me, for us to be in love before he beds me again." Heat flushed Rhona's cheeks. She couldn't believe she was actually voicing this to her younger sister. "But I'm beginning to think it's an excuse ... that he doesn't *want* me."

Silence fell in the solar, the hush broken only by the yips and grunt of the wolfhound pup as it rolled around the floor, the ball of wool clamped between its paws.

"I don't think that's the case," Adaira said eventually. Her voice was soft, pensive. "I've seen the way he looks at ye." She gave a sigh. "I'd love for a man to gaze at me like that."

Rhona huffed, reaching for her embroidery once more. She wished she hadn't said anything. Adaira was a maid and still believed that love was like the ballads Una sometimes sang in the evenings. Her head was full of silly notions. It didn't matter if Taran bestowed melting looks upon her. These days he treated her like a sister— and it was slowly breaking Rhona's heart.

Chapter Twenty-six

Things Unsaid

MACDONALD WARRIORS THUNDERED into the keep.
Pennants of the clan's plaid—green and blue threaded
with white and red—snapped and billowed. A hot wind
blew in from the south, sending dust devils spinning
across the bailey.

Rhona viewed the MacDonalds' arrival from the
window of Adaira's bower.

The sisters had been working at their looms together
when the horn announcing visitors echoed across the
keep. Putting down the tapestry beater—a wooden comb
that she used to push down the woven threads—Rhona
had crossed to the window. A heartbeat later, Adaira
appeared at her side. They craned their necks, watching
the sea of horses and men clad in plaid, leather, and
chainmail fill the bailey. At the end of the column, a
wagon rumbled in. A woman with hair the color of
summer wheat, a babe in her arms, perched on the back.

"Caitrin!" Adaira squealed. "He's brought her with
him."

Despite her low mood this morning, a smile stretched
across Rhona's face. Her sister's arrival was welcome

news indeed; so much had happened since she'd last seen Caitrin. She needed to talk to her.

The MacLeods, MacDonalds, and Budges would leave at first light the following morning. Rhona had barely seen Taran over the past day, for he'd been taken up with getting men armed, horses shod, and weapons sharpened before their departure.

The twists and turns of fate came at her so swiftly these days she could barely catch her breath. First this marriage, and now her husband was about to ride off to battle.

What if he falls?

Rhona's chest had twisted at the thought. She was angry with him for not letting her fight, and hurt that he didn't wish to lie with her, but the thought of losing him was like a dirk to her breast.

"He's grown so!" Adaira bent over the babe, tickling him under the chin. Her features tensed then. "He looks so much like his Da."

"That's not surprising, is it?" Caitrin's voice had a reproachful edge to it.

"Aye, but it's not the wee lad's fault," Rhona chimed in. "Some things can't be helped."

Eoghan MacDonald gurgled, his chubby hands reaching up to Adaira. He had a thick head of dark hair already, just like Baltair.

Rhona met Caitrin's eye. Her sister's lovely face was tired and drawn, although the dark smudges under her eyes had gone. She looked thin under the voluminous kirtle and léine, her collarbone more prominent than Rhona remembered.

"Are ye well, Caitrin?" she asked gently.

Her sister nodded. "I'm much stronger now, thank ye."

There was a formality to Caitrin's voice, an edge that warned Rhona from pressing further. The three sisters sat in the women's solar. The windows overlooking the hills to the east were open. The hot breeze breathed in, fanning their faces.

It was then that she realized Caitrin was studying her intently.

Rhona stiffened. "What?"

Her sister's mouth quirked. "Ye seem different ... I can't put my finger on exactly what."

"This heat has made me crabby," Rhona replied with a shrug.

Caitrin gave a soft laugh. "No, it's not that."

"It's obvious, isn't it?" Adaira spoke up. "She's a wedded woman now."

Caitrin smiled, although her blue eyes remained shadowed. "Of course. Taran MacKinnon ... I was surprised when Baltair told me."

Rhona cast Adaira a look of censure. Her younger sister had a wicked smile on her face as if she wished to say more. She'd kick her in the shin if she did.

The mood turned awkward. Rhona sensed Caitrin's curiosity. She knew her sister wanted to ask her about her wedding night, wanted to know if Taran treated her well. But to ask such questions would shine a light upon her own marriage. Caitrin didn't want to talk of Baltair—that much was clear. Once they were alone, Rhona had hoped to have a private word with Caitrin, but now she wasn't sure her sister would welcome such a conversation.

"Taran's not as frightening as everyone thinks," Adaira continued. She then gave a soft sigh. "The opposite in fact. Ye should have seen Rhona's face the day after the handfasting ... she looked like the cat that got the cream."

"Adaira," Rhona growled. "Enough."

"What?" Adaira favored her with a look of mock innocence. "It's the truth."

"Don't be a goose," Rhona snapped, rising to her feet. She couldn't believe Adaira was bringing this up, especially after their conversation the day before. Her sister hadn't understood a thing.

Adaira drew back, her features tightening. "I'm not a fool," she said quietly. "Don't treat me like one."

Rhona and Adaira stared at each other. Caitrin cleared her throat, breaking the tension. "Come ... let's not argue. I'm so happy to see ye both. Ye have no idea how lonely it gets in Duntulm."

Rhona tore her gaze from Adaira and forced a smile. "I'm glad ye are here," she said. "Wee Eoghan too."

As if recognizing his own name, the babe gave a squeal.

"Da said ye would get me a sword."

Taran glanced up from where he was sharpening a blade upon a whetstone, to see Iain MacLeod standing in the doorway to the armory. Even at sixteen winters, the lad carried his father's authority. Auburn-haired, with those penetrating MacLeod grey eyes, Iain wasn't someone Taran had ever warmed to.

The young man's aggressive tone, his pugnacious expression, didn't improve Taran's opinion of him this afternoon.

"Aye," he replied, rising to his feet and gesturing to the wall of swords behind him. "Did ye have a blade in mind?"

"I want a Claidheamh-mor ... like Da's."

Taran resisted the urge to raise an eyebrow. "Yer father has twice yer girth and strength," he pointed out. "Why not try a lighter long-sword?"

Iain's mouth twisted. "I didn't ask for yer opinion, *Beast*. Get me what I asked for."

Taran gave the lad a long, hard look before turning to the armory. There, he pulled a sword off the wall. It was a heavy weapon that had to be wielded with both hands, two inches broad with a double edge and a long, deadly blade. Taran's own sword was of the same make. Only, he was double the weight and strength of Iain MacLeod.

Taran handed the blade to the clan-chief's son, hilt first. The lad took it without a word of thanks. "Is it sharp?"

"Aye."

"Good ... ye will hear from me if it isn't."

Iain turned on his heel, intending to stride out of the armory, and ran into Gordon, who'd just entered the building. The lad bounced off the warrior's broad chest before snarling at him. "Watch where ye are going."

Gordon dipped his head and stepped aside. "Apologies, lad. I'll watch my step in future."

Throwing Gordon a black look, Iain stalked off, clutching the Claidheamh-mor in both hands.

"Jumped up pup," Gordon murmured watching him go. "I can't believe MacLeod's letting him fight."

Taran shrugged. "He thinks it's time the lad was blooded."

Gordon snorted. "God help us all then." He glanced over at Taran, his brow furrowing. "I hear Lady Rhona wants to join us tomorrow?"

"Aye," Taran growled, picking up the sword he was halfway through sharpening. "She's vexed with me for stopping her."

Gordon huffed a laugh. "I've seen her fight ... she's good."

Taran cast his friend a hard look. "The answer's still 'no'."

"More mutton, Rhona?" Taran held out a platter to his wife. Despite that he was hungry enough today to finish the lot, he'd left the last slice of meat for her.

Rhona's storm-grey gaze met his. "No, thank ye," she replied softly. "Ye have it."

Taran forced back a frown. Rhona hadn't been herself over the last few days. At first, he'd thought it was the shock of seeing Connel Buchanan gored by that boar, and then he'd put it down to anger at not being allowed to fight alongside him.

Yet it wasn't anger he saw in her eyes now, but something softer. She looked ... sad.

Taran stiffened, lowering the platter before him. What reason did she have to be unhappy? A chill feathered down his spine. Was she regretting their union?

Taran took a bite of mutton. Moments earlier he'd been enjoying the rich flavor of the meat, yet now it tasted like ash. In the weeks since their handfasting, he'd done everything to make her happy, to make her warm to him as a man.

And now that he saw melancholy in his wife's eyes, something deep within his chest twisted.

She wed the ugliest man upon this Isle, a cruel voice whispered in his head. *Why wouldn't she be regretting it?*

"I hear Rhona wants to join us tomorrow." Baltair MacDonald's voice intruded. Taran glanced up from his meal to see the clan-chief favoring him with an oily smile. "Why don't ye let her fight with us?" Beside Baltair, Caitrin stiffened. She cast her husband a warning look, but he ignored her. "Rumor has it that ye trained her in secret for years," Baltair continued, his smile widening. "Or maybe that was merely a ruse ... perhaps it wasn't a Claidheamh-mor ye were teaching her to wield."

This comment made Aonghus Budge choke on his mutton. Spluttering, the chief reached for a cup of mead. His pale blue eyes shone with amusement. However, at the head of the table, Malcolm MacLeod didn't look entertained.

"MacDonald," he growled a low warning.

Undaunted, Baltair shrugged, his attention still fixed upon Taran. "Maybe she can't fight at all."

Taran heard Rhona's sharp intake of breath next to him, felt the tension rippling from her. He knew that Baltair resented Rhona. She'd told him about the incident with Adaira. Taran wagered that, ever since, Baltair had been waiting for his revenge. He was trying to goad her into saying something that would humiliate her.

Taran wasn't going to let that happen. "My wife wields a sword as well as ye, Baltair," he replied. "I'm just doing what a husband does ... protecting her."

The MacDonald chieftain's mouth twisted. It wasn't the answer he'd expected or wanted. Taran held his gaze in an open challenge. Baltair would insult Rhona again at his peril.

Chapter Twenty-seven

Only a Coward

RHONA WAS SITTING at the window, staring out at the dusky sky, when Taran entered their chamber. It was shortly after supper, a tense meal during which she'd thought her husband and Baltair MacDonald might come to blows.

"Would ye take a walk with me?"

Rhona turned from the window and put down the embroidery she'd barely touched, to see Taran leaning against the doorframe. In his mail shirt and braies, stubble covering his chin, he looked rough—dangerous.

Belly fluttering, Rhona swallowed. Just the sight of him, the impact of their gazes meeting, made her wits scatter. She didn't seem to have the same effect on him though. Taran's expression was unreadable as he watched her.

"What ... now?" she asked, nervousness rising within her.

His mouth curved. "Aye ... it's a beautiful evening out, and tomorrow I leave for battle. I'd like to take a stroll in the gardens with my wife."

Wife. The way he said it made the fluttering in Rhona's belly increase tenfold. A walk would give them time together—time for her to broach the issue that loomed over them.

"Very well." She rose to her feet, smoothing her light linen kirtle. "I could do with some fresh air."

They left the tower chamber, traveling single-file down the narrow turret stairs. However, once they reached the wider stairwell below, Taran held out his arm to her. Wordlessly, Rhona took it, linking her arm through his. Together, they left the keep via the Sea-gate and made their way down the causeway. Turning off it, they took a path south to where the gardens lay, a riot of color against the stark outlines of the hills beyond. The dying sun had gilded the garden, and a wall of scent hit Rhona as they walked into it.

She inhaled deeply and tried to quell the churning of her belly. She'd forgotten how flowers released their scent in the evening.

"The garden is at its best this time of day," Taran said, echoing her own thoughts. "Yet few bother to visit it now."

"Ye are right," Rhona replied. "Thank ye for suggesting it."

He placed a hand over hers, squeezing gently. "We haven't seen much of each other these past days. I'm sorry for it."

Rhona heaved in a deep breath. "Aye, and tomorrow ye are leaving."

"I shall return."

She cast him a sharp look. "Sure of yerself, aren't ye?"

His mouth twitched. "A warrior has to be."

"But what if ye don't ... what if a Fraser sticks a dirk in yer guts, and I'm left a widow?" Rhona pulled her arm from his and halted, turning to face him. "What then?"

His gaze met hers. "That would be a shame."

Rhona gritted her teeth. Was he trying to vex her? "It would," she muttered, "and an even greater one, for I would have only had one night with my husband before losing him." She placed her hands on her hips, gathering the shreds of her courage. She had to speak now or she never would. "Are ye planning to shun me tonight as well?"

He loosed a sharp breath, his gaze guttering. "Ye talk as if I've treated ye cruelly, Rhona. I'm trying to show ye respect."

"By ignoring me? I'm beginning to think ye regret our handfasting."

He shook his head. "What I regret is the way it all happened. Ye were forced into wedding me. I'm just letting ye get used to being my wife."

Rhona scowled. "There's no time for that. I'm not a delicate flower that has to be handled gently for fear of breaking. Ye are starting to infuriate me, Taran MacKinnon."

His face tensed. "Then, I'm sorry."

Rhona clenched her hands by her sides. If he apologized once more, she swore she'd hit him. "I don't want ye to tell me ye are sorry," she growled. "I want ye to start treating me like yer wife. God's Bones, ye haven't even kissed me yet! What's wrong with ye?"

She regretted the words as soon as they left her mouth. Yet it was too late. She couldn't take them back.

Taran yanked back from her as if she had just struck him.

"Taran," she gasped. "I—"

Her husband took a step away from her, his big body tensing, and turned back toward the entrance to the garden. He might have stridden away from her then, if a man's voice, rough with anger, hadn't intruded.

"Ye will do as ye are told, woman. Is that clear?"

"But we just arrived here ... I don't understand why I have to go back to Duntulm so soon?"

"I don't trust ye in this keep ... not with yer sisters close at hand."

A pause followed, and the fine hair on the back of Rhona's neck prickled. They were listening to Caitrin and Baltair.

"What's wrong with that?" Caitrin's voice was sharp when she answered her husband. "Rhona and Adaira have done me no wrong."

"A blade-tongued shrew and that brainless chatterer. They're a bad influence on ye."

Caitrin's soft laugh echoed through the garden. There was no mirth in the sound, just scorn. "They're my *sisters*, Baltair. I will never forsake them ... not for ye, not for anyone."

A crack followed—the sound of an open palm striking flesh. "Ye will do as ye are told, woman."

Beside Rhona, Taran moved. He left her side and strode into the midst of the gardens. Rhona followed.

They came upon the couple, just as Baltair delivered another slap. Caitrin cried out, staggering back. They stood before a hawthorn hedge. The berries were just beginning to ripen, small red buds bright against the green foliage.

Caitrin glared up at her husband, eyes gleaming. Her left cheek glowed red as she raised a hand to it. Baltair loomed over her. He drew his right arm back to strike her once more. "I've had enough of being crossed by my own wife," he snarled. "I'll teach ye some manners."

"Baltair!" Taran's voice lashed across the garden, causing the two figures near the hedge to freeze. "Lower yer fist!"

The MacDonald clan-chief twisted, his gaze shifting to Taran and then Rhona. Behind him, Caitrin's frightened gaze widened. Baltair ignored Taran, his attention resting upon Rhona.

A cruel smile twisted his face. "Here's the shrew now, accompanied by her gargoyle."

Fury curled within Rhona's belly at his insults. She was sick of them. She carried no weapons, but her hands balled into fists at her sides. However, the words merely seemed to wash over Taran. His stride didn't check as he approached Baltair. He stopped before him, within striking distance.

"What's this?" Baltair met Taran's eye. "Ye shouldn't interfere between a man and his wife, MacKinnon."

"Stand back from Lady Caitrin," Taran ordered. He and Baltair were of a similar height, yet the weight of his presence made it seem as if he loomed over the

MacDonald chieftain. Baltair didn't back down though; there was a feral, stubborn glint in his eye. Unease feathered down Rhona's skin when she realized that he was the kind of man who enjoyed altercations with others. He wasn't intimidated in the slightest.

Baltair spat a curse at Taran. An instant later he lashed out at his wife once more.

Taran lunged, grabbing Baltair's wrist in motion. Caitrin cried out and cringed back against the hawthorn. Baltair's fist had stopped barely inches from her face.

Baltair roared and swung around to face the man who'd prevented him from striking his wife. Meanwhile, Taran cast a glance left at where Caitrin huddled. "Go to Rhona," he said.

Not needing to be told twice, Caitrin darted away from them, reaching Rhona's side moments later. Rhona reached out and pulled her sister against her; Caitrin's slender frame was quaking.

His right wrist still gripped by Taran, Baltair swung at him with his free fist. Taran brought his arm up, deflecting the blow easily. He then drove his knee into his opponent's belly. Baltair gasped, stumbled, and fell to his knees, winded.

Taran released him and stepped back, giving the man some space. He cast a glance over his shoulder, his gaze meeting Rhona's for the first time since they'd overheard the argument. His ice-blue eyes were cold. "Take Lady Caitrin away," he said quietly. "She doesn't need to see this."

Rhona hesitated. She didn't want to leave Taran with Baltair. Even winded he was dangerous. She knew he wouldn't leave matters here.

When she didn't move, Taran's face hardened. The scars on his face made him look frightening. "Go!"

Rhona swallowed before nodding. She knew his temper wasn't just directed at Baltair. The words she'd flung at him had cut deep; she'd wounded him.

"Come, Caitrin," she murmured, steering her sister. "Let's go back inside."

Caitrin didn't resist. Together, the two women turned and hurried from the garden without looking back.

Taran waited until the sound of Rhona and Caitrin's feet crunching on pebbles faded. Only then did he speak to Baltair MacDonald.

"Only a coward beats his wife."

Baltair struggled to his feet, still gasping for breath like a winded carthorse. "And only a fool interferes where he's not wanted." His dark-blue gaze met Taran's. "Ye will pay for that, *Beast*."

Baltair lunged again, even faster than earlier. Now that Taran had released him, his right arm swung at his opponent's head. It slammed into Taran's jaw. Taran staggered and bit down on his tongue. Blood filled his mouth, and his temper finally snapped. He reached out, grabbed Baltair by the collar of his léine, and head-butted him hard in the nose.

The MacDonald chieftain went down like a sack of oats. He sprawled back onto a bed of lavender, dislodging the bees that had been buzzing there.

Taran spat out a gob of blood and wiped his mouth with the back of his hand. It took all his self-control not to throw himself on Baltair and beat him senseless. He'd never been quick to anger, but his temper once roused was a dark, wild thing that took a while to settle.

Baltair groaned. His gaze, glassy with pain, met Taran's. Blood flowed out of his nose. His mouth worked as if he might speak, but Taran cut him off.

"Keep yer fists to yerself in future, MacDonald," Taran growled. "If I hear ye have mistreated yer wife again … I'll come looking for ye."

Caitrin dissolved into floods of tears the moment they were inside the women's solar. Adaira was in there, playing her harp by the window, when her sisters entered. One look at their faces and her fingers halted, cutting off the lilting music that greeted them.

Adaira frowned. "What's wrong?"

Rhona didn't reply. Instead, she led Caitrin over to a chair and let her settle there. Her elder sister covered her face with her hands, her shoulders shaking as she sought to contain her sobs.

After a few moments, Rhona met Adaira's eye. "Baltair," she said quietly. "Taran and I were walking in the gardens when we heard arguing."

Adaira walked across to Caitrin and knelt before her. She reached out and placed her hands on her sister's knees, squeezing. "I knew he was cruel to ye ... even though ye have never said anything. I knew."

Caitrin dropped her hands to look at Adaira. Tears coursed down her face, making the livid marks on her left cheek all the more evident. Rhona drew in a sharp breath at the desolation she saw in her elder sister's blue eyes. Caitrin had always been so strong. At this moment though, she looked broken.

"I hate him," she whispered.

Chapter Twenty-eight

Scars

NIGHT HAD FALLEN in a warm, dark blanket over Dunvegan when Rhona made her way down the steps into the bailey. She had not put on a shawl around her shoulders as the evening was sultry, the air soft against her skin. It was growing late, and the keep slumbered. Caitrin had finally retired for the night; she would share Adaira's chamber with her rather than return to the one she shared with Baltair.

Reaching the bottom of the steps, Rhona's gaze swept the shadowed corners of the yard. There was no sign of her husband here. She'd just come from their chamber; the only other place she could think to look was the stables.

She found him there, alone except for the rows of horses in the stalls. Taran had his back to her as she approached. He was in the tack-room, a partition at the end of the building. Taran was cleaning a saddle, buffing the leather with a soft cloth.

Rhona approached quietly, her tread silent in the slippers she wore. She was around four yards behind him when Taran spoke.

"Ye should be abed asleep, Rhona. It's late."

Rhona halted, surprised that he'd heard her. An awkward moment passed before she spoke. "I know it's late ... that's why I'm here. Are ye not going to join me?"

He shook his head, still not turning his face to look at her. "I'll make a bed for myself here in the stables once I'm done cleaning this."

His voice was low, weary. There was no sign of anger in it, although that just made Rhona feel worse. The words she'd thrown at him had tormented her all evening. Initially, she'd been preoccupied with Caitrin, but once she'd returned to their chamber—and found it empty—she'd been unable to settle. The more time stretched on, the worse she felt.

Heaving in a deep breath, for nerves had suddenly assaulted her, Rhona closed the distance between them and entered the tack-room. The rich scent of oiled leather enveloped her. She stepped up next to her husband so that their shoulders were nearly touching. "I'm sorry, Taran."

He cast her a glance. His gaze was shuttered, his expression impossible to read. "It doesn't matter," he replied. "Just leave things be."

A heartbeat passed. Rhona gnawed at her bottom lip. This was getting painful; she had no idea what to say to him, or how to put things right. But she couldn't walk away knowing she'd hurt him. Each time she opened her mouth, she wondered if she was just making things worse.

"I can't leave it," she said quietly, her voice barely above a whisper. "Taran ... I didn't mean what I said back in the gardens."

His gaze snapped back to her. "Yes, ye did."

Rhona's throat closed. "No ... I." She broke off here. The coldness of his gaze completely threw her. It wasn't like Rhona to lack confidence, yet at that moment she did. "I was frustrated," she admitted finally. "It was a child's tantrum, and I'm truly sorry for it."

He looked away from her and continued polishing the saddle. However, she noted his shoulders had tensed and his movements were jerky. Rhona moved back from him.

Nothing she said seemed to make any difference. The man before her was a stranger, so different to the husband of the past weeks who had made her laugh, and looked upon her with soft eyes. She should have let things be.

I've ruined everything. Her throat tightened, and tears pricked her eyes.

"I'll leave ye then," she whispered. "Goodnight, Taran."

She'd just started to turn when her husband moved. One moment he was standing at the bench, the saddle before him, and the next he dropped the cloth, took Rhona by the shoulders, and pushed her back against the far wall.

The movement was so sudden that Rhona gasped. His grip on her shoulders was firm, his fingertips digging in. When she raised her chin to meet his gaze, her belly twisted.

His pale-blue gaze glittered. His skin had drawn tight over his features, distorting the two thick scars that slashed across his face. He looked furious.

Taran leaned into her, his mouth twisting. "Take a good look at these scars, Rhona ... do ye think any woman would want to kiss a man with a face like mine?"

Shock fluttered through Rhona; she'd never realized he held so much anger inside him.

"Taran," she gasped his name in a plea. She'd never been afraid of him before, but fear coiled within her now. "I don't—"

"*Do* ye?" The question was a growl.

Rhona stared up at him, her gaze never wavering. "I don't understand," she whispered.

His mouth thinned. "Ye demanded to know what was wrong with me, why I've never kissed ye," he growled. "Why don't ye ask yerself if I've ever kissed *anyone*?"

Rhona stilled, realization dawning. She'd thought him experienced; the way he'd pleasured her on their wedding night had made her believe he'd lain with a number of others.

"I thought ye had bedded other women?" she whispered.

He stared down at her. A nerve feathered in his jaw. "Bedded, aye. Kissed, no."

The tension drained out of Rhona's body at these words. It was as if the fog had rolled back, and for the first time, she could see. Suddenly, everything was clear.

"Taran," she breathed. Rhona reached up, her fingertips tracing the deepest of the scars, the one that slashed vertically from his brow to jaw. He flinched under her touch but didn't move away. She traced the length of the scar before running her fingers along the one that slashed across his opposite cheek.

Then, she stood on tiptoe and stretched up to him, placing her lips upon the worst of the two scars.

His hands tightened on her shoulders, and she felt his body tremble against her. "Rhona ... no."

She ignored him. Instead, she trailed her lips along the ridge of flesh. "Yer scars are part of ye," she whispered. "I used to notice them, but after we wed, that changed." She drew back slightly so that their breaths mingled. "Since then, when I look at ye, all I see is the face of the man I love."

Rhona reached up to her shoulder and took one of his hands, drawing it down so that the palm lay flat over the top of her left breast. "Feel my heart," she said huskily. "Feel how it races. I'm telling the truth."

She watched his throat bob. His eyes had changed; they were no longer shadowed. Instead, they now gleamed.

Tenderness rose within Rhona. Taran MacKinnon wore his scars like armor, yet there were deeper ones inside him, ones that time had never healed. She'd ensure they never hurt him again.

She leaned toward him, her mouth pressing against his.

Truthfully, apart from a fumbling attempt by one of her suitors, Rhona had never been kissed. She had no idea what she was doing, but she felt compelled to take the initiative—to prove to him that her words were true.

Rhona moved her lips over his. She felt the rasp of stubble against her cheek, and a frisson of excitement made her stifle a gasp. She liked this. Tentatively, she traced the seam of his lips with the tip of her tongue.

Taran breathed a soft groan. His lips parted under hers, and his hands came up, cupping her face. His tongue slid into her mouth, exploring, tasting.

Rhona moaned and sagged against him. She felt as if she was drowning; Taran filled her senses, her world. The taste of him set her blood alight, and the kiss grew hungry.

When Taran gently bit her lower lip, she whimpered.

Breathing hard, Taran pulled away. His gaze fused with hers, never wavering. Trapped in his arms, Rhona stared up at him. "Kiss me again," she whispered. "Please."

He did, only this kiss was fierce, consuming. Rhona responded, the last of her restraint falling away as his mouth ravaged hers. Her hands slid up his chainmail vest to his neck. She wanted to feel his bare skin, but layers of clothing prevented her.

With a groan, Taran reached down, took hold of her skirts, and pulled them up around her waist. The warm night air brushed against Rhona's naked skin, and excitement pulsed through her. A melting sensation caught fire in the cradle of her hips. She reached down, her fingers fumbling with the laces of his braies.

When she released his shaft from the layers of plaid, her breathing caught. She wrapped her fingers around the thick column. The skin was smooth over the hard heat beneath. Her mouth went dry with need; she'd wanted this ever since their wedding night, had longed to be with him again, to touch him.

Taran gasped her name and kneed her thighs apart. Then his hands slid under her, grasping her buttocks as he lifted her to meet him.

Rhona guided him inside.

The feel of him penetrating her, the stretching, aching pleasure of it made her close her eyes, her head rolling back against the rough stone wall. He was big, but she took him in to the root, her legs wrapping around his hips to draw him in tighter still.

They stayed like that for a long moment, him buried deep inside her, and then Taran leaned into Rhona, trailing kisses up the column of her neck. She trembled under his touch before she offered her mouth to him once more.

He kissed her with languid sensuality this time, his tongue plunging into her mouth, before he started to move his hips to mirror the action.

The slick feel of their bodies moving together, the throbbing, building heat, was too much for Rhona. Her body started to quiver like a bowstring. Pleasure rippled out from her womb, and she cried out against his mouth.

Taran drove into her, deep and hard now, and Rhona clung to him, one hand digging into his scalp as she kissed him with abandon. The pleasure of it was almost too intense, and yet she would not prevent him. If her heart stopped from this, she would die willingly. Another spasm of throbbing, spiraling pleasure caught her, and she cried out, the sound muffled against his mouth.

Rhona clung to Taran, riding the waves that crashed through her. And then, his body grew rigid. Taran tore his mouth from hers, arched back, and let out a roar that shook the room to its foundations.

Taran lay on his side, staring down at the naked body of his wife spread out beside him. A single lantern burned on the mantelpiece on the opposite side of the chamber. It cast a soft light across the room, kissing every curve of Rhona's long-limbed, lush body.

He could have gazed upon her all night long. If only he didn't have to ride off to battle tomorrow. If only time could stand still.

Rhona's eyes were closed as she dozed. After their coupling in the stables, they'd returned to their tower chamber where Taran had torn off both their clothing, carried her over to the bed, and taken her once more. Their bodies were now slick with sweat in the aftermath. The shutters to the room were open, for the night was still and the air sultry.

Taran's gaze trailed up Rhona's body, taking in the auburn nest of curls between her thighs, the cradle of her hips, the dip of her waist, and the swell of her full, pink-tipped breasts. But when his gaze reached her face, it stayed there. Her dark-red hair fanned out across the pillow; she'd never looked so beautiful to him. Her lips, bee-stung from their kisses, were slightly parted, her cheeks flushed.

Gently, he reached out and traced her bottom lip with his fingertip.

She'd had no idea how much he'd wanted to kiss her, or how he'd worried she'd recoil in disgust. He'd barely been able to admit his fears to himself, yet with each passing day since their handfasting, they had grown.

But all his fears had been for nothing.

Rhona had given him her heart.

Feeling his caress, Rhona's eyelashes fluttered. She awoke, regarding him sleepily through half-closed lids. "Haven't ye slept?" she murmured.

"I dozed for a bit," he replied, "but then I realized I'd prefer to watch ye sleep."

Her mouth curved at this admission. "I hope I don't snore."

He huffed. "No ... but ye know I do."

Rhona held his gaze, her eyes darkening as she reached up and stroked his cheek with the back of her hand. "This has been the best night of my life," she murmured.

He captured her hand and brought it to his lips, kissing her knuckles. "And mine," he admitted quietly. "This feels like a dream. I fear that any moment I'll wake and ye will be another man's wife."

"Ye are not dreaming," she replied, her eyes shining. Her hand trailed down his chest to his belly. "This is real." Her fingers trailed lower still to where his shaft had already grown hard for her. She stroked him, her expression turning wicked. "Shall we see exactly how real?"

He groaned at her touch, closing his eyes and losing himself in the sensation. Then he sank down next to her and rolled over onto his back. A heartbeat later, he pulled her astride him.

Rhona laughed. "What are ye doing?"

"Just making sure ye are real, lass."

He lowered Rhona down onto him, and her laughter choked off. He opened his eyes to see her perched above him. His breathing caught at her loveliness: her breasts thrust forward, her auburn hair spilled over her shoulders.

He took hold of her hips and moved her against him, watching as she groaned and threw back her head, exposing a creamy length of neck.

Taran MacKinnon smiled. Aye, this was no dream. Rhona was his.

Chapter Twenty-nine

The Beast's Bride

"DO YE STILL wish to join us in battle?"

The question was unexpected. Rhona had been dozing against Taran's chest, her body languid in the aftermath of their lovemaking, when he spoke.

Propping herself up on an elbow, Rhona favored him with a level gaze. "Aye ... I do."

A shadow moved in those ice-blue eyes before he heaved a deep sigh. "My instinct is to keep ye here, safe within the walls of this keep ... but if to fight is what ye truly want, I'll not stop ye."

Rhona inclined her head. A strange blend of excitement and fear knotted under her ribcage. "Ye were dead against letting me ride with ye—what changed yer mind?"

He huffed a breath. "One of the things I've always loved about ye is yer wildness. Few women show an interest in learning how to fight. I've trained many men, and yer skills equal theirs. I'll not keep ye locked away for fear that ye will come to harm."

Rhona smiled. Reaching up, she caressed his cheek with her fingertips. "Thank ye, Taran. I'll not take any foolish risks, I promise."

His mouth thinned. "Ye had better not." He caught her hand and brought it to his lips, kissing her palm. "Today won't be pretty, lass. This confrontation between the MacLeods and the Frasers has been a long time coming. This battle isn't about land. It's about wounded pride. Morgan Fraser has wanted his reckoning against yer father for years. He'll never forgive him for taking Una."

Rhona nodded. She understood that. Her father had made a fool of his rival, and Morgan Fraser had been nursing his wounded pride for years. "I'll watch yer back today, my love," she promised softly.

His mouth quirked. "And I yers."

"This is madness." Caitrin put her hands on her hips and raked her gaze over Rhona, taking in the mail shirt, braies, and high leather boots she wore. "I can't believe Taran is letting ye fight."

"Well, he is," Rhona replied. She held out a pair of leather bracers to her sister. "Stop looking so disapproving and fasten these for me. I can't do it on my own."

Caitrin pursed her lips and took the bracers. She then cast a look at where Adaira stood behind them, her wriggling puppy in her arms. Their sister wore a composed expression, although her hazel eyes gleamed.

"Don't tell me ye agree with this?" Caitrin huffed. "Both of ye have lost yer wits."

"Rhona is as fierce as any man," Adaira replied.

Caitrin's jaw firmed. Her left cheek bore a red, swollen welt after the blows her husband had dealt the day before. But Rhona was pleased to see that her sister didn't look cowed or beaten this morning. Instead, she had a stubborn look in her eyes that Rhona welcomed.

"Ye might be able to wield a sword, but battle is something else entirely," Caitrin said, her voice tight. "I've heard that brave men have been known to lose their wits when the violence and death get too much."

Rhona's belly clenched at these words. "I've heard all the tales too," she replied, holding her sister's gaze firmly. "I'm not expecting an afternoon stroll."

She held out her wrist, and Caitrin stepped forward, fastening the bracer. She laced the leather arm guard with deft precision, and Rhona realized that it was likely a task she had done for her husband many times. Once Caitrin had finished lacing the bracers, she stepped back, her gaze shuttered.

"Will ye see Baltair before we leave?" Rhona asked.

Caitrin drew in a deep breath, tension visible in her slender shoulders. After a long moment, she shook her head.

"Do ye really hate him?" Adaira asked softly. Dùnglas had stopped squirming in her arms and was now licking her chin. She ignored the pup.

"Aye," Caitrin murmured. Her gaze glittered as she looked down, staring at the flagstone floor before her. "Every morning I wake and wish I'd never wed him."

"But Baltair was yer choice," Adaira reminded her. "Ye looked so happy the day of yer handfasting."

Caitrin's gaze snapped up, snaring hers. "Aye, and I've rarely smiled since. I made a terrible mistake." She paused here, a nerve flickering in her cheek. "His younger brother wanted to wed me, but I chose Baltair instead. A shallow, vain girl ... I chose the more handsome of the two brothers, the heir to the MacDonald lands." Caitrin's voice choked off. "And I have paid the price."

Rhona stared at Caitrin, shocked by her admission. She remembered the younger of the two MacDonald brothers: Alasdair. Sharp featured and lanky with a shock of raven hair that kept falling over one eye, he'd visited Dunvegan a number of times before Caitrin's union to Baltair. He'd been like a puppy around her sister, attentive and eager to please. However, Rhona didn't realize that he'd also been her sister's suitor.

Rhona cleared her throat. "Did Alasdair actually propose?"

Caitrin nodded, looking away.

Silence fell in the solar. It struck Rhona that the three of them really didn't know each other as well as she'd thought. They'd always been close over the years, but it seemed they held much back from each other.

"I always wondered why Alasdair left the isle so suddenly," Adaira mused aloud.

"He went to fight for the king against the English," Caitrin replied, her tone sharpening. "He didn't leave because of me."

Adaira gave her a pained look. It was clear that was what Caitrin wanted to believe. Neither of her sisters was going to contradict her.

Rhona tightened Lasair's girth and stiffened. She could feel the weight of someone's stare. It was stabbing her between the shoulder blades.

Casting a glance over her shoulder, her gaze met Dughall MacLean's. It was not yet dawn. Torches illuminated the bailey as the MacLeods, MacDonalds, and Budges prepared to ride out. Dughall sat astride a heavy grey stallion a few yards away. The warrior's face was cast partly in shadow. He watched her under hooded lids, his face stony. "What's this?" he growled. "The Beast's Bride dresses like a man this morning?"

"Aye, and she fights like one too ... so mind yerself," a male voice quipped. Rhona's gaze shifted to where Gordon MacPherson was leading his horse out of the stables. He cast Rhona a conspirator's look and winked.

Rhona glanced back to Dughall to see he was scowling. "MacKinnon clearly wants to be made a fool of," he growled. "Or maybe he'd like to see his pretty wife gutted on the battlefield."

The threat in Dughall's voice made Rhona tense. She was just about to spit out a cutting reply when Taran stepped up beside her. His face was hard as he met Dughall's gaze. "Mind yer manners, MacLean."

Dughall's face twisted. He then stretched out his neck and spat onto the cobbled yard between them. "Mind yer wife today, MacKinnon ... I'd hate to see her come to any harm."

"That's enough, Dughall," the rumble of the clan-chief's voice broke across the yard like thunder. "Threaten my daughter again, and ye will spend the rest of yer days in my dungeon."

Dughall paled, his jaw bunching. However, he did as bid. Malcolm MacLeod strode toward them, his bulk clad in chainmail, iron, and leather. Iain followed a few feet behind, his own armor clanking as he walked.

Surprised that her father had actually interceded on her behalf, for he barely even talked to her these days, Rhona met Malcolm's eye. Their gazes held for a long moment, and then her father smiled. Actually, it was more like a grimace, although his eyes held more warmth than she'd seen in a long while.

He stopped before her. "I never thought I'd see a daughter of mine ride into battle." His tone was rueful, but unlike the morning he'd caught Taran and Rhona training, there was no anger in it.

Rhona raised her chin. "I *can* fight, Da."

His gaze slid to the sword she carried at her hip. It wasn't a Claidheamh-mor—for that was a man's blade. Instead, Taran had given her a lighter longsword. She also carried a dirk at her waist. "I don't doubt it," he murmured. He reached forward and clasped a large hand over her shoulder, squeezing tightly. His gaze seared hers. "I'm proud to have ye fight with me today."

He released her shoulder and stepped back then, shattering the moment. Rhona swallowed the lump that rose in her throat. Never had her father spoken such words to her. The unexpectedness of it completely threw her.

Malcolm MacLeod moved away and started barking orders at his men. Iain followed him, although not before casting his elder sister a look full of jealous spite. Their father had praised a daughter while his first-born son stood forgotten in his shadow—Iain would never forgive her for that.

Rhona found that she didn't care.

They rode out of Dunvegan as the first glow of dawn warmed the eastern sky. It was a grey morning, and a chill wind blew in from the north, whipping up the surface of the loch and ruffling their horses' manes. The column of riders snaked out of the keep, bits jangling and shod hooves beating out a tattoo that shook the earth.

The MacLeods led the way, followed by the MacDonalds, and then the Budges. Rhona hadn't seen Baltair MacDonald since the previous evening and was grateful to be spared his baleful glare. Taran had told her what had happened after she led Caitrin away; the MacDonald chieftain would be nursing more than a broken nose this morning.

Nonetheless, Rhona found herself wondering if he'd been upset that his wife had not come out to see him off. Did he care for her sister at all?

"Why the fierce look, Rhona? We've yet to meet the Frasers."

Rhona glanced left to find Taran watching her. He'd reined in his bay gelding, Tussock, up next to her mare. They rode so close that their thighs almost touched.

"I wasn't thinking about them," she admitted with a wry smile, "but of Caitrin. I wish she wasn't wedded to that serpent."

Taran's brow furrowed, and he nodded. Silence stretched between them for a few moments before he answered. "It's hard to see someone ye love suffer," he said quietly. "I watched my mother grow from a laughing, beautiful woman to a frightened mouse ... but I was just a bairn and couldn't do a thing about it."

Rhona studied his face. She couldn't even imagine how it must have been, to see his mother slain in front of him. "Ye must have hated yer father," she murmured.

Taran's gaze guttered, his features tightening. "No ... I adored him," he replied. "That's what made it all the harder."

Chapter Thirty

Blooded

THE VALE OF Hamra Rinner lay in the cleft between two craggy peaks. A dark forest of pine and fir covered the lower slopes of the mountains, framing a wide meadow, where a burn wended its way over a bed of grey stones.

It was a lonely spot, far from the nearest village. The Fraser stronghold at Talasgair lay much farther south, upon the isle's western coast. Despite that this was MacLeod territory, the vale had always been the favorite hunting spot of both clans.

The MacLeod war party drew to a halt at the far northern end of the valley, tethering their horses amongst the trees. They would engage the enemy on foot, for it was cumbersome for the warriors wielding two-handed Claidheamh-mor blades to fight on horseback.

It had just gone noon; they'd ridden hard to reach the vale by the appointed hour. Would they find the enemy waiting for them?

Rhona followed the others out into the valley. The sun still hadn't shown its face. She glanced up at the pale sky and spied an eagle circling overhead. She'd never traveled to Hamra Rinner before. The resinous scent of pine filled the air. Up ahead, a stag bounded across the vale before disappearing into the trees carpeting the eastern slopes of the meadow.

"Remember all I taught ye," Taran said as they walked side-by-side. "Go for the throat, the belly, and the groin. Get in close so a man with a long reach can't use it to his advantage."

Rhona nodded, her stomach twisting as the reality of what was coming finally hit her. She was going to have to kill.

Part of her wondered if she was capable of it. What if she let everyone, herself included, down?

But she had no time to voice her worries, for it was then that she caught a flash of color to the south: the distinctive red, blue, and green of the Fraser plaid. Their pennants snapped in the wind.

Malcolm MacLeod raised his hand, signaling for them to halt. "There's that bastard," he growled. "Here to take what's mine."

"He won't, Da," Iain interjected. "We'll slaughter them all."

"That's the spirit, lad." Malcolm MacLeod tore his gaze from the fluttering pennants and glanced over at his son. His gaze narrowed. "Be careful with that sword today ... it's too big for ye."

Rhona watched her brother's cheeks flush. "I'm fine," he muttered.

Beside Rhona, Taran shifted. "I tried to warn him."

Gordon snorted. "Hope he impales himself on it." His comment was murmured, but Rhona heard it nonetheless. It didn't surprise or offend her; Iain might have been her brother, but he was growing into an unpleasant young man.

To the south, the Fraser war band approached. At first, Rhona could only see their banners, and then she caught sight of the men: rows of warriors clad in chainmail. Some wore helms that gleamed despite the dull day, while others went bareheaded.

When the two bands were a furlong apart, a tall, helmeted figure stepped out from the Fraser ranks.

Morgan Fraser strode out toward them, a cloak of plaid bearing the Fraser colors rippling from his broad shoulders. Rhona studied him with interest; he was the same height as her father but much leaner. Despite the heavy armor he wore, the man stalked rather than walked.

Malcolm MacLeod left the ranks of his men and lumbered forward. Unlike the Fraser chief, he wore no helmet. Rhona knew he found them cumbersome and complained that they limited his vision.

The two men stopped around five yards apart.

"MacLeod," Morgan Fraser's voice was a deep boom in the now silent vale. "We meet at last."

In response, Malcolm MacLeod spat on the ground between them. "Aye, Fraser. Ye have got what ye wanted all along."

"I knew I'd rile ye if I took yer land."

"Well, ye did."

"What's wrong? Don't ye like it when someone takes from ye something ye treasure?" The bitterness in the Fraser chief's tone cut the air.

MacLeod threw back his head and laughed, the noise rumbling like an approaching storm. "The lady chose the better man ... ye can't blame her for that."

"That *lady* was my wife, MacLeod."

Rhona heaved in a deep breath and spared a glance in Taran's direction. He was watching the exchange, his brow furrowed. Only blood would appease Morgan Fraser's wounded pride.

Malcolm MacLeod shrugged. "There's little point in talking then, is there?"

"No." The Fraser chieftain stepped back. "Get ready to taste steel."

The battle began with a swiftness that shocked Rhona.

A hunting horn shattered the stillness, its lonely wail echoing off the surrounding peaks. One moment the two bands had been standing, waiting for their chieftains to return to their ranks, the next they drew their weapons and ran screaming at each other.

Despite his girth and advancing years, her father was out front. He swung his Claidheamh-mor above his head bellowing. "Hold fast, MacLeods. Hold fast!"

Rhona's heart started pounding, and her skin prickled. This was it. She drew her sword and leaped forward. Half the band were already racing ahead, Taran among them. She risked being left behind.

The crunch of armored bodies, shields, and weapons colliding shook the earth as the first ranks met. Shouts, grunts, and cries rent the air.

Rhona tried her best to keep Taran in her line of sight, yet it was hard, for he plowed on ahead. She watched him raise his sword and engage the first Fraser warrior who came at him.

An instant later Rhona tore her gaze from her husband. A huge warrior bore down on her, Claidheamh-mor swinging.

Get in close.

Taran's advice rang in her ears. Gripping her longsword tightly with both hands, Rhona dove for him. During their years of swordplay practice, Taran had constantly told her that her biggest advantage was her speed and agility. There was no point trying to best a man of this size and strength. Instead, she went in low.

Her blade bit into the warrior's unprotected legs.

He roared and staggered. Rhona ducked away, narrowly missing the swipe of his sword. Before he had time to recover, she came at him again. She thrust her blade into his armpit, and he went down howling. Bile rose in her throat. Her belly roiled. Rhona swallowed, forcing down the nausea.

There was no time to react. She had to keep moving.

Rhona had heard many tales about battle, some terrifying. One thing she remembered, from the stories her father's men had swapped as they feasted in the Great Hall, was that a strange madness often took hold in the heat of battle. In such times a warrior lost all fear of death. Instead, the need to kill ignited like fire in a warrior's blood.

Rhona wished such a fury would take hold of her.

There was no such euphoria. Just a terrible bone-jarring effort. She was tall and strong, and yet the men who came at her were much bigger and stronger. It took every technique that Taran had taught her to fight them off—and it was even harder to kill them.

Her stomach twisted into a tight ball, while her hands—clutching the hilt of her sword—ached, as did her shoulders and arms. Sweat coursed down her back and between her breasts.

Her own viciousness sickened her. It was survival. The only way she bested the men who lunged at her, swords slashing, was to get in first, to stab them in places where armor and chainmail did not cover.

Throat. Belly. Groin.

Their screams, the stench of blood and worse, wormed their way under her skin, deep into her bones.

At some point, as the battle progressed, she became aware that it was shifting in the MacLeod's favor. There seemed fewer of the enemy to fend off now. She had long lost sight of her father and brother as they'd rushed to the front. The dead and dying lay scattered around her.

Half a dozen yards ahead she saw Taran, battling a huge man. She moved toward Taran, skirting around a Fraser warrior who lay groaning in a pool of spreading blood.

However, before she neared him, Dughall MacLean appeared. Blood splattered the warrior from head to foot and savagery twisted his face. Rhona had once thought him handsome, but she didn't now.

Rhona's step slowed. She expected Dughall to plow past her and into the fray once more. Only he didn't.

Instead, he ran at Taran and clubbed him across the back of the head with his fist.

"No!" Rhona's scream echoed across the vale, swallowed in the thunder of battle.

Taran, who'd just delivered a mortal wound to his opponent, dropped to his knees, his sword falling from nerveless fingers.

Dughall pulled a blade from his belt and raised it to deliver a strike to Taran's unprotected neck.

But he never brought the dirk down.

Dropping her sword and shield, Rhona flew at him. One hand fastened around Dughall's thick wrist, while the other grabbed a handful of hair near his brow-line and yanked, hard.

Dughall reared back, letting go of Taran. He and Rhona toppled backward onto the ground. He would have landed on top of her if Rhona hadn't twisted at the last instant. Still, the impact jarred her shoulder and hip.

Recovering swiftly from her attack, Dughall MacLean turned. When his gaze seized upon Rhona, and he realized who'd attacked him, a wild grin split his face.

Panic jolted through Rhona. There was madness in his eyes. He'd kill her, and then he'd finish off Taran. This was his revenge on them both for slighting him.

But to Rhona's shock, he tossed the dirk aside. "MacLeod bitch," he panted. "Ye have had this coming."

And with that, he lunged for her, his big hands fastening around Rhona's throat.

She reacted instantly the moment his fingers crushed her windpipe, driving her knee up into his cods.

Dughall let out a strangled cry and released her.

Rhona twisted out from under his heavy body and clawed herself away from him. However, he recovered from the blow to the groin faster than she'd anticipated. He landed upon her, flattening Rhona, face-down, to the ground. Air gusted out of her lungs. Winded, she scrabbled against the damp earth and tried to escape from under him.

But Dughall had pinned her fast to the earth; she wasn't going anywhere. His hands fastened around her neck, his fingers clamping down like iron claws over her throat.

Chapter Thirty-one

Shadows

TERROR REARED UP within Rhona. She would die here, throttled by her former suitor. She wanted to use one of the tricks Taran had taught her, but it was impossible, for Dughall's heavy body crushed her into the ground. She kicked and dug her toes into the earth, trying to push up against him, but it was no good. Her legs were useless.

A pressure grew in Rhona's chest, and her ears started to ring. Twisting her head to the side, choking as his grip tightened, she caught sight of the dirk Dughall had tossed aside.

It lay within arm's reach.

Her hands had been clawing at his fingers, trying to pry them free from her throat. Now, she flung a hand out to the dagger. Her fingers grasped the bone hilt.

She drove the dagger back, feeling it bite deep into flesh.

Dughall's roar deafened her, but at that moment the iron band around her windpipe released.

Rhona drew in gulps of air. Her lungs burned. She couldn't seem to breathe properly. That was because

Dughall was still sitting on her back, crushing her against the earth.

And then, suddenly he wasn't. The weight upon her chest lifted.

Still choking, Rhona rolled over.

Taran stood over them. His face was ashen, his eyes shadowed with pain. The short blade he held dripped with blood.

Dughall MacLean lay on the ground between them, thrashing as death came for him. His hands grasped around his ruined throat.

The hilt of the dirk Rhona had used against him protruded from his right thigh.

A sob rose in Rhona's chest as she struggled to her feet. Too close. Moments more and Dughall would have choked her. Rhona's legs trembled. A sob rose in her throat.

She tottered forward and collapsed into the cage of Taran's arms.

Crows circled over the Vale of Hamra Rinner, dark silhouettes against a dull sky.

The dead lay scattered across the meadow, their blood soaking into the peaty earth. Chainmail glinted in the watery afternoon light. The MacLeods had won the battle. The Frasers had retreated, hauling their injured with them.

"I stuck that bastard," Malcolm MacLeod announced. He limped toward where Rhona and Taran stood at the edge of the battlefield. Around them, MacLeod, MacDonald, and Budge warriors combed the meadow for survivors and spoils of war. "May Morgan Fraser's wounds fester before death takes him." To emphasize his point, the MacLeod chieftain spat on the ground.

"Da split him open from hip to knee," Iain announced. He followed behind Malcolm, his once shiny armor splattered with blood and gore. Rhona was impressed to see that her brother had proven his worth in the battle. He'd lost his sword though and had finished the fight with a dirk. "He won't survive such a wound."

"Good," Malcolm grunted. His gaze met Rhona's then. "I heard about MacLean ... treacherous dog."

Rhona swallowed. Her throat still ached in the aftermath. Dughall's fingers would leave livid bruises on her neck. Her father's gaze then shifted to Taran. The two men looked at each other for a heartbeat, and then Malcolm MacLeod nodded.

Rhona watched her father limp away before she glanced up at her husband. "I'm afraid that's the closest ye will get to a 'thank ye'."

He favored her with a weary smile. "Fortunately, I don't need his thanks."

"Taran ..." A warrior approached them. He was a young man, his blue eyes hollowed with fatigue. "Gordon MacPherson's been injured. He's asking for ye."

Taran's face blanched. "Where is he?"

"On the other side of the vale. Follow me."

The warrior led the way across the corpse-strewn field. Although Rhona was loath to walk amongst the dead, she doggedly followed her husband. She was fond of Gordon and would see him too.

They had nearly reached the halfway point when Rhona spied the body of Baltair MacDonald. She halted, catching hold of Taran's hand. "Look."

Taran turned, his gaze following hers.

The MacDonald clan-chief lay on his side, curled up around the blade that still protruded from his abdomen. The Fraser warrior he'd fought lay next to him, his throat slit. Baltair had managed to bring him down before dying.

Her brother-in-law's face looked different in death. He was a handsome man, even with the broken nose

Taran had given him, although in life his character had harshened his features. They appeared softer now.

"I'd say I was sorry to see him dead," Taran murmured, "but I'll not lie. The world's a happier place without Baltair MacDonald in it."

Rhona squeezed Taran's hand in wordless agreement. They continued across the battlefield.

Gordon lay propped up against a log on the far side of the valley. Ashen-faced, he still managed to greet Taran with a smile. However, the expression was tight with pain. Rhona drew in a sharp breath when she saw the deep slash down his right thigh. She could see a glint of white—the cut had gone to the bone.

They needed to get him to a healer.

Taran hunkered down before him. Rhona saw the worry in his eyes, although when he spoke, his voice didn't betray it. "Getting yerself into trouble again I see, MacPherson."

Gordon huffed. "One of those Frasers got under my guard," he rasped. "Didn't even see him coming."

Rhona knelt down next to Taran, her gaze shifting to where blood still ran from the gash upon Gordon's thigh. "I need to bind that for ye," she muttered. Rhona pulled up the edge of her mail shirt and grabbed hold of the hem of the léine she wore underneath, ripping a strip free. She was making a habit of this of late.

Gordon's gaze widened. "Lady Rhona ... don't worry yerself over me."

Rhona cast him a quelling look before she shifted closer and started winding the length of linen about his thigh. "I'm not," she replied. "I'm ensuring ye don't bleed to death before we get ye back to Dunvegan."

Gordon's throat bobbed. He shifted his attention back to Taran. "If I don't make it, will ye give Greer a message from me?"

Taran's brow furrowed. "No need for that ... we'll be back home tomorrow. Ye can tell her yerself."

"We've got a live one!"

The shout, a few yards away, made Rhona glance up from her work. A cluster of warriors were forming around a figure that lay prone upon the battlefield.

"It's Morgan Fraser's eldest!"

Malcolm MacLeod lumbered across to join them. He was limping heavily, having strained something during the battle, but his face was set in determination. "Let me have a look at him."

The MacLeod chieftain elbowed his way through the gathering crowd and peered down at the unconscious man. Rhona was too far away to make out the young man's features, yet she caught sight of a shock of red hair—a brighter shade than her own.

"Aye, that's Lachlann Fraser, all right," Malcolm MacLeod growled. "I haven't seen him since he was a lad, but he's got his father's looks."

"What will ye do with him, Da?" Iain had pushed his way in and was now standing next to his father. The young man withdrew the dirk from his belt, his expression turning feral. "Do ye want me to slit his throat?"

Malcolm MacLeod cast his son a cool look. "Ye are a bloodthirsty pup, aren't ye?"

The comment brought a few smiles from the surrounding men. Iain's cheeks flushed, his mouth thinning. Ignoring his son, the clan-chief turned his focus back to the unconscious warrior at his feet. "What's wrong with him?"

"Took a blow to the back of the head by the looks of it," one of the warriors replied. "Knocked him out cold."

A slow smile spread across MacLeod's face. It wasn't a pleasant expression, but one filled with cunning and malice. Rhona's breathing grew shallow at the sight of it; her father was not yet done with punishing Morgan Fraser.

"Pick him up and put him in the wagon with our injured," Malcolm ordered. "We're taking Lachlann Fraser back to Dunvegan, where he will rot in my dungeon for the rest of his short life."

Rhona exhaled sharply. She didn't envy the man his fate; the dungeon in the bowels of the keep, carved out of dark rock, was a sunless, fetid place.

She'd never heard of anyone who'd survived it.

Rhona sat before the hearth, shivering.

They'd made camp for the night around fifty furlongs north of the Vale of Hamra Rinner. A mist curled in, wreathing like smoke across the craggy hills and in-between the tightly-packed tents. Autumn was approaching; the air had a bite to it. But it was not the temperature that made Rhona tremble.

Ever since the battle she'd been on edge. Now, as the day drew to a close and she was able to rest, her limbs wouldn't stop shaking.

"Here." Taran appeared at her side with a steaming cup in his hands. "Some hot spiced wine will settle yer nerves."

Rhona cast him a rueful look. "Does it look like they need settling?"

"Aye … I've seen more color on the face of a corpse."

Rhona took the cup, her chilled fingers wrapping around its warmth. The rich scent of hot bramble wine filled her nostrils, and she felt a little of the day's tension ebb out of her. She took a gulp of wine, letting its heat burn down her throat, and released a shuddering breath. "That's better," she murmured.

"Did I make a mistake letting ye join us?" Taran asked quietly.

She glanced back at her husband to see him watching her. A deep groove had formed between his eyebrows, and his gaze was shadowed. She could feel his worry for her.

Rhona shook her head. "It was my choice."

Silence fell between them for a few moments before Taran spoke once more. "Many men would have quailed at today's slaughter. But not ye. I watched ye fight. Ye did yer father proud ... ye did yerself proud."

Rhona held his gaze. "And what about ye, Taran," she murmured. "Were ye proud of me?"

He reached up, his palm cupping her cheek as he gazed into her eyes. "I was terrified the whole way through that battle," he admitted. "The thought of losing ye is like a blade to my guts. I'd never have forgiven myself. I'm not sure I want ye fighting alongside me again."

Rhona drew in a trembling breath. She could feel the tension in the hand that cupped her cheek, see it in the lines of his face. He expected her to argue with him, to insist on riding out with her father from now on.

"I'm not sure I want to see another battle," she admitted, her voice barely above a whisper. "One was enough. All that death sickened me ... even Dughall's."

Taran loosed a breath. "Thank the Lord." He moved closer to her, his fingers tracing the lines of her face. "Yer eyes look so haunted tonight. So empty."

Rhona swallowed. "Chase the shadows away, Taran," she said softly. "Please."

His gaze widened for an instant, and then he nodded. Gently, he took her cup of wine and set it aside. Then, he rose to his feet, pulling her with him.

Taran picked her up as if she weighed nothing and turned, carrying her away from the smoldering hearth. Their tent sat just a few yards behind them. Taran ducked into it, and they entered a warm, welcoming space lit by a small brazier in the center. A deerskin lay upon the floor; it would be their bed for tonight.

Taran lowered Rhona so she stood before him, and his mouth claimed hers for a deep, hungry kiss. Rhona groaned, her lips parting as she surrendered to him. Her arms went up, interlocking around his neck.

Their clothing came off—blood-encrusted mail shirts, braies, léines, and boots—until they both stood naked. Rhona entwined herself around Taran, gasping when his hands slid over her body, claiming every inch of her as his own. She pressed herself hard against him, desperate for his strength, his warmth. His love.

Chapter Thirty-two

How Things Change

CAITRIN DIDN'T WEEP when Rhona told her Baltair was dead.

She showed no reaction at all.

Rhona hadn't expected tears, but this carven figure before her, devoid of emotion, of life, made concern flutter up within her. "Caitrin," she said gently, taking a step closer to where her sister stood. "Did ye hear me?"

Caitrin held Eoghan in her arms; the babe had gone still, his blue eyes huge, almost as if he understood what Rhona had just said. Caitrin swallowed before she gave a curt nod.

Across the chamber, Adaira shifted. She had followed Rhona into the solar upon her return to Dunvegan. Unlike the other women, Caitrin hadn't come out to welcome the returning warriors.

"So, the Frasers were defeated?" Caitrin asked finally; the faint rasp to her voice was the only sign of the emotion she was keeping in check.

"Aye," Rhona replied. "Morgan Fraser was badly wounded ... it's likely he'll die."

"Who was that man they dragged down into the dungeon?" Adaira asked. Her blue eyes were full of curiosity. "He has hair like flame."

"Lachlann Fraser, the chief's eldest son," Rhona answered.

Adaira pulled a face. "I almost pity him. The pits down there are foul."

Rhona shrugged before turning her attention back to Caitrin. Her elder sister had not moved. Her gaze seemed unfocused, as if she was lost in her thoughts. "Caitrin?"

Her sister blinked. "How did he die?"

"A blade to the belly." It would have been an agonizing death, but there was no need to tell Caitrin that. "They have brought his body back and laid it out in the chapel."

Caitrin's features tensed. "I will go to him later."

Rhona nodded, relieved that she had come to life. Still, her sister's lack of emotion, her detachment, concerned her. Caitrin carried too much within; even with her sisters, she couldn't seem to share what lay within her heart.

"Da wants us all to join him in the Great Hall tonight," Rhona said after a pause. "There will be a feast to honor our victory ... and our dead."

Caitrin's mouth pursed. "Tell him I'm not well enough to attend."

Rhona shook her head. "I'm sorry ... but he's insisting. He says he wants *all three* of us to join him."

Caitrin looked away, her jaw clenching. "I tire of having men tell me what to do," she growled. "All my life I've had to mind them. I look forward to returning to Duntulm, to being left in peace."

Rhona didn't reply. She understood Caitrin's frustration, for she'd endured much of late at her father's hands. And yet, because of him, she was now wed to Taran. Warmth flowed through Rhona at the thought of her husband. Last night he'd made slow, tender love to her; she'd wept in his arms afterward.

She knew too that her sister would find no peace at Duntulm. The MacDonalds of Duntulm were now without a chieftain; sooner or later Caitrin would be subject to the orders of another man. Rhona tensed at the thought.

Caitrin had suffered enough. Couldn't they just leave her in peace?

Taran watched the healer apply a poultice to Gordon's thigh. His friend bore the treatment stoically, although his face had gone grey, and sweat beaded his forehead and top lip. Greer stood beside Gordon, her fingers grasping his. Her eyes glistened.

"Well," Gordon grunted as the healer drew back and reached for a strip of linen to bind the wound. "Will I keep my leg?"

"It's a deep wound," the man replied. Old and bent, with a thick mane of white hair, the healer's bright gaze fixed upon Gordon. "Even if it doesn't fester, ye will bear a limp for the rest of yer days."

Gordon's face tightened at this news.

"*Will* it fester?" Taran asked.

The healer glanced at him. "It's too early to tell ... for now the flesh is healthy. I will return tomorrow to tend the wound."

Taran watched the healer bind Gordon's thigh. Then the elderly man collected up his basket of healing herbs, powders, and tinctures, and bid them all good day. Gordon was one of many warriors he'd have to see today.

When the man had gone, Gordon loosed a long breath, leaning back against the mountain of pillows that Greer had propped him up against. "Great ... I'm going to be a cripple."

Taran's mouth twisted. "A limp hardly makes a man useless."

"MacLeod won't see it that way. Such a warrior isn't much good on the battlefield."

"That doesn't matter to me," Greer spoke up, her voice husky. "Stop complaining Gordon MacPherson. Ye are alive, aren't ye?"

Gordon's gaze met his betrothed's, and the pair of them watched each other for a long moment. Taran suddenly felt as if he was intruding.

"I thought I was done for after the battle," Gordon replied, his gaze never wavering from hers. "All I cared about was not seeing ye again, not being able to tell ye how much I love ye, bonny Greer."

Greer's cheeks flushed. Taran was surprised by his friend's admission. Gordon wasn't a man for emotional talk.

Taran cleared his throat. "I'll leave ye both then."

Gordon nodded, yet his attention never strayed from Greer. Likewise, she stared back at him. The atmosphere in the small chamber inside the guardhouse grew charged.

Taran departed with a smile on his face.

Caitrin MacDonald entered Dunvegan's chapel. Inhaling the scent of incense and the fatty odor of tallow, she let the door thud shut behind her, finding herself within a cool, shadowy space.

Caitrin drew in a deep breath and reached up to the small crucifix she wore about her neck. Kirks and chapels gave her a sense of peace, a calm in a world where she felt controlled by the will of others. There were no booming voices of men here. There was no one to make demands upon her.

She'd left Eoghan with Adaira while she visited her husband. It was a rare moment of solitude.

Moving across the pitted stone floor, Caitrin's gaze shifted to the altar at the far end of the space. Sunlight filtered in through high arched windows on the western wall, dust motes floating down like fireflies. Just beyond the pooling sunlight lay a corpse upon a stone bench.

Baltair.

Caitrin's step slowed. She studied his profile, his dark hair brushed back in a widow's peak. From this distance, he looked as if he were sleeping.

It was hard to believe Baltair MacDonald was actually dead.

Reaching his side, Caitrin stopped. Someone had dressed him in clean clothing, for there were no signs of war upon him. The mortal wound to his belly had been bound and covered. He wore a long mail shirt, plaid braies of MacDonald colors, and a wide leather belt with the clan crest upon it. His hands rested on the pommel of his longsword, which lay upon his chest.

Caitrin's gaze slid up the length of Baltair's body and rested upon his face.

Death had softened it.

She'd once thought him so handsome; just the sight of him before their handfasting had made her knees grow weak. Yet it hadn't taken her long to fear him, for her stomach to knot whenever he walked into a room.

How things change.

Her husband's eyes were closed; he really did look as if he were sleeping. It made Caitrin nervous, and she took a step back from the bench. Even in death, she was afraid of him.

Swallowing the lump in her throat, Caitrin wiped sweaty palms against her kirtle.

Coward.

Her younger sister had just come back from battle, where she'd wielded a sword as well as any man. But here *she* was, scared of a corpse.

Caitrin's hands balled into fists. She was tired of being afraid, sick of jumping at shadows. This man had turned her into a mouse. Once she'd been proud and full of spirit. She'd laughed and flirted with her father's warriors. Smiles had come easily, and when Baltair had asked for her hand, she'd felt smug that such an attractive, charismatic man would want her for a wife.

She barely recognized the woman she'd become.

Steadying her breathing, Caitrin stepped back to the edge of the bench and stared down at her husband.

"Ye no longer have any hold over me," she whispered. Her voice was low, yet it seemed to echo in the empty chapel. "The Devil take ye, Baltair MacDonald."

"To all those who fell defending the MacLeod name and honor." Malcolm MacLeod raised his drinking horn high into the air. Rhona noted the ruddiness of his cheeks; her father was already well into his cups and the night was still young. "Ye will be remembered."

A chorus of 'ayes' went up across the cavernous hall as men and women stood up and raised their cups.

"Yesterday the Frasers discovered that they cross us at their peril," MacLeod continued. "They learned that the MacLeods, MacDonalds, and Budges stick together." The clan-chief's eyes shadowed then. "Brave Baltair MacDonald lost his life in that valley, leaving my daughter a widow. We share her grief, her loss."

Opposite Rhona, Caitrin sat still and silent. Dressed in a charcoal-colored kirtle and veil, as befitted a widow, her sister's gaze was downcast. She didn't acknowledge her father's words. Seated between Caitrin and Aonghus Budge, Adaira cast Caitrin a worried look.

"The MacDonalds of Duntulm must keep strong!" Malcolm MacLeod boomed. He swayed slightly on his feet as he thrust his drinking horn high into the air once more. "I will send word to the mainland, to where Baltair's brother fights for our king. Alasdair will return and take his place as chieftain." These words brought forth a cheer from the MacDonald warriors gathered at a nearby table. But Rhona noticed that Caitrin blanched, her pretty mouth thinning.

Her father was oblivious to her displeasure. Instead, he turned his attention to Aonghus Budge.

"The Budges of Islay have proved their loyalty and quality. Thank ye, Aonghus ... yer friendship is dear to me."

The Budge chieftain acknowledged MacLeod's words with a wide smile. Despite his advancing years and stout figure, Aonghus Budge had fought against the Frasers.

He bore minor injuries from the battle: his right arm was in a sling, and he bore a shallow gash to his forehead.

"I seek a way to repay ye," Malcolm droned on. "The Budges and the MacLeods must endure."

Rhona stifled a groan. Drink always made her father loquacious. She wished he'd sit down and let everyone resume eating and drinking. She shared a pained look with Taran beside her. Under the table, he squeezed her hand. Soon enough this feast would be over, and they'd be able to retire to their tower chamber. Excitement fluttered up within Rhona at the thought.

"I have decided that our clans must be united in marriage," Malcolm MacLeod slurred. "I have one daughter not yet wed. Aonghus, I give ye the hand of my youngest, Adaira."

Chapter Thirty-three

A Fine Wife

ADAIRA GASPED, HER face turning ashen. "Da!"

Malcolm MacLeod waved her protest away, his attention still upon the man beside her. Aonghus Budge's grin looked wide enough to split his face.

"A generous gift, Malcolm," Budge replied, "and most appreciated. Adaira is a lovely creature and more biddable than her elder sister. She will make a fine wife."

"Aye." Malcolm MacLeod's brow furrowed at the mention of Rhona's refusal. It hadn't happened that long ago, but to Rhona, it seemed as if a year had passed. She didn't feel like the same person, and yet she would still be loath to wed that toad.

"Ye can't do this, Da." The words were out before Rhona could stop them. Under the table, Taran's fingers tightened around hers. It was a warning, but she didn't heed him. "Adaira can't wed Budge. He's nearly thrice her age!"

Aonghus Budge's grin slipped.

Her father looked her way. His face turned thunderous. "Hold yer tongue, lass."

"Please, Da," Adaira choked out the words. "I don't want this ... I can't—"

"Silence!" Spittle flew as their father leaned across the table. Una reached out, plucking at her husband's sleeve to calm him, yet he shoved her hand aside. "I will not have my daughters defy me. Ye will do as ye are bid."

Tears streamed down Adaira's face. Her hazel eyes were wide, desperate. "I won't do it," she gasped. She gripped the edge of the table as if it was her anchor in a stormy sea. "I won't."

"Ye will!" Malcolm MacLeod launched himself forward and threw the contents of his drinking horn in Adaira's face.

The Great Hall of Dunvegan went silent.

Blood-red wine dripped down Adaira's cheeks, staining the pale blue kirtle she wore. Beside her, even Aonghus Budge looked taken aback by MacLeod's outburst. Wine splattered the clan-chief of Islay's cream-colored léine. "I have agreed to the match, Malcolm," he growled finally. "There's no need to lose yer temper."

MacLeod collapsed into his chair. His face was dangerously red now, and he wheezed as if he were out of breath. Una watched him, her face taut with concern. "Malcolm?"

"I'm all right," he mumbled. "Just give me a moment." His gaze remained fixed upon Adaira. She made no move to wipe the wine off her face; instead, she merely stared back at her father, her expression stricken.

The look in her sister's eyes made an iron band fasten around Rhona's chest; it was a look of utter betrayal. Out of the three daughters, their father had always been softest with his youngest. He'd called Adaira his 'fairy maid', his 'wood sprite'. He'd indulged her over the years.

It made his treatment of her now even harder for Adaira to bear.

Across the table, Caitrin met Rhona's eye. Her elder sister's face had gone hard, and her blue eyes bore a flinty look that Rhona had never before seen.

"Ye would do this to Adaira, Da?" Caitrin's voice echoed through the now silent hall. "Wedding her to Budge will kill her."

MacLeod's barrel chest was still heaving, although his eyes narrowed. "So ye have a tongue, after all, lass? I was beginning to think Baltair had cut it out."

A muscle feathered in Caitrin's jaw, but she continued to stare her father down. "Would ye have *yer* fate determined by others?" Her voice was hard and cold. "Would *ye* not fight to choose whom *ye* wed?"

"Women don't get to choose," Malcolm MacLeod snarled back. The glint in his eyes warned them all that his temper was kindling once more. "Ye are fit for breeding and little else." Una cast him a dark look at that, but heedless, the clan-chief plowed on. He reached for a ewer of wine and refilled his drinking horn. "One more word on this subject and I will have all three of ye whipped."

"I loathe him." Adaira choked out the words against her pillow. "He's a beast!"

Rhona sat next to her sister, gently stroking her back while Adaira sobbed upon her bed. She'd said little since following Adaira up here; there weren't any words that could undo their father's decision or lessen the shock.

She was still reeling from it herself.

Guilt pulsed through Rhona. Her belly ached from it.

If I'd agreed to wed Budge, Adaira would have been spared.

Aonghus Budge was a brute, but Rhona was physically tougher than her sister. She'd have endured his cruelty easier. Instead, she'd defied them all and ended up wed to Taran MacKinnon. She should have been miserable now, for that was what her father had wanted, in order to punish her for running away. And yet fate had taken an unexpected twist.

Instead of misery, she'd found love.

But what about her sister?

Rhona heaved in a deep breath. Her sister's shoulders shook from the force of her sobs.

Adaira was gentle and kind, a lass with a giving soul. Rhona had never been that good. Compared to Adaira, she felt selfish and difficult.

"I'm so sorry, Adi," she whispered, using the name their mother had favored Adaira with as a bairn. "If I could undo it, I would."

Rhona glanced across the chamber at where Caitrin sat next to the fireplace. She was nursing Eoghan. Usually, Caitrin wore a serene expression when she was feeding her son, but tonight her expression was harsh. Her gaze smoldered. With a jolt, Rhona realized she'd rarely seen her elder sister so angry. She bristled with it. Baltair's death had unleashed something in her, a fire that had long been smothered. Rhona was glad to see it, although misgiving stirred within her as well.

She knew from bitter experience what happened to women who rebelled.

"Will ye stay on at Dunvegan awhile?" Rhona asked.

Caitrin shook her head. "Baltair must be buried on MacDonald lands. We leave at dawn tomorrow."

With a gasp, Adaira sat up, pushing her walnut brown hair out of her eyes. "No, Caitrin ... ye can't leave. I need ye!"

Caitrin's gaze guttered. "I'm too angry to be of any help to ye. The very sight of Da makes me want to scream. If I stay here, he'll only have ye whipped because of me." Caitrin's gaze shifted to Rhona. "Ye will look after Adaira?"

Rhona swallowed, her throat suddenly tight. "What makes ye think I'll be able to hold my tongue?"

Caitrin's mouth twisted into a rueful smile. "Ye still have fire in yer belly, Rhona—but now happiness has tempered it. I've seen the love and trust between ye and Taran." Her smile faded, and she dropped her gaze to where Eoghan suckled hungrily. "I've no idea what that's like."

Rhona returned to her chamber later that evening with a heavy heart. Taran was there already, waiting for her, although he'd fallen asleep. Still fully clothed, he was stretched out upon the bed, his face gentle in repose.

Shutting the door quietly behind her, Rhona padded over to the bed and gazed down at him. When he was asleep, his scars were less evident; they seemed smoother against his skin, not so disfiguring. When he was angry, those scars made him look terrifying.

The past weeks had taught her that a very different man lay beneath the forbidding exterior that had earned him his reputation as the Beast of Dunvegan. His big heart, his kindness, and his respect for her still awed Rhona.

Her breathing hitched. *What did I do to deserve him?* Guilt writhed in her belly once more as she imagined her sister cringing in bed while Aonghus Budge took her maidenhead.

Rhona felt sick at the thought.

With a heavy sigh, she sat down on the edge of the bed. Feeling the mattress shift, Taran groaned, his eyelids flickering. His gaze settled upon her. When he spoke, his voice was husky with sleep. "How is Adaira?"

"Upset ... terrified."

A shadow passed over his face. Taran propped himself up on an elbow and reached for her hand. Wordlessly, he entwined his fingers through hers and squeezed.

"I feel so useless," Rhona whispered, her vision blurring. She'd managed to keep her upset to herself while with her sisters, but somehow Taran always made her defenses crumble. It was as if he saw right through her shield, to her heart; there was no point in hiding her feelings from him. "It should have been me to wed Budge."

Taran made a sound in the back of his throat. "And ye would never have been mine."

Rhona met his eye. "I can't bear the thought of Adaira going back to Islay with him ... he'll kill her, Taran. Just like he did his last wife."

Taran's gaze narrowed. "He swears her death was an accident."

"And ye believe him?"

A beat of silence passed before Taran shook his head. He watched her, his expression tender, before he released her hand and reached up to push a lock of hair off her cheek.

"Ye are so fiercely protective of yer sisters," he said after a moment. "Why?"

Rhona drew in a shaky breath and scrubbed at a tear that escaped, trickling down her cheek. "Just before my mother died, she called the three of us to her bedside."

The memory of that day crashed over Rhona as she spoke. The sight of her mother, frail with sickness, her once lustrous blonde hair strawlike and spread over the pillows that propped her up in her sickbed. The heartbreaking sadness in those hollowed eyes.

"She told me I had Da's fierce heart … that she would rely on me to look after my sisters. I remember her final words to us as if she spoke them yesterday: 'Ye will be women one day, in a world ruled by men. And as such ye will have to be doubly strong, sharp, and cunning to survive.'" Rhona broke off there and closed her eyes. "I didn't know what she meant at the time. But I do now."

"Yer loyalty does ye credit," Taran said, brushing away a tear, with his thumb, that trickled down her chin. "It is one of the many things I love about ye … but be careful that it doesn't tear ye up inside." He paused there, and Rhona opened her eyes, meeting his gaze once more. "Ye can't protect yer sisters from the world, any more than ye can hold back the tide or keep death at bay. Things seem bleak for Adaira now, but none of us know what lies in store for her."

"Ye mean Aonghus Budge might die in his sleep before the handfasting and spare her?" Rhona asked, her mouth quirking. There was wisdom in her husband's words, and she knew in her heart that he spoke the truth. Only, it was hard to let go of a lifetime's habit.

"Aye." Taran smiled back. "Don't underestimate yer sister either. Ye have seen the change in Caitrin since

Baltair fell. Life molds and shapes us, forges us into who we're meant to be."

Rhona caught his hand and raised it to her mouth, kissing his fingers. "Taran MacKinnon ... how did ye get to be so wise?"

He raised a sandy eyebrow. "Are ye mocking me, wife?"

"No ... I'm serious. I think I know who ye are ... and then ye say something that surprises me. There are depths to ye I never suspected."

He huffed a laugh. "There are to most of us ... I just choose to share my thoughts with ye." He sobered then, gazing up at her with a tenderness that made Rhona's breathing constrict. "I didn't have an easy start to life, mo chridhe. It shaped me differently to other men."

My heart.

Rhona's gaze misted once more; her heart ached with love for Taran. His words eased the guilt and worry that stole away her happiness and cast a shadow over the world. He was right. She would always be there for her sisters, but she couldn't control their fate. Even their father, powerful as he was, couldn't foresee all ends. He'd not been able to see that his wayward daughter and the scarred warrior who'd loyally followed him for years were meant for each other. Perhaps his decision to wed Adaira to Aonghus Budge would take a twist none of them expected.

Rhona bent down and kissed Taran, her lips parting his. He groaned against her mouth. When she pulled away, they were both breathless, and the weight that had settled over her shoulders had lifted. "It shaped ye into a wonderful man," she murmured. "I'm blessed to have ye as my husband."

The End

From the author

I hope you enjoyed the first installment of THE BRIDES OF SKYE.

THE BEAST'S BRIDE was new territory for me, both for its setting (my first Medieval Romance!) and for the 'Beauty and the Beast' theme at the heart of the story. I wanted to put my own personal twist on the theme, which meant going deep into the characters. As always, the story I planned wasn't entirely the one I ended up writing. Taran and Rhona's story took me in directions I didn't expect, and some scenes were gut-wrenching to write. Until now I'd say that Galan (from BLOOD FEUD) has been my favorite hero ... although now I've written this book, Taran might be in first place!

Of course, you'll be wondering what happens to Adaira and Caitrin now? Fortunately, you won't have to wait long to find out. Books #2 and #3 are both coming soon!

As with all my books I really enjoyed the historical research that went into this story. The MacLeods are a dominant clan on the Isle of Skye, and they reside at Dunvegan to this day. Malcolm MacLeod was an actual clan-chief, who did steal the wife of the Fraser chieftain, resulting in a bitter feud! History doesn't record Malcolm MacLeod, who apparently did get very fat in his later years, as having any daughters—but since I know that history often forgets such details, I decided to give him Rhona, Adaira, and Caitrin.

The historical backdrop to this novel is real too. In the year of this story, 1346 AD, the Hundred Years War between the English and the French had begun, and King David of Scotland took the opportunity to try and win back Scottish independence. However, things don't work to Scotland's favor. There will be more on the unfolding historical events in Books #2 and #3.

See you again soon, with THE OUTLAW'S BRIDE!

Jayne x

About the Author

Award-winning author Jayne Castel writes epic Historical and Fantasy Romance. Her vibrant characters, richly researched historical settings, and action-packed adventure romance transport readers to forgotten times and imaginary worlds.

Jayne has published a number of bestselling series. In love with all things Scottish, Jayne also writes romances set in Dark Ages Scotland ... sexy Pict warriors anyone?

When she's not writing, Jayne is reading (and re-reading) her favorite authors, cooking Italian feasts, and going for long walks with her husband. She lives in New Zealand's beautiful South Island.

Connect with Jayne online:
www.jaynecastel.com
www.facebook.com/JayneCastelRomance/
https://www.instagram.com/jaynecastelauthor/
Email: contact@jaynecastel.com

Printed in Great Britain
by Amazon